NEMESIS

STERLING FALLS ROGUES
BOOK 1

S. MASSERY

INTRODUCTION

Hello dear reader!

Artemis's story deals with some very difficult subject matter, including drug abuse, sex trafficking, rape, suicidal thoughts, and self harm.

If you'd like to know a bit more about some side characters and Artemis's history, dive into the short prequel story, Terror (available here: https://BookHip.com/HMPRACQ).

Happy reading!

xoxo,
    Sara

PROLOGUE

Artemis

PAIN ECHOES THROUGH ME. It's my only constant in an ever-changing landscape. It keeps me company while I sleep, when I am awake. It is the steady beat of a drum against taut, hollow skin. They may have carved me out and forgot to replace my insides.

Whoever *they* are.

The truck rumbles to a stop. There's only a creak of warning, then the floorboards beneath me tilt. I slide, unable to stop myself, my body knocking against others and tumbling to the ground. I land on top of someone, and another's weight presses on my legs.

I blink through the hazy aches. There's a huge black building in front of us with an open, waiting door. I glance around, temporarily pushing aside the pain. We're in an alley, hemmed in by a chain-link fence and another brick building at our backs, and the truck blocking our only escape.

Immediately, men with guns come forward. They

untangle and haul us up, half dragging us when our legs don't work, and into the black building.

Down a long, dimly lit hallway. They use a key to unlock a set of double doors. I check over my shoulder. One of the girls who huddled against me in the back of the truck, her chin wobbling and tears staining her cheeks. Now, she can barely keep her footing. Two guards hold her by her upper arms, pulling her along.

They've holstered their guns, but it doesn't make me feel any better. Just the fact that they're *there*, at their hips and probably ready to use them, sends ice down my spine.

"Here," someone says. A woman?

Another door opens, and the brightness of the room forces my eyes closed.

I'm shoved into a chair, my wrists locked at my sides, before I can adjust.

A hand—cool, dry—grips my chin and forces my head up.

"Age?"

"Fifteen," someone else answers the woman.

"Hmm." She turns my head to the side, then releases me. "Strip her."

When I fight, a fist lands in my gut. I almost throw up, but there's nothing in my stomach to eject. I grit my teeth and double over while they cut off my clothing. All of it.

Someone grabs my hair at the base of my neck and yanks me into a straighter seated position.

"No tattoos," the woman says. "Limited scarring. Bruising..." She tsks. "I tell them to be gentle around the face."

"Makeup," the man behind me suggests. "Aren't you always saying makeup can cure anything?"

"It doesn't hide a split lip or swollen eye," she counters.

"I give your guards an inch, they take a mile. So, no inches. These girls are more valuable when they're pretty."

I shudder.

"Lean her back."

Suddenly, the whole chair tilts. I shoot upright—try to—but the man never released my hair. My scalp burns, and I arch. I cry out until they stick something in my mouth, and a heavy strap cinches across my torso just under my breasts.

There's a click, and my legs are lifted.

Spread.

I close my eyes.

The man above me chuckles. "She's blushing."

The woman snaps on gloves, and suddenly she's touching *there*. Between my legs—

My stomach rolls.

"Virgin," she declares. "Her hymen is intact. Get her into the shower, then back to me. We need to take photos for the auction. Oh, wait."

She's suddenly beside me, swabbing a spot on my upper arm.

Pinch of pain, and then warmth radiating up my shoulder and down to my fingers.

"A little something to make her more compliant," she says to the guard. "So you won't have any more excuses if she comes back more broken."

Her face swims above me, blocking those terribly bright lights. If I expected any sort of compassion, I am sorely mistaken. Her expression is fucking cold.

"Welcome to Terror, beauty."

1 ARTEMIS

(nearly) ten years later

I'D LIKE to punch whoever said eyes are the window to the soul. I hate my eyes. I hate looking at myself in the mirror, especially lately. If that saying about eyes being a window is true, my soul is tarnished. Practically burned to ash.

My strategy lately has been ignoring the issue, which is why I'm up and out of my condo bright and early this morning. I'm supposed to meet my twin brother in an hour, but I decided a nice, relaxing sunrise on the cliffs would do me good.

Except for the cloud cover that has ruined my view. That seems to be on par with everything else going to shit in my life. I've been occupying myself in the meantime by tossing rocks over the edge, because watching the sky go from dark gray to light gray is just depressing.

"You're early." Apollo approaches from Olympus, the looming building just down the sloped pathway from the cliffs. Olympus, which I skirted around in favor of the wind lashing at me.

Olympus is a building straight out of Ancient Greece, a Pantheon-esque temple that my brother and his friends use to host masked fight nights. Dress as your favorite character from Greek mythology. Just don't wear flowers, or else you'll be marked. Hades doesn't take kindly to someone imitating his beloved Persephone.

I still remember the opening night, although it was years ago. It was everything they—and I—hoped it would be. More, even, because it turned into something that seemed to escape reality.

It was *Olympus*. Home of the gods. It was luxury and grandeur, and it catered to those with a thirst for anonymous violence. The indulgence of the place, and the brutality of fist fighting, doesn't fail to draw a crowd.

Apollo has been my near-constant companion since before we were born. We're thick as thieves—sometimes to a scary level. We know each other inside and out. And sometimes that's terrifying, because I feel like he can know what I'm thinking just by looking at me.

I meet him halfway, stopping just shy of hugging him. Unlike mine, his eyes aren't tarnished. Even with everything he's done and gone through, his eyes are kind.

There's something wrong with me lately. More than just avoiding my own gaze in the mirror. I just can't put my finger on *what*.

"How's Saint?" he asks.

I wrinkle my nose. "He says he's fine."

He's not fine. In fact, Saint Hart is less fine than me—and that's saying something. The love of his life died right in front of him, and then he more or less threatened to kill himself and follow her into an early grave.

I've been playing babysitter at the request of Apollo's best friend. Although, when I agreed to this nearly twelve months ago, I never could have predicted that Saint Hart would *still* be living with me.

"I've got a project for him." Apollo appraises me. "Something you could help with, too, if you want."

"No." I scoff and face the cliffs again. Olympus is situated on some of the highest cliffs in Sterling Falls, and the view at the edge is unbeatable... even when it's cloudy. "No, I'm good. If it'll get Saint out of my hair, he can have at it."

"Hmm."

My brother annoyingly tall, and while I got *some* height in the genetic lottery, I didn't get six-foot-something. For me, puberty was a bitch. Suddenly I had to contend with breasts and hips, which further separated my brother and me in appearance.

We do look alike, though. Dark hair, tanned, olive-toned skin. Our dad's grandfather was, fuck, I don't know. From somewhere in the Middle East. Our mother had Spanish blood. That's what she used to say, but it could've been a drop for all I know. Our ancestry kind of got lost on us somewhere around the tender age of fifteen. That's when both Apollo and I were thrown to the wolves...

Different kinds of wolves, but their hunger was the same. They tore away our innocence, and it was a miracle we both came out on the other side.

"Tem." Apollo takes my hand.

I slip away before he can get a good grip, making a show of kicking a few loose rocks over the cliff edge.

The ocean is mighty today, far below us. The resounding *crash* of waves against the rocks sends spray almost high enough to reach us. The wind picks up the faint mist of it, giving us the smell of the sea.

We're halfway into September, which means we'll get our fair share of storms rolling in over the next two months, and then winter will sweep in like a freight train, bringing snow and ice and freezing blasts of wind.

It's the best time of the year.

When he doesn't reply, I sigh. "I'm in no mood for it."

"It?"

"You trying to make things better." I squint out at the horizon.

"What are you in the mood for, then?"

I don't know. If I could figure that out, maybe I could work out what's been off. But nothing I've tried so far has helped. Or made me feel more like *me.*

"I'm going for a drink." I meet his gaze, daring him to judge me.

But he doesn't, he just... nods. I can't read his expression. Another first. Another oddity. I brush it off before I can get too sucked into it.

I cast one more look out at the ocean and contemplate jumping. The waves are cracking so hard against the cliff face, a jump would probably end in broken bones.

The last thing I need is for Apollo to feel the need to save me.

We've done that before.

His attention stays trained on me as I hurry down the sloping lawn and climb into my car. The engine revving is comforting, and I speed down the driveway in a shower of gravel.

It occurs to me, halfway to Bow & Arrow, that I didn't get what I was coming for. Which was *help.* With Saint.

He's been in a fucking mood, and I can't deal with it anymore. Apollo's household should be out of their honeymoon stage by now, which means they can take him. Or, better, Saint can stay at Olympus. There are plenty of rooms with beds.

And he wouldn't really be *alone*, because someone is always coming or going at Olympus.

I hit the steering wheel.

I had a whole speech planned out, and instead, when he asked? I said he's *fine*. Or rather, that he thinks he's fine. Which is true enough. I've been watching him spiral for a while now, and he's done nothing to save himself.

Apollo said he had a project for Saint, though. Maybe it'll be a big enough distraction to get him out of this funk.

Bow & Arrow, my saving grace, comes into sight. I bought the building a year after Olympus opened. The fight club was so successful, and my brother insisted on paying me for every little thing I did to help, that I was able to save up for this place in North Falls.

It's a nightclub with a rooftop restaurant, designed to attract the tourists and locals alike. It's a blend of luxury and mystery. The club portion opens at nine, but the restaurant on the top level serves dinner starting at five. On weekends, we offer brunch service, too.

In the summer, reservations are nearly impossible to get at the last minute. During the off season, which started approximately two weeks ago when schools went back into session, we remove the reservation option.

I park in my usual spot and swipe a keycard to enter in through the back. The entire building was brought back to the studs when I first bought it, but I still shiver passing through the heavy metal double doors.

I'm not sure I'll ever get over it.

There's an industrial staircase immediately to my right, and I take it all the way up to the top floor. It deposits me into a hallway that leads straight into the kitchens. On the left is my office, the door closed and locked, and on the right is Antonio's office.

It's open, the light on.

I swing in without knocking and drop into the chair across from his desk.

Antonio has been a constant in my life since I was sixteen. Far more constant than my parents, who gave up on me when I was a teenager. My brother tries to be there—and tried harder back then—but he was in a gang that tore him away from me in more ways than one.

It's Antonio who put me back together after the worst few months of my life. And the months I suffered is nothing in comparison to what others face.

He's bent over his desk with slim, rimless glasses perched on the end of his nose. His pencil scratches across a page in his notebook.

Until his gaze lifts, we don't speak. Finally, he finishes the page and sets down the writing utensil, frowning at me.

"You look like shit."

I wrinkle my nose. "Thanks."

"What's wrong?"

I shrug. "What're you working on?"

He slides the book to me. I scan the page he was just working on, a smile slowly blooming across my face. I didn't think I'd be smiling today, but...

"Chocolate cake?"

He watches me. "Your birthday is coming up."

My smile slides away, and the frown I've been staving off comes back. "No."

"We're celebrating," he says. "With this. The perfect chocolate cake. I've been working on the ingredients for months. It's your favorite, so you can't say no."

I scan the pages again.

"My sixth iteration," he adds.

Birthdays? Add it to the list of *sore subjects*. And the

fact that he's been working on it long enough to ditch five probably perfectly reasonable cake recipes... it means he cares about it. About me. I already knew he cared about me, but I often like to ignore the fact that it's there. It's easier when we're just existing as... business partners.

"Well." A lump forms in my throat. "That's... Okay. Fine."

He grins, then takes the pages back. He glances at the digital clock on his desk. "Kitchen should be ready to go. Time to put on my chef hat."

I stand. "Let me know if there are any issues."

"Always."

I head across the hall into my office. Owning your own business comes with its fair share of paperwork. Antonio takes care of the restaurant, our club manager basically runs the nightclub aspect, which leaves me to pay the bills.

Which is what I end up doing for over an hour. My eyes are tired and my hand cramped when one of the club hosts knocks at my office door.

I lean back in my chair and smile at her. "Everything okay?"

"Sam called out sick."

Sam is the nightclub manager. She isn't usually known for calling out... *ever*. And with only two hours until the club opens, she's cutting it a little close. The woman is seriously like a superhero. She probably had awards from school for perfect attendance.

"How about Jackie?" I ask.

The girl in front of me, Mel, shakes her head. "She's in Emerald Cove for the week. Doing that training thing and visiting her sister."

Right.

"Sorry." I pinch the bridge of my nose. "I knew that."

"I didn't know who else to ask..."

"No, it's not your fault. I'll finish up here and be down in a few moments."

She hesitates.

"What else?"

"Paul has a scheduled day off, and Barry isn't here yet."

Fires, fires everywhere. Paul is one of our security guys. He basically wanders around and makes sure people aren't causing trouble in the club. Barry is the club's door bouncer. To have them both out? Not good.

I wave off Mel, assure her I'll be downstairs soon, and reach for the phone.

What feels like fifteen thousand phone calls later, I've got everything sorted. Barry has been located, plus another on the security team will be coming in to assist. Mel will have help on the floor, and I will be behind the bar. Which just leaves one missing piece.

I head out to find Antonio and give him my best, award-winning smile. Well. I don't know if it would win anything, but I'd like to think so.

"You have a scheming face," he calls across the counter. He's got little slips of paper in his hands, pausing in his orders only to spare me those words and a quick glance.

"How do you feel about managing the nightclub tonight?" I force a bigger smile. "I've volunteered to be behind the main bar, so you can give me shit for moving too slow."

He rolls his eyes. "Done."

I pump my fist.

"But only if you call the missus and tell her why I won't be home until dawn."

Fuck.

I head back to my office to tell Vittoria, Antonio's wife.

She's strong as nails and twice as scary, but their relationship is pure gold. They have three children, only one of whom is still living with them. But not for long.

Soon enough, she'll be heading to college, and they'll be empty nesters.

"Tony?" she answers when I call.

"Better," I greet her.

"Tem! To what do I owe this surprise?" She pauses. "You're keeping him late again."

I wince. "Is that okay?"

"I suppose it will have to be. We'll be seeing you by the house this week, right? I have some new plants to show you, plus some nodes for you to take home. They're rooting already."

"Yes, of course. Thank you."

She makes no mention of any birthdays, for which I am relieved.

"I'll be over soon," I promise. "The club is closed Mondays..."

"Excellent. Talk soon, dear. And keep my husband safe while you work together."

I tilt my head. The tone of her voice makes me think...

Nah.

"Bye, Vittoria." I hang up and stare at the phone for a long moment. The weird feeling is creeping back, and I stand abruptly. This is the last place I want to get caught up in that.

I lock my office door and head for the stairs. I have an apartment downstairs for emergencies. My brother's used it before to hide from his enemies, but now I mostly use it to stash extra clothes. And sometimes I sleep there when the condo feels too cold.

The apartment is empty. I change into a slinky gold

dress and release my thick hair from the clip it had made its way into, then slick on even more makeup. I trade my tennis shoes for heeled boots that grip at my calves, plus necklaces, earrings, bracelets, rings.

Full-body transformation.

I meet my gaze in the mirror and try not to cringe.

Just get through tonight, I tell myself. That's all I need to do.

2 ARTEMIS

I STARTED WORKING for Antonio when I was seventeen. It was at Antonio's first restaurant, actually. We were both out of sorts, kind of floundering with what to do with our lives. He fell into the restaurant business, and he said he couldn't take my moping. So he put me to work. First as a busser, then a bartender when I turned eighteen.

I didn't speak to a single person other than him. Eventually, I started talking to my co-workers. But not to any real extent. The lead bartender talked to the *real* customers, while I made the drinks that came in on the tickets for the tables.

There was a learning curve, obviously. But once I figured out that everything has an exact amount, it became more about science and less about alcohol.

A year later, Antonio put me in front of *people*. At that time, they were scary. The prospect of them anyway. But he must've said something to the other bartender, because he worked alongside me, letting me interact with customers at a crawling pace.

Making drinks? Fine.

Conversation? I'd rather not.

After what I went through, everyone was seen as dangerous. It took a long time to unwind that fear and learn that not all of them were evil.

And from there, other people seemed pretty easy.

Now, I'm grateful for the loud, thumping music. People crowd around the bar, but they're not looking to chat with *me*. They're barely able to talk to the person beside themselves without tonguing each others' ears.

Just the way I like it.

"Artemis," Antonio calls from the side.

I make my way to him, although it's a little slow. I drop off drinks along the way and collect the cash they slide me, until finally I reach the older man.

Cassandra is just behind him.

"VIP bar needs an extra set of hands... and some guidance." He quirks his lips. "Mel is drinking with the guests."

I groan. "Cassie's replacing me here?"

"Yep."

I nod and gesture for her to get back here. I lean in and tell her, "Tom just went to restock garnishes, so you're only on your own for a few more minutes."

Antonio and I watch her settle in for a moment, but there's really no need. Cassandra's been around almost as long as Bow & Arrow. The only reason she's not a manager is because she's refused the promotion twice.

"You good?" he asks me.

I jerk my head up.

Bow & Arrow's aesthetic is moody. While the restaurant portion is light and open, with spectacular views, the club is dark. There are different levels, with caged dancers floating above the dance floors. Mirrors, dark marble, lights.

It's all an illusion to keep my idea of luxury and mystery alive.

The fight club, Olympus, does the same thing in a different way.

It's part of the draw. People realize they'll never uncover what's hiding in all the shadows at this place, but it doesn't stop them from trying.

I get to the upstairs VIP section, nodding to another of our security on my way by. It's almost midnight. And as soon as I step in, I spot Mel taking a shot at one of the booths.

Fuck my life.

I head straight to the bar. It's quieter up here, with less demand. Or should I say, less crowd and twice the demand. The rich always expect more—and it's one area I avoid as much as possible.

"Artemis! I'm so sorry." Mel leans on the bar. "I—"

"Are you drunk?"

She shakes her head once. Too fast. She's wide-eyed, for the first time showing a speck of fear.

"Stand up straight," I order.

She's all dolled up to work the VIP floor. Short dress, dark makeup. Her stance is even on both feet—in heeled boots—and steady.

I grab a pack of mints from under the bar and toss it at her. "If I see you drinking on the job again, you're done. Got it?"

"Yes, ma'am. Sorry."

Who would've thought I'd get ma'amed at twenty-five? Almost twenty-five. Even more fucking disgruntled, I wave her away and focus on the man sitting alone at the bar.

"What can I get for you?" I ask, stopping in front of him.

He looks up from his phone and... glitches? He stops moving for a long moment, just staring at me.

And I stare back. Because, one, he's hot as fuck. And two... he seems familiar—but not in a normal Sterling Falls way, where the locals all recognize each other on a certain level. This is different.

The more I stare, though, the less I can narrow down *how* he's familiar. Greenish eyes, maybe hazel, and blond hair, muscular... Where do I know him from?

"Fireball," he says. "And Dr. Pepper."

I wrinkle my nose. "Really?"

He frowns. "I thought bartenders weren't supposed to judge drink orders."

"I couldn't help myself with that one."

He laughs. It bursts out of him, and I don't know how to react for a moment. Until he stops and returns to watching me.

I just weirded out a customer.

"Coming right up." I clear my throat and turn away. *Coming right up.*

Ice. Shot of fireball whiskey. I fill the rest with Dr. Pepper from a can and set it down on a napkin in front of him.

He slides me a credit card.

"You want to close out now or open a tab?"

"Tab. Why'd they bring up the big guns?"

I tag his card and put it with the few others, then stop back in front of him. "Am I the big guns?"

"You seem like you're in charge."

I smirk.

Mel catches my eye at the edge of the bar. When I give her my attention, she nods toward a new incoming group. It seems almost automatic to take stock. They appear to be a bachelorette party, a single girl in a skimpy white dress and pink sash surrounded by equally dressed-up girls wearing black sashes across their chests. There are a few guys in the group, too.

"Want me to take them?" Mel asks me.

I don't have time to respond—they come straight to the bar.

And in less time than it takes to get their drink order, the rest of the bar is packed.

It's good, though. It keeps me busy, and my mind just kind of goes staticky. It's exactly what I need, and three hours later, I'm sweating, my feet hurt, and all I want is to sit down.

"Last call in ten," Antonio says over my shoulder. He pats my back and moves past me.

"Thanks."

I go down the remaining patrons and ask if they need anything else, finally pausing at Fireball and Dr. Pepper.

"Back again," he says.

"Indeed. Can I get you another?"

"Only if you have one with me." He raises an eyebrow. "Or a drink of your choice. On me."

I smile. "On you, huh?"

"It's called buying a gorgeous woman a drink."

"Flirting?"

He smirks. "Something like that."

"Lucky for you, my boss would be okay with *something like that*." I tip my head. "I'll come back once everyone is closed out."

"Do that."

I make myself a drink and keep it behind the bar, adding it to his tab. Belatedly, I actually retain his name. It's typed in raised print on the credit card.

Reese Avery.

I squint at it. My chest is so tight, I can't draw in a single breath. He can't be... *him*. He's different than how I last knew him. Taller? Older, obviously. More filled out.

White spots flicker around the edges of my vision, and I slowly look back over my shoulder.

"Figured me out?" he asks.

I touch my temple.

That weird feeling comes back tenfold, rearing its ugly head like a wave cresting over me. The white spots are replaced with encroaching darkness—a sure sign that I'm about to pass out.

The last thought I have before I faint is: *I never should've gotten out of bed today.*

3 ARTEMIS

THE BOY CUPS *his bleeding nose. He stares at me with a baleful expression. Like I'm the violent one. I touch my split knuckles and cover them with my other hand. I'm not violent. I'm just trying to survive.*

"I wasn't going to touch you without permission," he says to me.

His gaze flicks over my shoulder. To someone beyond us.

I glare at him. "Whose permission?"

He doesn't have an answer to that.

I GROAN. My head pounds. It takes too long to force my body into motion. I'm halfway up before I open my eyes.

A hand grips my shoulder.

"Easy," a gruff male voice says. "Take it slow."

I blink hard, the white spots from before receding, and Antonio's face swims into view. Familiar, gruff, steadfast Antonio. He seems vaguely worried, though, and he pushes me back down.

"Just rest a second, Tem," he says. "You hit your head."

"Ugh."

"Yeah. Sounds about right." He leans over me, a pen light suddenly glaring into my eyes. "You might have a concussion."

I lick my lips. "What happened?"

"Fainted," Mel says, somewhere near my feet. "One of the customers helped me get you into the back, but you were coming to and he left."

Reese?

My breathing hitches, and I automatically reach for Antonio's hand.

"What is it?" he asks.

I shake my head. Not in front of Mel. Not in front of anyone. He glances over his shoulder at my employee and dismisses her. The door closes behind her, and I rise back up on my elbows. I sigh when it registers where we are.

We're in my freaking apartment, the one tucked away in Bow & Arrow. It makes sense that we didn't leave the building, but...

"He carried me all the way here?" I squeak.

"Who is *he*?"

My mouth dries.

I sit up and swing my legs off the couch. This place underwent a *serious* sterilization after my brother stayed here. I even got a whole new freaking couch because I didn't trust him.

And then he snickered and said I should've bought a new dining table, too.

Fucker.

Anyway.

"I just, um, recognized him." I avoid Antonio's gaze.

"From where?"

I clear my throat. "You know where."

He goes quiet. Then, without warning, he jumps up and rushes out of the apartment.

Well, that's not good...

"SEEMS like you're the one who needs to be watched now."

My shoulders automatically creep up. "Can't a girl make it all the way into her own condo without being accosted?"

I should've expected this. Antonio called and said he was going to take care of it. He told me to stay at the apartment, seeming to forget that I have the equivalent of a pet at home. So I grabbed my jacket from my office and drove back to the high-rise in downtown Sterling Falls, and now I'm home.

But I should've remembered that this *pet* likes to bite.

"You don't give me much of a choice most days," he says. "Figured you'd like a taste of your own medicine."

I flip the lock and slowly turn to face Saint Hart. Dead best friend's... whatever he was to her. Lover, partner, boyfriend. Although that latter one seems too shallow a word to describe their relationship.

Soul mate?

He sits at the breakfast bar in workout gear. A tight white shirt that's nearly translucent, stuck to his skin with sweat and showing off his myriad of tattoos. He literally has almost no real estate left, minus his face. And under his shorts, probably. Is his ass tattooed? His dick?

Something I've only questioned a few times in my life. But luckily, I've never seen either one.

Maybe the tattoos stop mid-thigh. Except when he

scratches his leg and drags up the hem of his shorts, and the ink just keeps going up and up and up...

I shake myself out of that line of thought. What helps is to picture Nyx's face, particularly how soft her eyes got when she looked up at Saint. She was tall and thin, like a graceful willow, and absolutely covered in tattoos.

But when I first met her, she had none. The artwork she displayed was all Saint's handiwork. And then she died, and Saint fell apart. Which is how he ended up here. In my condo.

Annoying the shit out of me day in, day out, while I try to keep him alive.

It's been an exhausting year.

"Who told you?"

He raises his eyebrows. "Who told me what?"

"That I need watching."

He shrugs.

I grit my teeth and move past him. It's late. Late enough that he should be sleeping. But, no. Instead, he waits up for me like some sort of psycho. Just to aggravate me.

"So?" he questions. "You're not really a fainter. Although I can picture it. I've seen you pass out before, when you lose your fights at Olympus..."

I'm going to kill whoever told him.

I yank open the fridge and peer inside. I'm starting to hate this place. Like, serious hate. It's more than just the decor is wrong, or the couch is uncomfortable. Both of those things are untrue anyway. I love the way I decorated the unit.

It's the giant motherfucker sitting on my barstool that makes it unsavory.

"Do you still think about killing yourself?" I ask, bumping the fridge door shut with my hip. A long coat zipped up to my throat covers my gold dress. While I'm starting to overheat, I don't want to reveal what's underneath.

Saint has a problem with a lot of things, and the way I dress is high on the list.

He glowers at me. "Why the fuck would you ask that?"

"To see if you still actually need to be here." The *obviously* hangs unspoken between us.

"That's not up to you or me." He rests his chin on his hand, smiling slightly.

Fucker.

He's right, though. Jace King, my brother's best friend, asked if Saint could move in. There was no stipulation on how *long* Saint would have to stay, or who would decide when it was time for Saint to fly the nest.

Although he might need shoving at this point. I'd love to be the one to do it, too. Just a quick, hard nudge...

He's got a mug in front of him and a black metal water bottle beside it. The more I take him in, the more I realize he might not have been waiting for *me*, and just drinking himself into an oblivion.

That only happens when he dreams about her.

God, the dreams. Nightmares, one might classify them as. One of the first nights he was here, sleeping on the couch because the other room wasn't ready for him, the sounds of his hoarse yelling woke me.

And when I woke him up? A hand on his shoulder?

He nearly took my head off. The moment his eyes opened, I'd never seen such hatred. And that was only the beginning of our war.

But living with Saint is like stepping onto the platform at Olympus. We wear our masks, and we do our best to inflict mortal blows.

And after a year of it... I fear the lashes have turned to scars across our backs. Irreparable damage.

I drift closer to him, until my hips press to the counter and we're within reach of each other. There's no chance of us touching, though. Jace knew he was putting Saint with the one person he couldn't hate-fuck his way out of his emotions.

I lift my chin.

And then I move.

I snatch the mug and leap backward at the same time that Saint lunges for it. He barely misses, his fingers snagging my coat sleeve.

I sneer. "If there's liquor in this, you owe me."

He narrows his eyes.

The liquid is amber. The mug is ice-cold.

So it's either tea or something else.

I sniff, and the smokey, pungent scent of scotch assaults my nostrils. I make a face, and he reaches out again.

I swallow it down. *Yep*, it fucking burns a path down my esophagus. I set the mug in the sink and point at him. "You're not supposed to be drinking."

"Okay, *Mom*."

"Fuck off. Where's the bottle?"

"Who scared you so bad you fainted?" he asks instead.

I frown.

"Ah, see? You don't like me pressing on your bruises either."

It's got to be around here somewhere. I yank open cabinet doors, drawers. Saint watches me, his gaze like a laser on my skin, until I get to the refrigerator.

The freezer.

I find it tucked under a bag of frozen peas, half empty. The glass is frosted.

He grabs my wrist. His hand is so hot, it might scald me. But his grip is tight enough that I can't just pull away. I gape at him, tugging, but he holds fast and draws me upright. He kicks the freezer door shut.

"Just leave it," he says.

"You—"

"I'm not going to get drunk and throw myself off the balcony," he interrupts. "I've had plenty of opportunity to do that, Artemis, and I haven't."

"You think I like being on suicide watch?" I hiss. "You think Nyx would—"

"*Don't say her name.*" He pushes me against the refrigerator and slams his hand to the door to the left of my head. "Don't. How about we cut you open so *your* secrets can spill all over the floor? I'm sure they're just as ugly as mine."

My mind goes to Reese, and I choke on my laugh. That's where we're at—it's either laugh at our trauma or fall to it.

"Uglier, Saint," I whisper. "You can count on that."

He drops my wrist, drops his other hand. It's like he suddenly realizes how close we're standing. One big inhale from both of us, and our chests would brush.

My face flames, and he steps away fast.

"I'm going to bed," I murmur.

"Who scared you?" he asks under his breath as I'm retreating.

I am not going to answer that. The answer is way too fucking complicated to even start.

By the time I've showered and changed into pajamas, the sun is rising. I take a particular joy in closing my blackout shades and crawling into bed. My body is running on empty, and my mind is buzzing with nothing-thoughts. Sleep should come easy.

It does, but it's far from restful. Instead, I dream of dark hallways and pain. I'm just on the edge of consciousness, tossing and turning, but the burn of ropes against my skin, the crack of my nose breaking, the constant darkness, holds me hostage.

And when I finally wake, I'm alone. Free of everything except the sheets twisted around my legs. I kick them off and curl on my side, the panic so visceral I can taste it.

I breathe deeply, touching the bridge of my nose.

That dream was too real, too close to the real hit that broke it once. Doctors were quick to set it, but no one cared that I had a pair of black eyes. I learned fast that I was pretty with or without bruises.

And only pretty girls are of value.

There's sunlight peeking around the edges of my curtains.

I hop out of bed, shivering, trying to literally shake off the dream. I let the sunlight in, then dress fast and slip from my room. Saint's bedroom door—it *was* an office, but was converted when he moved in—is shut. It tells me absolutely nothing. He could be in there awake or sleeping, or gone. Probably gone, since it's the middle of the day.

In the elevator, my phone rings.

It takes me a second to fish it from my pocket. I frown at the name scrolling across the screen.

"Why are you calling me?" I ask instead of a hello.

"I'm not allowed to check up on you?" Wolfe James asks. My brother's other best friend, besides Jace King. The trio are inseparable.

"You are," I allow. "But it's suspicious."

"I was mainly just calling to find out if you're still fighting tonight."

I pinch the bridge of my nose. "Right."

"You forgot."

"I... didn't."

He scoffs. "Antonio's got a security photo of some guy printed out. He wants it plastered everywhere. He was in the sheriff's office first thing this morning."

"Shit." I drop my hand when the door slides open on the parking garage level. "Who did he talk to?"

"Bradshaw."

That, at least, is a blessing. I mentally shift around my to-do list to include an urgent visit to our friendly neighborhood sheriff.

"I'll be at Olympus tonight," I tell Wolfe. "But I'm not fighting."

"Suit yourself."

"Who is?"

He pauses.

"Wolfe?"

He's always been straight with me. When he and Apollo were kept separate, *I* was the one holding them together. That's a whole different story, though. That was when Sterling Falls was no better than a warzone. But the point is, he owes me honesty.

"Don't shoot the messenger," he warns. "But... Saint is fighting."

I stiffen. "I'm not going to shoot the messenger. I'm going to shoot *him*."

I contemplate turning back around and storming into Saint's room. I'd love to start another fight with him, this one about how fucking stupid he is.

"It's been a year, Tem." His voice is soft. "You both—"

"Don't," I whisper. "It's not me, Wolfe. Jace put Saint—"

"You and I both know Jace asked *you* because you were her best friend."

Were. Why is one word so painful?

I get in my car and throw my head back against the seat. Because when I think about Nyx, my insides go all funny. Kind of numb and nauseated all at once.

"I don't want to talk about it. What I do want to talk about is Antonio."

Antonio, who is taking the appearance of Reese a lot more seriously than I am. Antonio, who loves me like his child, who would do anything to keep me safe. He's not going to let me handle this on my own. Not after what happened last night.

"Right." Wolfe sighs. "I'm getting on my bike now. I'll meet you at the sheriff's station."

I allow a tiny smile. "Yeah?"

"I can't let you interrogate Brad alone."

More like, he can't pass up an opportunity to help interrogate him.

"See you there," I manage before he hangs up.

Nathan Bradshaw has been the sheriff forever. Wolfe, Jace, and my brother like to call him Brad to irritate him. The sheriff holds an elected position, and I kind of thought he might lose it—or retire at the tender age of thirty-something—after Sterling Falls slipped back into a time of peace. Wartime leaders are usually replaced once the war is over...

But peace doesn't usually last either. It has reigned for a year, though. A year of rebuilding. Sterling Falls has been putting itself back together, and I've watched tourism come back. Shops that were boarded up and closed out of fear have reopened. The oppressive curfew that forced Bow & Arrow, amongst many nighttime businesses, to temporarily close was lifted.

Now... that *off* feeling is back.

Maybe it's just a vibe, but I have a suspicion that something bad is about to happen.

I leave the parking garage and drive through the financial district. The buildings here are tall, all glass and steel, but it's the only area of the city that truly feels this way. The rest of it is older, more spread out. The buildings outside of the financial district were designed to savor the views of the tree-covered hills to the west and the ocean to the east.

Olympus is all the way east. The sheriff's office, however, is around the corner from the university in the center of town. It's only a ten-minute drive from my highrise, and I pull into the parking lot a few minutes before Wolfe.

He turns off his bike and flicks down the kickstand beside my car. When he yanks off his helmet, he rakes his hand through his dark hair and grins at me.

"How's the family?" I ask him.

His blue eyes gleam. "Busy, per usual."

"Of course."

He sets the helmet on the seat and gestures for me to lead the way. We go up the wide marble steps and into the building, skipping the elevator in favor of the stairs. First floor is reserved for the officers and detectives under Nathan Bradshaw's command. Second floor houses the city council and his offices.

The sheriff's secretary takes one look at us and goes pale. She presses a button, murmuring something through her intercom system.

And thirty seconds later, Nathan Bradshaw himself strides out of his double-doored office.

"Artemis," he greets me.

His hair is so short, it appears light brown. But his beard

is shockingly orange-red. He's in his regular dark-green uniform, sans hat, and I can't help but glance at the gun strapped to his hip.

"And Wolfe," he adds.

"Brad," Wolfe says.

I make a face. "We're here about Antonio."

"Ah." He tips his head, silently inviting us into his office.

Wolfe immediately drops into a chair and kicks his legs out, gazing around. The windows on the far wall let in a lot of light, and his large desk is relatively uncluttered. And there's space, so it's not a matter of that. But it still feels cramped.

That weird feeling comes back when Bradshaw extends a printed photo of Reese.

I stare hard at it. Antonio took a screengrab of the security feed when I was passed out in that gold dress. And, as suspected, Reese was the one to jump to my rescue, because he's carrying me in the photo. My stomach knots, and I swallow hard. It's like, seeing it now, I can *feel* his hands on me. One arm under my knees, his fingers pressing into the side of my thigh.

Bare skin, my mind whispers.

And the other supporting my back, his hand on my ribs.

"Antonio said he was dangerous. That we should arrest him on sight." Bradshaw leans toward me. "And judging from your expression..."

Wolfe snatches the paper from him and slams it facedown.

I let out a slow breath.

"I don't have an expression," I finally say. *Lie.* "Because he's not dangerous. I just felt sick, passed out, and that guest happened to be willing to help. Antonio assumed the worst."

"Uh-huh." Skeptical would be an understatement. The sheriff turns his attention to Wolfe. "What do you know?"

He shrugs. "Just that Tem wouldn't lie to you. Antonio is protective of her, you know that."

"I know jack shit," Bradshaw replies.

I scowl. "You—"

"Quiet," he snaps. "You're giving me a different story than Antonio, but neither of you have given me a name. Or a reason for these dramatics." His gaze softens. "You passed out, Artemis?"

I push my shoulders back. "I'm *fine*. We came down here to stop whatever bullshit manhunt you're dreaming up to hunt for this guy."

Nathan Bradshaw holds both hands up, a mockery of a surrender. "Me? I'd do no such thing. Especially not when it's Antonio asking a favor... for you."

I wince.

"Artemis," he repeats. "You don't look okay."

"Jesus." I shake it off. "Everyone's just wound up so tight."

"A storm is brewing," Wolfe murmurs.

My attention shoots to him. He's still the picture of relaxed in the fucking chair, his ankles crossed. And he gives me a lazy smile.

"What makes you say that?" Bradshaw asks.

"It's been too quiet, Brad. It means there are schemes being slotted into place under the radar, and those are the fucking worst." He stands. "We've done our part squashing the power vacuum Kronos and Cerberus left behind. But a month ago, the squabbles went radio silent. No more issues. Our sources turned up empty."

A chill sweeps down my spine.

"Something is coming," he finishes.

He yanks open the office door, and I scramble to follow him. The last thing I want to be is trapped in a room alone with Nathan Bradshaw.

Wolfe and I walk side by side back to the parking lot, and I finally glance at him.

"You meant that," I murmur.

His blue eyes fix on me. "Two of our informants are missing."

"*Missing*-missing, or..."

"Presumed dead." Wolfe shifts. "Don't mention it to Kora. Or Antonio. Or, fuck it, anyone. This guy..." He pulls the paper out and holds it between us.

It's jarring to see it again.

Him again.

I hadn't realized he took it.

"Is he trouble, Tem?"

I take the paper from him. I could get my own, but this seems so much more convenient. I fold it up so I don't have to see it anymore and shove it in my back pocket. And it sucks that Wolfe is so fucking perceptive, because he seems to know exactly what I'm doing.

The answer to his question is *probably*, but I can't make myself say that out loud. So I land on, "I have no fucking clue."

I can't condemn Reese without having a conversation. But that means digging in and actually finding him.

Luckily for me, I know just the person to locate him.

4 ARTEMIS

STERLING FALLS, to the locals, is divided into four main quadrants. North Falls for the tourists, the beaches, and mansions. South Falls for the industrial district, the harbor, and marina. West Falls is mostly residential, with the reservoir supplying water to homes up in the hills just outside city limits. The Titans covered those neighborhoods, although most have gone underground since the gang was... beheaded.

East Falls used to be ruled by the Hell Hounds. There's a compound on the southeast side of the city, abutting the industrial district, where the Hell Hounds ruled their roost. They were primarily a motorcycle club, although over the years they evolved into something else.

Much to the sheriff's dismay, the gang didn't dissolve with their leader's death last year.

Instead, a new leader stepped into Cerberus's shoes. He's been shifting the club toward the right side of the law, although I think they still get up to their mischief. Wolfe, Cerberus's son, makes sure the new leader doesn't drift the club back to where it once was.

For the record, I avoid them when I can...

But now, as I bump down the gravel driveway toward the Hell Hounds' compound, I can't help but imagine it the way it used to be. The Hell Hounds were feared. Cerberus caused his fair share of damage while he was alive.

And yet, he managed to shape three teenage boys into something normal.

Wolfe, as Cerberus's only son, should've taken over. But he wanted nothing to do with it. Jace King was brought into the club as a young teen, and Apollo...

My brother was sold into it.

So that's where the trio was formed, and they've been together ever since.

Finally, I round the corner and come up on the club-house. It's a massive, sprawling building that's been remodeled in recent years. There's a long row of bikes out front, and one of the Hell Hounds sits on the porch, smoking a cigarette.

I park on the end and climb out of my car.

"Club meeting," the Hell Hound informs me. "You can't go in until they're finished."

I blow out a breath. The kid looks young. I'd be surprised if he had tipped over into his twenties yet. The scruff above his lip strikes me as the first hair he's been able to grow on his face. And because of it, he's unwilling to fucking shave.

He stares at me.

I stare back.

If there's one thing I can't stand, it's waiting.

"Tell Malik to find me when he's done." I hop off the porch, ignoring his protest, and go around the far side of the building.

There's a gravel pathway that leads to the residencies.

At one point, they all used to be in the same building. And the only way in was through that front door they have the puppy guarding.

This is better. Both in my interest—for breaking in—and just simple privacy reasons.

Take Saint, for example. He hears everything, which has made nighttime activities a thing of the distant past. Even solo activities.

Separate is better.

I find Malik's unit with ease. He's the leader, therefore he has the largest and nicest accommodations. His window isn't even locked, which makes my break-in job that much easier. I've scaled buildings before, but climbing through a window into his apartment is nothing.

Once in, my boots solidly on his laminate flooring and the window left only a crack open, I take a breath. It smells faintly of wood shavings in here, a remnant of the reconstruction. But overwhelmingly, it smells like Malik.

And that is an unexpected comfort.

The place is neat, but not un-lived-in. He's got a kitchen, which I'd bet everyone else doesn't have, and there's a plate and cup in the sink. A collection of framed photos hung on the wall in the hallway leading to the bedroom. The three-cushion couch faces a television, and a crumpled blanket has been haphazardly thrown over one of the arms.

I let my fingers trail along the back of the couch, debating if it's safe to take a seat.

Who knows what Malik brings home nowadays.

When I was younger, I was obsessed. He killed that crush relatively fast, but the shame of it still simmers low in my gut. I *threw* myself at him, and all he had to say was that I couldn't. Shouldn't. Blah, blah, blah.

To a sixteen-year-old girl, it was devastating.

The front door opens, and Malik strides in. His gaze finds me immediately, and his severe expression softens.

"Shit," he mutters. "Kid didn't tell me it was you."

"Your pup should learn the important faces."

"Kind of hard when you're never around," he counters.

"Come to the club, old man. Bring your gang. Spend some of your money."

He eyes me, then slowly shakes his head. "You don't need them scaring away your North Falls rich tourists."

I crack a smile. "I think a little danger would intrigue them."

His hair is long enough to need to be tied back. He keeps it contained at the nape of his neck, although right now he tears the leather strip out and rakes his fingers through his hair. A sign of agitation? Wolfe does the same thing sometimes, although his hair is managed. Probably Kora's doing.

But as far as tells go...

"Is this about you passing out?" he finally asks. "Do you need to sit down?"

"For fuck's sake," I groan. "How did you hear? Antonio—?"

"Mel," he says, smirking.

I don't like his smirk.

I also don't particularly like that my host is associated with the Hell Hounds. Something I *should've* known but missed. I'll figure that out later—who she's fucked, how deep in she is, if she's been hanging around the Hell Hounds recently or if I made a bigger mess with her by not uncovering it sooner.

"She ran here after her shift," he supplies. "Couldn't stop talking about it."

"And what did she say?" My voice is tight.

She's freaking fired.

"Just that the big, bad Artemis swooned so hard she passed out." His gaze sharpens. "And her hero carried her back to her apartment in the club."

I scoff. "I swooned, huh?"

"Are you capable of such a thing?"

No. I'm criminally broken when it comes to romance.

I turn away from him and investigate his fridge. If he was polite, he would've offered me a drink. But he's just standing in the middle of his apartment like he's the guest, and he watches me make myself at home.

The fridge is mostly stocked with beer.

Typical.

I grab two cans and toss one to him, then jump up to sit on the counter.

He comes forward and cracks his, leaning across from me. We drink for a long moment in relative quiet, and I try to forget that the whole reason I'm here is because I need help.

I do not like asking for help.

I set the beer aside and shift my weight to one hip, pulling the paper from my back pocket. It's still folded, and I hold it out to him.

He takes it from me.

"I need to find him."

He scans the page. "You look unconscious, Artemis."

"I was doing a realistic swoon, remember?"

He scowls. "Right. Who is he?"

Ugh. I bite my lip. "Do I have to tell you?"

"You want me to find him? I need his fucking name."

He refolds the paper and tucks it in *his* pocket, glaring

openly at me. "I think you know it. And, if sources are correct, Antonio *and* the sheriff know it, too."

Fuck.

They scan IDs at the door. Of course Antonio uncovered it—*and* told Bradshaw. The asshole sheriff didn't bother revealing that much. Bradshaw lied to me.

Our security office would've been the first place Antonio went, both to get that photo and his name. He wouldn't go to the sheriff with half-cooked information.

"Reese Avery," I finally say. "And you're on a fucking clock, Malik."

He smirks again. "What will you give me when I find him?"

"A favor."

"You're not your brother."

Because Apollo, with his friends, gift favors to those who win at Olympus. Anything within their long-reaching power.

"No," I allow. I hop off the counter and saunter closer, until he's stiffening up in front of me. "I'm not Apollo. I'm better. So find Reese before the sheriff and Antonio. *And* my brother."

"You're asking a lot." His voice is low. "One favor might not cut it."

"Either you find him," I murmur. "Or I do, and you get nothing."

I step back.

"My phone's on." And then I head out the way I came, slipping through the window. My boots hit the gravel, and I stride away from Malik Barlow with a smile etched in place.

Even if I feel a bit like throwing up.

5 ARTEMIS

REESE AVERY IS A GHOST. I spend the rest of the day trying to track him down and come up painfully empty. I don't hear from Malik or the sheriff. Or Wolfe, Jace, or Apollo. *Or Antonio.* But then the sun sets, and I am due at the fights, so I head back to my empty condo to get dressed.

I arrive at Olympus on time—as in, with everyone else. The hired hands are wearing their raven masks. They haven't worn those in a while, as Apollo likes to have them rotate in new ones. But I like them best of all, with their sharp beaks and blue-black, glistening feathers.

The man at the door waves me in without hesitation. And without payment. I adjust my mask. It's made of bone, although there isn't really an animalistic shape to it. Not like Apollo's intricate deer skull mask.

My gold dress swishes around my thighs, and I slip easily through the crowded atrium. There's no end to the luxury of Olympus on a fight night, although at once I long for the emptiness of it during the day.

I find a spot at the back and lean against the vegetation-covered wall. It's practically alive with blooms and vines and moss. It's meant to represent Persephone. It was a gift for her when they took Olympus back from the Hell Hounds.

Raven-masked employees weave through the room, dressed all in black, holding trays of champagne. I resist the urge to snatch one off and chug it.

Eventually, the huge doors boom shut. The chatter rises sharply, anticipation clawing at the room, until Apollo appears. Like usual, he wears only brown leather pants. The gold deer skull mask obscures his whole face. There are beaded leather cords that hang down, brushing the tops of his shoulders, and golden antlers protrude from the top of the mask.

He carries a staff that he uses on the marble floor like a gavel.

Boom, boom, boom.

"Welcome to Olympus," he calls to the hushed crowd.

I can't help the prickle of excitement that travels through me.

"I'm your host for the evening, Apollo." The mask can't obscure the edges of his wide smile. "We have some great fights planned for you tonight. Winners will walk away with not only their dignity... but glory."

The crowd cheers.

"Who will have to be scraped off the floor? Who will persevere?" He raises his arms. "Only time will tell. Enjoy yourselves, gods and goddesses. The doors are now open."

Because I'm looking for it, I see his foot twitch on the marble. There's a sharp *pop*, and smoke bursts up from the floor. People gasp and cry out, and when the smoke clears, he's gone.

Some go upstairs, to where there are better views down to the fighting ring. Others flood around the wide center staircase, preferring to be up close to the action.

I wait.

I don't know why I linger in the atrium, hanging back until the room is empty.

Almost empty.

Someone's on the steps, near where Apollo stood. A man in a black dress shirt and pants. From the back, his dark hair is close-cropped on the sides and a longer on top. He's scuffing his foot across the step.

To figure out how Apollo disappeared?

"Some tricks should be left a mystery," I call.

He straightens and pivots. His mask is inky black. It's surprising how much depth it has, and from here, I can't tell if it's fabric or something else. And for a moment, I'm stumped on who he represents.

"I like figuring out how the world works," the man says. His mask comes all the way down to his jaw on his right side. On the left, his high cheekbone and sharp jawline are visible. His lips quirk. "Don't you?"

"I know how it works," I say. I climb the steps slowly, until I'm even with him. And it's startling how much taller he is than me. "Olympus tells me its secrets."

Not as much as it speaks to its hosts.

"Hmm." His eyes are nearly as black as his mask. "Artemis?"

I almost flinch.

"There are tiny arrows in your mask. Like the bone's been chiseled."

Oh.

"I... yes."

"The gold is a giveaway, as well. You matched your brother."

I tell myself that he's speaking of the gods.

"You're going to miss the first fight," I say.

The half-smile never leaves his lips. "They can't start without me."

I tilt my head. "Is that so?"

"That's what they tell me."

"Who are you fighting?"

He eyes me and doesn't answer. My throat tightens, and when he remains silent, I turn on my heel and leave him to figure out his mystery.

Fighters generally stay in their area until it's time—it's rare for one to go wandering.

I work my way through the crowd on the first floor, ducking and weaving and somehow avoiding getting elbowed or drinks spilled, and finally make it to the front.

Nyx and I used to stand here to watch. Not exactly front and *center*, but close enough. If neither of us were fighting.

She was a better fighter than me.

The thought knocks the wind out of me. My muscles lock up, refusing to bend in front of so many people. Apollo's on the platform, and I feel his gaze linger on me for a moment. Vaguely, I realize he's introduced Wolfe and Jace —Ares and Hades. And Persephone. They're up on the second level, on a balcony all their own.

My heart gives a weird extra-hard thump.

And then the first pair of fighters are emerging.

I recognize the man. He goes by Minos here, and he's a regular like me. He gets up next to Apollo and flexes, and the audience eats that shit up. And then another guy I haven't seen before steps onto the platform.

"Hypnos," Apollo introduces. "Perhaps he'll put Minos to sleep?"

That gets a laugh.

Apollo asks them to bump fists, and then he hops off the platform. He lands beside me and glances down. "You don't look great."

I scoff. "Why does everyone keep saying that?"

He hums.

It's only a matter of time until he asks if I've been sleeping, eating enough, *whatever*. He's always cared, and I love that about my brother. But sometimes it can be suffocating.

Minos gets the first hit.

Hypnos's head whips to the side, and he staggers. Minos goes for him again, not one to give an opponent a moment to breathe. But it seems almost like Hypnos is ready for it, because in a split second, they're grappling and twisting, and then Minos is crashing like a felled tree to the platform.

Hypnos stands still and waits.

It seems to take ages for the other fighter to drag himself up, clearly shaken at having lost the upper hand. In comparison to Minos, Hypnos is small. Probably still taller than me by a few inches, but lean. Nearly slender but for the cords of muscles packed on his thin frame.

Deceptive if Minos is only comparing sheer size.

"You can talk to me," Apollo says under his breath.

I elbow him.

Five minutes later, Minos falls for the last time.

Apollo taps the bottom of his staff against my leg and hops up. He declares Hypnos the winner, lifting his arm over their heads.

Hypnos looks at me. Through the black fabric mask that cuts across the upper portion of his face, his eyes...

I suck in a sharp breath. His gaze moves on, coasting across the crowd, then higher. To the second floor. He pauses on Ares and Hades. The three will convene with the winners after the last fight, but for now, there's only the thunderous applause.

And then it's over, and he's being ushered out by a raven-masked man while two more struggle to pick Minos up off the floor.

"Well," Apollo calls in the following hush. "That was a thrilling opening. Did anyone see that coming?" He laughs. "Next up are two new fighters. Although if you're a regular, you might recognize one as an occasional host..."

Saint.

I ball my fists.

"Please welcome out our first fighter, Hermes!"

The doors open, and a path is created. Saint strolls down with his arms loose at his sides, and he hops up onto the platform. His fabric mask is white, shot through with gold threads. I find myself leaning forward, analyzing how he moves.

He's shirtless. Of course he's shirtless, most of the guys who fight are. He's somewhere between Hypnos and Minos in terms of stature. Packed with muscle but not overdone with it. He touches the galaxy tattoo over his heart and glances to the ceiling.

My jaw clenches.

"And a visitor to Sterling Falls," Apollo's voice booms. "Atlas!"

The titan who held the world on his shoulders in some myths. He was charged with keeping the heavens from crashing to earth in others, a punishment after losing a war against Zeus.

I just don't expect the man I met in the atrium to come out of the fighters' quarters.

I should. He practically admitted to fighting—

When he finds me in the crowd, he smirks. I frown in response, ignoring the flush that creeps up the back of my neck.

Atlas. A heavily burdened titan for the mystery guest.

He is shirtless, as well. The black mask he wore outside has been replaced with a softer one that molds to his face. His body ripples with muscles, although there's not a speck of ink on him. When he gets up close to Apollo and Saint, he's taller than both.

My body goes cold when Apollo hops down from the platform. He comes to stand beside me, and I grip his wrist. I'm practically vibrating with the urge to shut this down. Not tonight, not even the fighting—just *this* fight.

"This is wrong," I whisper urgently. "Stop them."

Apollo scowls. "Artemis."

"*Apollo.*"

He shakes me off, never taking his eyes away from the circling men. "Saint is a grown up. He can make his own decisions."

"Clearly not, if he can't be trusted to live by himself."

Apollo sighs. "He's not going to die here."

Something in me isn't too sure. I don't want to name this fear that's crawling higher and higher up my throat. And it isn't just Saint. It's all of it. The past twenty-four hours, or maybe longer.

Maybe since Nyx...

I force myself to stand and watch.

Saint—*Hermes*—makes the first move. His jaw is set, his expression burning hot. Atlas, on the other hand, is frigid. They meet each other blow for blow, not bothering to duck or defend themselves.

There's something feral about it, more so than any of the other pairings. Often, a person finds themselves reduced to some sort of primal, survival instinct. The kill-or-be-killed feeling can take over. But this is worse. There's no slow easing into it.

The way they attack each other would make me think it's personal. Saint's eyes gleam, and every hit seems to create waves of fury inside him. While Atlas takes and receives just as brutally, there's only cold... Relief? *Joy?*

And when Atlas puts Saint flat on his back, I close my eyes.

6 ARTEMIS

THE THREE HOSTS OF OLYMPUS—HADES, Ares, Apollo—have not removed their masks. I keep mine on, too, lingering in the shadows. This back room, separate from the fighters' area, is for the winners.

And one at a time, those winners are called forward to receive their prizes.

As is tradition, they offer favors. All the fighters get paid, but the winners...

What was Saint planning to ask for?

Freedom from you, a little voice whispers.

I accept the blow and straighten. Saint will just have to keep trying if that's his aim.

There were four fights, and they've been receiving the winning fighters in reverse order. Atlas and Hypnos are left, waiting in the hallway with a raven-masked man. Another employee opens the door and ushers out the previous, who asked for help with his sick mother. Getting her in to see a specialist.

Done, Apollo stated.

Atlas strides in and stops before them. He's changed his clothes. His black dress shirt and pants

"Congratulations, visitor," Ares says. *Wolfe.* It's sardonic, a tone I don't quite expect from him. Perhaps he's feeling Saint's loss as much as I am?

"For your win, you receive a favor," Hades explains. "If it's in our power to grant it, it's yours."

Atlas inclines his chin. "I want to know more about the woman behind us."

There's a breath of silence, no one moving or breathing, and then they all turn to me.

Me?

I glance around. Of course he's talking about me—I'm the only one here.

There was a time when the winners' favors were heard aloud right after a fight. When their wants and desires were laid out for the spectators to judge, as well.

Thank goodness that's a thing of the past.

"You want to know more about her? You could just ask her out," Hades murmurs. "Why waste a favor?"

Atlas's inky-black mask is still freaking me out, in the way that I want to touch it. It hides so much of his face, it's impossible to decipher who he is. All I know is who he's not.

"You better not mean in a sexual manner," Apollo says stiffly. "She is—"

"Your twin," Atlas finishes. "Some things do translate. And I want for nothing else. I'm a mere spectator to the workings of Sterling Falls. You graciously allowed me to indulge here tonight. The only thing I wish to ask is that she stay with me for a full day."

Shock.

Shock?

Yes, shock.

"It's not our favor to grant," Ares finally decides. "Artemis?"

I catch his pointed look. He wears red contacts at Olympus, and it seems to lend to his violent character. And he's translating that if it *isn't* okay with me, they'll go to pains to give him something else.

Or toss him over the cliffs.

But either way, the choice is mine.

Atlas faces me.

"Why?" I question.

"You intrigue me."

I don't like that answer.

"If it helps, I will stipulate that you won't be harmed. I will not touch you. Not unless you ask me," he adds with a wicked grin. "And we will stay within the bounds of Sterling Falls."

"In two days," I find myself saying, although I don't know why the *hell* I'd agree. "Come back here at dawn."

He nods. "It's a date."

"It ends at sunset," I add. "A full *day*, as you said."

"That is acceptable." Atlas's gaze lingers on me.

My brother's jaw is clenched so tight, he might crack a tooth.

But it's Hades who inclines his chin.

Atlas strides away without a word, and I lean back against the wall with a rushing exhale. But there's no true time to contemplate it, because Hypnos is the final winner to be received. My muscles ache so deeply, even my bones protest. I want to slip away, but then he's in front of them.

I stay close to the shadows.

"Hypnos," Ares says. "What favor do you seek? If it's in our power, we will grant it."

The fighter changed into an unassuming black sweatshirt and jeans, his hands in his pockets. Like this, he looks… almost normal. Like he didn't take down one of Olympus's best regular fighters.

It's losses like this that bring Minos back.

But besides the somewhat normal clothes, he wears a full-face mask. It's black, although not as deep as Atlas's. It covers everything except his eyes and holes to breathe from his nose. There's a garish slash across the mouth area, too, and metal stitches seem to hold it closed.

Decoration.

Symbolic?

"I've been contemplating what favor to ask the mighty gods of Olympus," Hypnos says.

I slowly stand straighter. His voice… his voice scratches something in my brain, even muffled behind the mask.

"And what have you decided?" Apollo asks.

My gaze bounces between Hypnos and Hades. The latter seems to be sharpening, his attention like the tip of a blade. He senses something, too.

Hypnos lifts his chin. "It's in your power to grant it, but I fear you will turn me down anyway."

Why does his voice sound so familiar? And distant at the same time. I forget Hades and stare at the side of Hypnos's head, the black mask hiding his distinguishing features. Even his lips and jaw are hidden.

"Ask," Hades demands.

Hypnos points at them. "I want ruin."

Silence. My breath is trapped in my lungs.

"War is coming to Sterling Falls," Hypnos whispers. "And I want everyone to *fall*."

Hades makes some movement with his fingers, or maybe his foot. I've never seen this version of an alarm. But suddenly Hypnos is surrounded by raven-masked men who catch his arms and drag him away. Not out the main door, but past them to the side.

Closer to me.

Hypnos's bright gaze lands on me, and he laughs. "There you are, Artemis. Sticking to the shadows like always."

He's not even struggling against the men, seemingly resigned to the fact that he's being escorted none too gently to the exit. His feet drag on the marble floor, and his eyes burn into me.

"Your demise will be the sweetest," he promises. "Always the hunter. But now, you will be the hunted."

"Get him *out*," Apollo orders.

Hypnos laughs. It's a laugh that seems to echo in my ears even after the doors slam behind him.

I rip my mask off and let out a shaky exhale. I turn away from my brother and his friends, touching my cheeks. They're hot. My whole body is engulfed in flames.

"What the fuck was that?" Ares asks.

I glance over my shoulder. They've removed their masks, too, exchanging dark looks.

I need to get out of here.

Haphazardly tying my mask back on, I shove out into the hallway and through the main corridor that leads along the fighting room to the front atrium. The right side of the hall is open arches, revealing the now-empty platform.

Wonder where Saint slunk off to.

If he's smart, he'll be holed up here until my anger runs out. Although I *think* it'll stay fresh as a freaking daisy until my date with Atlas has passed.

I should've refused and had him thrown over the cliffs.

I'm not sure where Hypnos went either. If they escorted him all the way to the edge of the property or threw him off the cliffs or simply let him walk away. That alone gives me an extra boost of adrenaline slipping out of Olympus and hurrying to my car.

Nothing bad happens. The wind tugs at my dress and mask, the ocean is a *shush-shush* noise far below the rocky cliffside, and I am alone. Which is perfectly fine by me. I glance back toward the door and spot Apollo.

He lifts one hand in a wave.

I grimace and wave back.

I guess I'm not *truly* alone. My brother would never let anything bad happen to me, not if he could help it. Which makes me think this date with Atlas will not be alone.

What makes it worse is that I don't really have anyone to talk to about this. In another lifetime, I'd call Nyx. Or, better, she would've been beside me to witness it. Instead, she's six feet fucking under.

The drive home is routine. I park in the garage, in my usual spot, and take the elevator to my floor. My unit is locked, same as always, and the scrape of my key against the pins is better than any cheesy welcome mat.

And yet.

The moment I open the door, I register that Saint was not smart. He came back to the condo, and he's seated on his regular stool at the breakfast bar. His dress shirt is unbuttoned.

His mask is on the counter, and he has a pack of peas—the same that hid the liquor just yesterday—pressed to his face. That bottle is also present, along with a single glass.

"Didn't anyone ever tell you it's in poor taste to drink alone?"

Saint glances at me.

Jesus. His face is really fucked up.

I creep in closer for a better look, but he just turns away.

His cheekbone might be broken. It's definitely bruised and swelling—as well as the rest of him. His skin is a patchwork of bruises and cuts and drying blood.

I circle around him, shaking my head.

Idiot, I want to say.

"You can't judge me." He squints. "You know what's coming up."

I drag the bottle across the counter and take a sip. "A lot of things are coming up, Saint."

My birthday being one of them. My past is another.

With a start, I realize I scheduled my "date" with Atlas —henceforth only referred to in quotes, the sham that it is— on my twenty-fifth birthday.

Stupid. And here I was, planning on hiding at Bow & Arrow or spending the day in bed.

At least I'll be able to avoid the celebration that's undoubtedly coming... The chocolate cake that Antonio will be baking. Apollo's family will no doubt loop me into their celebrations, too.

Overall, not feeling great about this year. Ten-year anniversary of being sold into a sex trafficking ring will do that to a girl.

"Elora's death," Saint spits.

I stop and stare at him. Elora is Nyx's real name. He doesn't call her Nyx anymore, not in private. As painful as it is, I go right back to that day. I wasn't there—another thing he blames me for, I'm sure—but I remember it. I can't scrub it out of my head.

He's watching me just as intently, and I *hate* it. That his gaze catches everything, and the knowing sneer creeps across his face. He's realizing that I either forgot or blacked out the date, and now it's another thing he can lord over me. It's not my fault I've been focused on other things.

I inch closer. "Speaking of Nyx."

Saint's brows lower.

"How do you think she'd feel about you living on the brink of death for a *year?*"

I'm close enough to touch him, so I fucking do. I press my finger into one of the bruises at his temple, pulling from him a long-overdue wince.

He catches my wrist. His hand, like his gaze, is a furnace.

"Don't," he says.

"Don't what, Saint? Don't hold a mirror up so you can see how ridiculous you look?"

He rises. He's still got hold of my wrist, and he turns us so I'm between the counter and him. "Ridiculous? How about you, Artemis? When you fight and come back covered in bruises, you don't find me touching all your sore spots."

"Well, Saint, maybe I *want* you to."

My throat closes.

I didn't mean to say that.

I didn't mean to admit that I've been sorely deprived of touch in the last year—through his fault or mine, I'm not sure. It's not like I was dating anyone. Flirting with men isn't the same as being cared for by them.

"Maybe I want someone to fucking care," I admit softer, twisting my wrist until his grip loosens. "*Maybe* I've just been languishing in this fucking town. I've had to watch you spiral like a sad little balloon, and I'm the sucker trying to keep you afloat. It's consuming my life."

"Shut up."

"She's not coming back." *Going all in on the hate today, Tem.* "Nyx is dead and buried, and you're acting like she gives a shit about anything that happens here."

"Artemis," he warns.

I scoot to the side, and his hand on my hip stops me.

"She's dead," I repeat. "She's not coming back. She's not going to storm in through the door—"

"God, shut *up*." He covers my mouth with his other hand.

Another point of contact. His palm is warm and dry against my lips. Calloused in spots. His focus, though, is on my hip. The hand there that slowly bunches up the fabric of my dress. Until it's all the way up, and his fingers dig into my bare skin.

"Do you like walking around in these dresses?" He hums. "They show off so much of your goddamned legs, it drives me insane. *You* drive me insane. You're so different from her, a glowing beacon in the dark, and I just want to smother you."

My heart hammers, but I'm caught in a moment of trying to figure out what he means. And what I want.

His touch is drawing out a fire in me, and I can't tell if it's a good or bad thing. Maybe that's why, when he turns me around, I move willingly. I catch the edge of the counter, although he pushes my head down anyway. My cheek touches the cool surface.

I've been in this position before, a thousand times in different places, with different men groping at me and taking without asking, but this is unusual. My body is practically vibrating with the way I need someone to touch me.

The bottle of scotch is inches from my nose.

And when Saint shoves my dress up and my panties down, I don't tell him no. If this is how he wants to cope, fine. The battle of my own will is raging in my head. That this is wrong *and* inevitable at the same time.

That this moment has been coming for months.

Didn't I say I was the only one he couldn't hate-fuck his emotions out on?

I'm a big, fat liar.

The zip of his pants opening is loud in my ears. And then something touches me—a finger between my legs?—drawing through the heat that's been pooled there since we first started arguing.

Sue me. My relationship with sex is fucked up and twisted, and for once I'm not running away from it.

"You disgust me," Saint whispers.

I make a noise. I don't mean to, but one minute my throat is locked and the next a low whine comes out. I jerk, embarrassment flaming my cheeks, but there's nowhere to go. So instead, I lean into the uncomfortable bits. The way the counter digs into my hips, my toes stretching down to remain in contact with the floor.

His finger slides into me. Just one exploratory digit, and then it's gone. He kicks my legs wider, and then something *bigger* is pressed to my slit.

It hurts when he pushes in. I close my eyes and breathe through the pain, but it just keeps washing over me with every millimeter. Until he's fully seated inside me, and I don't really know if I can breathe.

All I know is that I deserve this kind of pain. I relish it, *welcome* it.

But I hope it hurts him, too. That this is the kind of agony he needs instead of fighting at Olympus—that this satisfies something more.

He barely waits for me to adjust. His hips jack, and his dick slides almost all the way out. Then he shoves back in. I grip the counter and let him punish me for this latest transgression. The fight at Olympus wasn't enough.

Bending me over the kitchen counter might not be enough.

"Harder," I snap.

"Slut," he replies. "You're a fucking whore for my cock."

"Yeah." My voice wobbles as he hits my G-spot. "What else?"

Rough memories grasp at me, dirty-fingered things that threaten to throw me back into Terror, but I force myself to remember who put me in this position. It's his voice, his cold voice, that drags me back to the present.

"I hate you," he mutters.

"You're sure acting like it."

He growls and pulls out. There's an immediate ache of emptiness between my legs, but he spins me around and lifts me onto the counter. My bare ass barely makes contact before he's right back in position, thrusting into me.

This time looking me in the face. I keep my gaze on his parted lips. Eye contact seems forbidden and dangerous. The tattoos on his neck, the dragon tail curling over his shoulder, move with every flex of his muscle. My attention wanders down his throat, to his chest. The seared brand dead center, the scar disfiguring the tattoos underneath. The galaxy over his heart that represents his lost love.

Lower.

He grips my hair and tugs my head back suddenly, so I can't even see if his cock is tattooed. I look down my nose and stare at his face.

The pain in my scalp and between my legs is wicked. I wrap my legs around his hips, digging my heels into his ass.

"You're the absolute worst," I say to him. Or the ceiling. The pressure on my scalp is, surprisingly, keeping me grounded.

This isn't the first time I've had sex since... *before.*

When sex was a negative connotation. In the decade since, I've learned a lot about myself. Shed the view that it's all bad, that I'm a dirty creature... although here Saint is, telling me everything bad about myself.

And I don't mind it.

He's not gentle, he's not tiptoeing around my trauma.

I think I like it...

He grunts.

"You're a parasite," I breathe, although it's more of a moan. "You come into my home and keep terrorizing me."

He runs a finger over my clit, and I nearly jump out of my skin. I focus on the stupid recessed light above me and try not to actively groan. He's working wonders on me, eliciting *pleasure* when I'm pretty sure all I deserve is pain. Especially from him.

The dichotomy is going to ruin me.

"Am I terrorizing you now?"

He's more of a mess than I am, darkened skin around his eyes, his face swelling. And he never stops moving, like fucking me is just something his body needs.

"Ask me in five minutes," I manage.

He presses on my clit again, rubbing the little bud until my mouth gapes open and pleasure zings through me like a lightning bolt.

"You think this is going to take that long?"

There's a flush making its way up his neck.

He plays me with expertise. I blame my lack of sexual activity lately, but I come on his fingers and cock too fast, and every moment of it feels like watching a train wreck. I imagine if someone were to shove me off a cliff, instead of just jumping, that's what this would be like. It's the surprise of it more than anything. My back arches, and I squeeze my eyes shut against the feeling.

He grunts again, although it's very pointedly fucking snobby.

Just when I think he's going to come inside me, he pulls out and fists his length. It *is* tattooed. I catch a glimpse of it through his fingers, the head red and wet with my arousal. *Fuck me, that's hot.*

Three jerks later, and his cock erupts.

It hits my still-throbbing core, the insides of my thighs. We're both breathing hard.

In the silence, my mind comes back to me. I didn't just have sex—which is not the problem. It's that I finally broke and fucked *Saint Hart.*

My skin crawls.

When he comes back to the present, he meets my gaze.

He's equally horrified.

7 ARTEMIS

I SHOW up at Olympus on my bike, so as not to give this Atlas character any impression of being a freaking chauffeur.

On most days, I like my car. It's not particularly flashy, although it's new to me. It has all the bells and whistles. The guys gave it to me a few months ago when they spotted me walking around town. It didn't take them long to figure out I had sold my other one. That vehicle reminded me of Nyx, and blood, and the freaking war that took over the town.

Up until my brother and his friends swooped in, I didn't particularly care about my lack of transportation. My own two feet carry me just fine.

The bike, though. That was a gift to myself.

I dressed in a black body suit fit for riding a motorcycle. It's mostly leather, with matte black metal buckles around my thighs, abdomen, and chest. The leather pants tuck into sturdy boots, a black leather jacket zipped up to my throat and straps secured horizontally across my abdomen. It hides a rather plain black blouse underneath... and a concealed gun at the small of my back.

The outfit is meant to downplay my features. I'm more curvy than I'd like to be, especially in the last year. I gained a few pounds during this peace time in Sterling Falls. Like the stress of war fell away and I could relax. As much as I could living with Saint anyway.

My breasts came out of nowhere when I was fourteen, hips and an ass that made an appearance in the same year. I went from passing as my brother to *not*. Unless I'm dressing up for Bow & Arrow or Olympus, I like to pretend the curves don't exist. I slimmed down quite a bit after the first initial growth spurt, although it's worse lately.

My hair is in a thick braid over my shoulder, my makeup practically nonexistent. We're going down the I'm-not-trying-to-impress-you route.

It doesn't help that I woke up this morning dreading today. My eyes opened before my alarm, and I immediately got dressed like a zombie. Today is my birthday.

I try not to think about my fifteenth birthday. Waking up with a mixture of happiness and wariness. Apollo was already gone at that point, and I had plans of sneaking out of the house to go celebrate with friends.

That never happened, and instead... *Terror*.

Forcing myself to consider today like any other, I got on my bike and zipped along the mostly empty roads to Olympus.

Once parked, I consider going inside. It stands still and dark, the sun not yet peeking over the horizon. But if I go in, I'll miss the best part of the morning. The sky robbed me the other day, and I hope it gives me *something* better today.

I take the path up the sloping hill to the cliffs, my footsteps sure even in the low light. At the edge, so close my toes almost hang off, I take a deep breath.

The salt air, the low rush and crash of waves below, flood me with strength.

I sit and swing my legs over the edge. The heels of my boots kick loose little bits of dirt and gravel, and they fall a long way into the churning, dark water below.

In front of me, the sky is lightening in slow increments. It's clear of clouds today, which will hopefully grant me a good omen in the form of a perfect sunrise.

Saint is back to avoiding me. And he and I... After our, uh, sexual misadventure, he rather calmly went into his room and emerged a minute later with a bag slung over his shoulder. And then he walked out with a weird expression.

It allowed me to freak out alone, but he'll be back.

He always comes back, whether it's by his choice or Jace's.

Besides, my sources say he's holed up at Starlight, his tattoo shop. A few months ago, I accidentally discovered a cot set up in the corner of his back office. When Jace finds out—which he will, because the bastard knows everything—he'll put an end to it.

But until then, it's not my problem. He's dealing with the approaching anniversary of Nyx's death, and I'm dealing with my birthday and Atlas and that terrible *off* feeling that I can't shake or pinpoint.

So, yeah.

He left me with a mess—mental, physical.

I can't say I didn't lie in bed and bring myself over the edge a few more times at the thought of his dirty talk. Although maybe *dirty talk* is a stretch. More like degradation.

Am I into that sort of thing?

I don't *want* to be into that sort of thing. I want to be cherished like a fucking princess, because that's what I deserve after the life I've led. But Saint knows exactly how to get under my skin, and I hate him for it. I hate him for who he is, and how much he loved Nyx, and *all of it*.

Great freaking start to my birthday.

I sweep my hand along the gravel beside me, sending another shower down to the water.

"Aren't you afraid of falling?"

My shoulders hike up.

Normally I'm good at keeping my awareness up, constantly cataloging my surroundings. It's one of those survival instincts that I've apparently retired today.

Atlas slowly lowers himself down beside me, then leans forward and peers down. "Do you drink tea?"

I glance over at him. Today, his dark hair is a bit shorter. There's a curl that flops down across his forehead, very rockstar-ish, and his dark eyes stay fixed on the water below. His whole persona seems rockstar-ish. Kind of slouching in a confident, I-don't-care vibe.

Hot, too.

I should've pegged it from Olympus, the fight. He's not what I'd call classically handsome, but the slope of his jaw, his high cheekbones, make him stand out. He's more startlingly, devastatingly pretty... and it's completely at odds with his muscular frame. I'd put his age at late twenties. No ring on his finger, though.

That doesn't really matter when it comes to intentions. I learned that early.

"I do like tea," I say.

The corner of his lips lift, and he holds out a travel thermos. He unscrews the cap and pours some, passing me the makeshift cup. His jacket is army-green, open to expose a black t-shirt. Jeans. Work boots. It's a normal outfit that gives me zero clue about what we're going to be doing today.

I bring the mug to my nose and inhale. It smells spiced, and steam curls off the top of the liquid.

"It's not drugged, right?"

His jaw tics. "I don't drug women. And it would be a poor way to spend our day."

"Ah, yes, about that." I set the mug aside. "We're officially on the clock."

He chuckles. When he doesn't move, though, I pick the mug back up.

I sip the tea, mildly impressed by the amount of flavor packed into it. I wait for him to ask something of me. For him to goad me to rise and take me... wherever he has planned. But instead, he leans back on his hands and watches the sunrise with me.

And it is certainly a brilliant one.

Happy birthday, Artemis.

My phone buzzes. I fish it out and scan the text from my brother.

APOLLO

Beautiful sunrise today. Chin up, sister.

I stuff it back in my pocket without replying. He's got his family to help him usher in the day. They've made no attempt to corral me into their plans, which is fine by me. Antonio will want me later. But for now, I've got...

I glance sideways. "What is your name?"

He frowns. "Perhaps we should stick with Atlas."

"You know *my* real name."

"Artemis is your birth name?" Surprise colors his tone.

"My mother was very invested in Greek mythology." I shrug. "She had odd quirks."

"Had."

"Indeed." I tip forward and once again contemplate jumping. It wouldn't be so bad. At this time of year, perhaps the water would even be warm. Warmer than the chilled bite in the air this morning.

She's still alive, but he doesn't need to know that. He doesn't need to know that I haven't talked to her since the morning of my fifteenth birthday. The last image of her burned into my brain is her sadness as my dad drove me away.

"Kade."

"Friends call me Tem," I offer. "Not that we're friends."

When the sun finally peeks above the waterline, Kade stands. He seems to be waiting for something, and finally holds out his hand. "Come. We should begin."

"Begin?" I look up at him. "You've barely told me anything. Just offered me tea and sat here in silence."

He pinches the bridge of his nose. "I'll tell you in the car."

"Because I am your *favor*." I rise without his help and undo the buckles of my jacket. Then the zipper. I drop it to the grass and unbutton my pants next. I take more care with the gun, still strapped in its holster, then kick off my boots and peel away my socks. Pants next, shaking them out and making an effort to fold them on top of my boots.

He watches me, his dark eyes seeming to get even blacker. "That's not what I meant, Artemis."

I roll my eyes, but I don't stop. My blouse is next, until I'm standing in just my underwear. The wind whips at my hair, tugging strands loose from my braid and threatening to push me off that cliff. Not that I would mind—it's been my impulse since the very beginning, after all.

And somehow, I need to get the feel of Saint off me.

It's been two days, and I still *feel him*. His fingers left bruises on my hips where he gripped me, but it's worse than just that. There's guilt associated with his touch that I can't rid myself of, no matter how many showers I take.

Does it remind me of my past, or am I just losing my mind?

Is this a betrayal to my best friend?

I don't have an answer—and I've taken a shit ton of showers in the last two days.

Atlas, aka Kade, is giving me nothing.

I suddenly want to give him nothing in return. The trick with this particular cliffside is to push off at the jump. There's a cropping of rocks at the bottom that will absolutely snap bones if you hit it wrong. It's why throwing people over is so tempting. No launch from the start means they fall straight down.

I listen for the *shush* of water rushing back out to sea. When there's a slight pause in the oncoming waves, I jump.

I take two big steps, ignoring how the rocks stab into the soles of my feet. I swear Kade reaches for me. His fingers graze my arm. But he's not fast enough, and the wind carries his alarmed shout away.

I leap into the open air, holding my arms out for a brief moment. Then I cross them and straighten my body, hold my breath, and hit the water like an arrow.

The chill of it wakes me up, and I shoot down, down, down. My bare toes brush the mossy rock underneath, and the water feels more like a gentle squeeze down here than a washing machine's spin cycle. I look up and watch the roll of a wave overhead. It's white-capped and angry, but it can't touch me.

I release a slow stream of bubbles.

In a minute, I'll swim away from the rock face. There's a ladder I'll eventually need to get to. But not yet.

This is the first time I've felt like myself, and I don't want to let it go.

A second later, another body enters the water.

Kade hits feet-first, but he turns underwater and dives down. He seems to think I'm stuck or incompetent, maybe, because he grabs at me.

I shove him away.

Eye contact is really not easy underwater. And neither are pointed looks... or glares. It's like saying, *if looks could kill*, but the receiver took off their glasses.

He catches my hand, intending to drag me up, but I hold fast. My lungs have begun that delicious ache, the burn for oxygen. I can last another minute, maybe. Thirty seconds comfortably. But that's all we need.

Another wave moves over us, the last of a swell, and I relent. I push off and kick for the surface.

We breach at the same time, a good fifteen yards from the cliff. I suck in a lungful of air, the burn in my chest immediately easing.

"What the *fuck*?"

I slick the water out of my face. "You joined me."

To say I'm surprised is an understatement.

His gaze darkens. "Because you didn't come up."

Aww, he cares.

I roll my eyes, both at the passing thought and the idea that he wanted to save me. It all comes back to whatever he needs me for. He went to the effort of fighting at Olympus, of winning... and maybe he just made it up on the spot after talking to me before the fights.

I don't believe that, though.

He has a motive I have yet to uncover.

A wave comes toward us. A big one, already foaming white at the top and beginning to curl.

"Go under," I order.

I take a breath and dive down, and he follows a second later. I tug at his arm, making him swim lower, and I count to twenty in my head.

We pop back up, and I frown at the *crash* of the wave against the rocks.

The ocean is a bit more volatile today than usual—but that makes two of us.

"How do we get out of here?" He treads water carefully, his gaze flicking from the cliffside to the incoming waves.

He shed his jacket and shirt, too. Maybe even his shoes and socks—I can't see from here. His hair is plastered down. The smooth, curved lines of his shoulder muscles, down to corded biceps, draw my attention. Not that I should be watching him like that, but... you know.

Sex with Saint seems to have awoken that part of my brain. The lust side.

It was easier when that part of me was dormant.

To answer his question, I point to the metal runs drilled into the rock behind him. The ladder hugs the uneven terrain, making it an adventurous climb.

Back in its infancy, Olympus tested the fighters' desires to compete by asking them to do insane things. Like jumping off this cliff. Although after a few broke their legs in their attempts, the cliff kind of shifted to represent something more ominous.

Now only the seasoned cliff jumpers attempt it. There's another spot farther up the coast with a lower cliff and an easier route up. That particular spot is also protected by the curve of the land, blocking most of the ocean waves from coming in directly.

This is more fun.

He exhales.

"No one said you got to dictate how today was going to go," I point out. "Fine print, my friend."

I ride the back of the next swell, paddling hard to reach one of the rungs. My fingers catch on it, and it seems to take herculean effort to drag myself up. Kade follows right behind me, his breath literally hot on my heels until we get to the top.

I flop onto my back.

Kade drops to his knees beside me, laughing quietly. "You're something else."

Goosebumps prickle at my skin, although I can't tell if it's because of the salt water still clinging to my body or something else. I glance over, taking in his bruised abdomen —where Saint got a few hits in—and tight, obvious six-pack. Hell, eight-pack. There are no visible tattoos above the waistband of his now-soaked jeans.

His shirt and jacket and boots were discarded a lot hastier than mine, belying his urgency.

Can't say that doesn't make me feel a *little* better.

When the watched sensation doesn't ease, and I can't pinpoint it to Kade, I crane my head back. The lawn becomes the sky, and an upside-down figure stands near my bike.

Maybe it should surprise me, but it really, *really* doesn't. Because I know him from his silhouette alone.

I sit up and crane around, eyeing Saint Hart right-side-up. Who has no right to be glaring at me like he is.

"My sore loser?" Kade guesses.

He takes my wrist and pulls me to my feet. I can't seem to break my staring contest with Saint, while the man beside me gathers our clothes. I sigh and start toward him, leaving Kade to follow.

Saint meets me halfway. His gaze rakes up and down my body, a flush overtaking his neck and face. "What the fuck, Artemis?"

"I thought friends called you Tem," Kade interjects.

"We're not friends," we both say at the same time.

I wrinkle my nose. I don't like having anything to do with him, including saying the same words at the same time. Like we're on the same page? *Nope.* He's been acting like a jerk and avoiding me since I saw his dick.

So why did he come?

Or more aptly—who forced his hand? My brother, ever the worrier, or one of his best friends?

"I don't suppose you have a reason for being here," I say after a beat.

"Well." He lifts his chin. "As a matter of fact, I'm your chaperone for the day, *Tem.*"

Kade laughs. "Yeah, no."

"You don't get to decide that."

The big guy beside me hooks his thumb in my direction. "Do you see her face? What part of that says, '*Oh, please follow me around all day like a lost puppy?*'"

I snort.

I changed my mind. Between this and actually jumping, this guy is growing on me.

"Let's get dry," I say to him. "There are showers in Olympus. And then we can figure out how to ditch the Debbie Downer."

Saint scowls. "Seriously?"

"I seriously don't want you following me around, asshole," I snap. "Go run back to the guys and tell them we got away from you. Whatever."

"Just don't come crying to me when something bad happens to you."

I gape at him. Kade's watching me, I can feel his gaze like a white-hot poker. It would take too long to explain my issues with Saint. To cover the last year...

"Why don't you go jump off a cliff?" I retort, forcing a sweet smile. "Make sure to aim for the rocks."

With that, I turn on my heel and stride toward Olympus.

Because *fuck him*.

Well, not really. We're not doing that again.

8 ARTEMIS

OUR DARING ESCAPE from Saint isn't as thrilling as I hoped it would be. By the time we emerge from the fighters' area—there are separate shower rooms for the men and women, and I keep a box of my things in my brother's quarters—changed and dry, Saint is nowhere to be found.

Seems he took me at my word.

"Now," Kade says. "My turn."

I sigh. A tendril of unease winds through me, but I shove it down. The last thing Saint can be is *right*.

Kade's blacked-out SUV is parked beside my bike. And since I purposefully took the bike to not be a chauffeur... I suppress my vocal groan and follow him to the SUV. As we walk, I find myself analyzing him like I would a fighter. How he moves, how he holds himself.

But then I get distracted. His ass is dangerous in his jeans. In the light of day, he seems overall different than the man who fought Saint two days ago.

There are less demons clinging to his skin, for one.

Maybe the ocean water washed them away, not the fight, like it erased the feel of Saint's hands on my body.

I climb into the passenger seat and look over at him. His dark hair is still damp. I unbraided mine and dried it before rejoining him in the hallway, all my armor put back together. Although, isn't it strange? I felt more at ease underwater, mostly naked, than I do right now.

Fuck these favors.

If Saint had won, would he have asked to be rid of me? Or was he planning on asking for something worse?

Kade pulls out onto the main road, heading toward North Falls. There's a road that follows the cliffs up toward the more popular, touristy neighborhood of Sterling Falls.

We pass the spot where town folks regularly cliff jump. Although empty today, it's a popular spot because of how the coastline is. There's a little protected pocket where the water is considerably calmer. Plus, a staircase carved out of the rock instead of the insane ladder.

I face forward. We crawl past Bow & Arrow, dark and silent this early in the morning. Halfway down the boardwalk, the pristine white-sand beaches that the tourists flock to is empty minus a few runners. It's weird seeing it at this time of day. Usually, I'm leaving Bow & Arrow just before dawn, with everything cast in shadow.

"Where are we going?"

He doesn't reply.

We continue down the road, and my throat gets tighter as soon as we move off the main strip of businesses and into the high-end residential neighborhood. People who paid an extraordinary amount of money to have mansions built with an ocean view—but not the cliffs. They wanted sandy, private beaches.

Somehow, I know what house we're going to before we arrive at it. Because of course. It couldn't be easy, right? It couldn't be a rental farther east, toward the reservoir. It couldn't even be Kade bringing me to the forest to do wicked, cruel things to my body.

I might enjoy that more.

But when he turns into the exact driveway I predicted, all I can see is blood spilling across it, and her body—

I didn't see her body, though. I wasn't here when it happened—I was trying to avert another disaster and nearly got blown to pieces in the process. Not that it matters. Nothing matters when her death is thrown in my face over and fucking *over* again.

"What's wrong?"

The house is different. It was all dark, bulletproof glass and stone before, kind of ominous in the way it had been fully morphed into a fortress. Not to mention riddled with bullet holes and blood.

It was sold. Changed. But they'd have to bulldoze it and cleanse the land to erase the death that sticks to this place.

I ignore his question and ask one of my own. "Why are we here?"

He climbs out. I let out a long sigh—again—and follow. I skirt the pavement where Nyx's blood once stained it. In the year following, someone's gone to a great amount of trouble to either refinish it or replace the slab entirely. There's not a trace of her anymore.

It still makes my hackles rise when Kade and I go inside.

Whether this has been redone or left the same is a mystery. I didn't venture into the house, my curiosity sated by standing in the driveway. But he leads me down a hall to a kitchen in the back and grabs a folder from the counter. He tosses it across the island to me.

"What's this?"

"I haven't been entirely honest with you," he says.

I scoff. "You've told me nothing, so..."

"I didn't want a *date*, per se. More like, I wanted your expertise in a matter."

I inch closer. Sunlight streams through the huge windows, giving the room a bright and airy feel. The ocean is just outside the door, the sand smooth and free of footprints. This house sits at the end of the neighborhood, after all. To my left there are huge sand dunes, and going right along the water would lead me back to the boardwalk.

What I mean to say is: I'm not trapped.

I flip open the folder and stare down at a photo of a side profile of a man. My stomach drops, but I try not to show my hand to Kade. I keep a blank face and scan the rest of the short write-up about Reese Avery.

Parents: deceased.

Siblings: none.

Occupation: unknown (last documented doing construction).

His bank accounts are active, but only in the form of monthly payments from a trust set up by his grandparents. There's the occasional withdrawal of cash from a small bank chain in Emerald Cove, the next town over.

"I don't understand," I say, my gaze flicking back to the photo.

It looks like a screen grab from the bank security feed, slightly grainy and the angle all wrong to have been taken by a normal camera. It could've been zoomed and cropped from one on the ceiling. His expression doesn't reveal anything. There's no sense of fear or urgency, just a stoicism that seems foreign to me.

"I need you to find him."

I don't want to find him.

"Why?"

Kade rests his hip on the counter. "He's been missing for two years."

I scoff before I can help myself. "Missing?" I wave my hand over the folder. "Missed by who? No one wants to find him."

Anger flashes across his face. "I want to find him."

I scowl. "No."

"What do you mean, *no*?" He steps closer. "I asked—"

"You asked for a date. If you wanted to find him, you could've just—"

"No."

He could've asked Jace for help. Between Jace, Wolfe, and Apollo, they've got the whole city covered. Informants, alliances, bribes.

Maybe not so much of the latter, with the lack of gang wars in Sterling Falls, but still. They've got the network to make a search possible.

Me? Not so much.

And more importantly, I will not be digging up old wounds. Owning the building where I used to be regularly forced to have sex is bad enough. Knowing Terror is still right there, under the club, has given me equal amounts of grief and peace over the last few years.

If I keep it, it's like a tourniquet. It stops the bleeding... for a price.

Sacrifices the limb.

The better method would've been therapy, but fuck that.

Kade exhales. "I have reason to believe you're the only one who can find him. He talked about you."

He knows.

Panic constricts my throat.

I don't want him to know. I don't—

The front door opens. And I *must* be on edge, because I draw my gun and spin.

And end up pointing it straight at Saint.

He stops dead, his focus going from the barrel to my face and back. His expression is as distressed as I feel, and another bout of guilt washes over me. He followed me. He didn't want to come here any more than I did, but he followed me anyway.

"We're leaving," I inform Saint.

I holster my weapon and storm up to him, grabbing his hand. His fingers automatically thread through mine, and he allows me to pull him out of the house. Past the driveway, where Kade's SUV nearly hides the very spot...

I keep us moving all the way to Saint's fucking motorcycle. Of course he couldn't drive a car. I climb on and scoot back, allowing space for him.

He wordlessly hands me his helmet and swings his leg over.

I slide the helmet on and buckle it, my fingers trembling. It takes me too long, and by the time I'm ready, the bike has roared to life under us. I glance at the house, where Kade stares at us with a dark expression.

"Go," I urge Saint. "For God's sake, just get us out of here."

He grabs my wrists and drags me forward. I've got no resistance in the leather and slide down the seat easily, my chest colliding with his back. I dig my fingers into his abdomen, and I think I catch a faint groan.

There's no time to analyze it, though—he hits the gas, and we shoot away from the house of horrors.

We end up at his tattoo shop, Starlight. He has his own parking spot in the back, out of sight, and he dismounts faster than me. He slips inside and leaves the door open for me.

I move slower, although I'm officially spooked.

When I enter, Saint's got most of the lights on. The front is chic maximalism, dark walls covered in gold-framed prints, a white couch, a neon sign. Plants. Those were my contribution, since I spent many nights in the beginning waiting for him to be done with clients. Afraid that he was going to do something stupid like leave Sterling Falls altogether, maybe, or stab himself in the eye with his tattoo machine.

"Sit," he orders, pointing to the tattoo chair. The piece of furniture is a work of art all its own, nearly every part of it adjustable. Right now, it's a chair without a headrest, and the leg portion is up. Meant for a recline, I guess.

He once mentioned how much it cost, and I felt sick inside.

Bow & Arrow isn't cheap, by any means. And I certainly know how to support myself. But I don't like to be frivolous.

It isn't until I sit in it and lean back that I get it.

He sits on the stool to my left, rolling closer. He's snapping on gloves and wheeling a tray with his tattoo machine closer.

"What are you doing?" The alarm in my voice gives me away.

He smiles.

Dark, tortured, broken Saint Hart... *smiling*. I haven't seen the man smile since before the love of his life died in his arms.

His gaze runs over me again. "Hmm..."

"What. Are. You—?"

He stands and comes around the front of me. He points to my jacket. "Off."

"I'm not—"

"You take it off or I cut it off."

He's freaking serious.

For the second time today, I roughly undo the buckles and zipper, shrugging out of it. He touches my blouse, hooking his finger along the collar and tugging.

"This, too."

"Fuck off."

He sneers. "You've evolved from 'fuck you,' I see."

"Clearly a mistake," I counter. "Worst sex of my life."

"Yeah? So going another round solo in your bedroom wasn't you trying to relive it?"

"I did no such thing," I hiss.

His sneer morphs into a smug smile, and he grabs the hem of my shirt without warning. He yanks it up, my arms automatically lifting to help him.

Goosebumps prick along the backs of my arms in the cool air. I belatedly cover my chest, although my bra isn't super revealing. It's one that I had lying around Olympus, since my original was wet.

He sits and scoots his stool closer.

"Here." He presses on the ball of my right shoulder. "This is payment for me saving you earlier."

I roll my eyes.

"Are you going to tattoo a realistic dick on me?"

He pauses. "Um..."

"Because if you do..." I lean over and tap his chest. "I'll flay off your favorite tattoo."

Saint turns away abruptly, finished readying his equipment and my skin. And then something soft drops into my lap, and I pick up the strip of my blouse.

"Did you seriously just cut my shirt?"

"Yep. Tie it around your eyes."

I growl.

"Or I will tattoo that realistic dick on your face when you're sleeping."

"I'd never sleep through that."

He chuckles. "You'd be surprised at how much drugs can hold you under."

He doesn't know.

My shoulders creep higher, but I force myself to remain calm. It seems like everything lately is a reminder of my past. Dark hallways, bruises, pain. And then floating along the bottom of the river, swept away by a powerful undercurrent... Some days the longing to go back there is stronger than the horror of what I faced.

It's those days that I fight at Olympus.

I let out a slow breath and tie the scrap of fabric around my head. I go still, every muscle tensing. It's silent in the shop, and the first touch of something against my skin makes me jump.

He laughs at me. "It's a marker."

He continues for some time, switching to a sharper one, and then, *finally*, the tattoo machine buzzes to life.

"Tell me what he did." Saint's voice curls in my ear.

"I..." I lick my lips. "He brought up past trauma."

The needles bite into my skin at the same time that I finish my sentence, and I suck in a sharp breath. My abdomen clenches, my hands ball into fists.

"Past trauma," Saint questions.

"There was a boy from... a dark time in my life."

"You have a dark time in your life?"

I don't like not being able to see. I don't like not knowing if he's mocking or serious. And the bite of the needles as he drags them across my skin is surprising. It hurts, yes, simultaneously worse and better than I would've expected.

Better because it scratches that itch. The one that wants me to float along the bottom of the river, half unconscious, or stand at the bottom of the ocean and wait until my lungs are bursting.

Worse because the pain just goes on and on and on...

"Was this past trauma why you fainted at the club?"

I clear my throat. He lifts the machine away from my skin, wiping at it, but he doesn't restart.

"Yes," I admit. "And now I have to find him."

"The boy? Why?"

"Kade wants him found." And I'm going to do it. I've already decided. It was an unconscious decision. Subconscious. *Whatever* it is, I know in my bones that I won't go back on it.

"Fuck him." Saint resumes the tattoo.

I sink farther into the chair at the next pause. "This is weird punishment."

"Payment," Saint says. "When else do I get to pry into your head?"

I frown.

"Don't scowl, you'll get wrinkles."

"Okay, Mom." I don't stop, though. If anything, it just intensifies.

Because when was the last time Saint and I had a real conversation? Before Nyx...?

"What about you?" I ask.

He sucks in a breath.

"Any past trauma I should know about?"

"Just Elora," he says softly. The tattoo machine goes silent. "We're done."

9 ARTEMIS

I SIT at my desk in Bow & Arrow and work up the nerve to peel off the bandage on my shoulder. I've been trying—and *failing*—to do so for the past hour. Which means, yes, I still haven't seen what he put on me. It's a permanent mark that I'll either have to pay to get covered, if it is indeed a phallic symbol, or...

I don't want to think about the or. The idea that Saint might've been nice or thoughtful for such a brief moment in time.

Doubtful.

He could've tattooed his name on my shoulder, for all I know.

Or slut.

I shiver and pull the short sleeve of my shirt down again. I don't want to know right now.

My attention goes back to work, and I open the security feeds. Scanning to make sure everything is okay...

"Holy shit." I lean in close to the lower screen.

Kade. Sitting on a stool, drinking something in a short

glass. He's looking around. Maybe looking for me? Or Reese. If he knows Reese was here...

But Reese was upstairs in the VIP section.

So maybe he doesn't know as much as he let on.

I dial Apollo's number, tapping my pencil on the desk until he picks up.

"Atlas is here," I say without preamble.

"Aren't you on your date? The sun hasn't set. He should be where you are."

I bite my lip. "Everything he said pretty much relates back to..." God, I can't even say its name. "He's in this building and he might have no idea what went on here, or he knows everything and he's fucking messing with me."

"Okay. What do you want to do?"

Great question.

"Get him out without making a scene," I say. "My security guys will just throw him out on the street... this needs a more delicate approach."

He hums. "Okay. We'll be there in twenty. Stay out of sight."

"Thanks," I whisper.

He said... what had Kade said? That I'm the only one who can find Reese? And is that because of Terror or something else...?

My cell rings. I glance at the caller ID and allow a teeny, *tiny* smile at Nathan Bradshaw's name scrolling across the top of the screen. He's an asshole in the worst of times and a life saver in the best of them.

"Hey," I answer.

"Are you at Bow & Arrow?"

"Yeah...?"

"Fuck." Behind his voice are sirens. Not just one cop car, but a few. The sounds all overlap, like wolves howling at the start of a hunt. "Any chance of you getting out of there?"

"Did my brother call you?"

He pauses. "Should he have?"

I wince. "No, no. Why are you sounding so freaked out?"

"There's been a bomb threat."

My stomach swoops, and I swivel back to the security feeds. "Did they say where?"

"They said, 'Where everything began.'"

Oh.

Fuck.

I hang up on the sheriff. I grab my holstered gun from my purse and tuck it in my jeans, shove away from my desk. At the last second, I shrug on the hoodie that was hanging on the back of my door. It conceals the handle of the gun. No need to alarm my staff, right?

It could be a moot point, because as soon as my hair is out of my face, I sprint out of the office. I take the service stairwell down past the club and say a silent thanks that I wasn't planning on going into the club tonight.

That decision led me to keep on the leather pants and boots I wore earlier. Although after my visit to Starlight, I had to walk home in my bra with my jacket zipped up to my chin to cover it. My ruined shirt was tucked in my pocket.

At home, I couldn't control my frown as I changed into a shirt and replaced my jacket.

I bypass the club's levels and reach the lowest floor in this stairwell.

And there, standing in front of a heavy metal door that I make every effort to avoid, my heart skips.

Beyond this door lies Terror. Some of it anyway.

This part of the building has been sealed off for years.

But even as I reach for the handle, pulling it open on squealing hinges, I know someone else has been here.

Not me.

Reese?

Someone else?

The space in front of me is pitch-black. I reach blindly to the left, my fingers tripping on a light switch. A row of dim bulbs flicker on, one after another, revealing the long-abandoned hallway. Grime clings to the walls. The air is stale.

There are doors every so often, all closed up tight. They have deadbolt locks on the outside of each one.

Memories of my time here surge up. Guards shoving us into the rooms, the scrape of metal on metal as they locked. The pungent fear overlaying despair.

I draw my gun and step into the hall. I creep down like something is going to leap out and bite me. I pause in the doorway of the room used by a sadistic doctor. It's empty and weathered, the chair equipped with stirrups and restraints tipped over on its side and covered in dust.

She was the only woman who worked on this level—the only one I saw. She inspected us when we arrived, examined us after particularly vicious sessions, patched us up or drugged us when necessary, all with a cold, alien expression.

The tile floors are cracked, the glass cabinets over the counter broken, medical supplies strewn about. She didn't bother to take anything of value with her, not the vials of drugs or anything else.

My throat tightens. I can't breathe in this space, but my mind must've warped it, too. Because while it looks bad, it felt worse. And feelings dictate nightmares.

I step away. The more I explore this level—there's an

amphitheater at one end and two different shower rooms—the more I'm certain there's no one here.

But there is another level.

To get to it, I have to take another staircase. It remained separate. The door acted as a warning to everyone trapped here, and a symbol of worse things if we were disobedient.

It's been kicked inward, the metal door hanging at an odd angle, only attached by one hinge.

Fear coats my skin like sweat.

I really, *really* don't want to be down here.

I get to the bottom of the stairs and inch out into the huge room. There are old, broken cameras mounted on the walls, directed at furniture that has long since been torn apart by rats... Or someone furious enough to rip them all apart.

My toe hits a glass bottle. It clinks as it rolls out in front of me. My stomach twists, and the fear rises up my throat. It chokes me, threatens to spill out if I let it. They kept so many boys and girls down here, got them addicted to drugs, and profited off their bodies.

And it was fear of ending up *here* that kept us obedient upstairs.

"I knew you'd come here."

I shriek and spin, raising my gun and flashlight together.

"Hey. It's just me." Apollo steps out of the shadows, a gun in his hand. It's lowered down to his side, and his other hand extends to me.

I force myself to breathe and stuff mine back in its holster. While I'm getting more wound up, he exudes calm concern.

"Sheriff called me after he talked to you. Hinted about you doing something stupid after he mentioned the basement. This place..." He winces. "I wasn't good enough to find you. It took me days to figure out you were gone, and weeks to beat it out of Dad. And then you were..."

My stomach twists. As much as it kills *me* to be here, knowing Apollo knows what went on here is even worse. I was here for months—but it wasn't just *here*. I was shuffled around like my importance was noteworthy. A prize hidden under a shell, kept just out of Apollo's reach.

I approach him. "It wasn't your fault."

"This bomb threat, Tem..." He takes my hand. "You don't think they'd come down here, do you?"

Reese knows it.

Maybe Kade does, too.

"I think I'm going crazy," I whisper.

He drags me into a hug, tucking my head under his chin. Of anyone in the world, my brother gives the best hugs. It doesn't matter that we're in the darkest place I've lived through, it doesn't matter that he holds a gun, all that matters is the wash of safety that comes over me.

But...

It doesn't.

The longer he holds me, the more I feel something terrible is going to happen.

Or maybe already happening.

I pull back and look up at him, and I open my mouth to put it into words... Except nothing comes out.

Hypnos threatened ruin.

Kade wants to uncover old, vicious memories.

Reese is supposedly in hiding, but I suspect he's up to something, too. Why else would he come back?

Sterling Falls just got through one war... how will we possibly survive another?

After my mini existential crisis, Apollo and I split up to

search the rest of this level. He seems hesitant, but I brush him off. I can do this.

More like, I *have* to do this. If only to prove to myself that I'm fine.

Except every step invokes memory after memory—an onslaught of things I desperately shove out of my mind. Things I've spent the last ten years trying to forget. Officially a decade, now that I'm twenty-five.

When it gets to be too much, I allow myself to return to the floor above. There are areas still to be uncovered and relived.

I find Reese in the amphitheater.

I don't want to go farther in. To stand on the stage, even as dimly lit as it is. The emergency lighting, the little strips along the stairs and around the platform that must've come on with the hall's switch, don't do much to beat back the shadows. All that's missing is the spotlight. The people hidden in shadows. The cruel, cutting gazes and the voice that calls out numbers...

I touch the heavy curtain at my back. It's one I'd stepped through a long time ago, countless times, with burning eyes and fear locking up my chest.

After a moment, I push forward and step onto the stage.

Reese sits halfway up, a few seats in from one of the aisles. The plush seats are faded either with disuse or dust. The air in here is stale, as well, but at least it's more open than the hallway below.

There are no windows. The gridwork of lights overhead are untouched, and they might even work if I found a switch...

Definitely don't want that.

"We were here under a very different set of circumstances," he says sadly. His voice travels the distance, and the silence, easily.

He looks like he hasn't slept since I last saw him, with dark circles under his piercing eyes. His light-brown hair is spiked, as if he keeps running his hands through it. What would cause that? Frustration?

He does it again, his nails scratching his scalp. "We were both forced into different roles."

I don't have a reply for him, if that's what he wants.

I wet my lips and inch farther out onto the stage, turning in a slow circle. The audience chairs are arranged in pairs, with slim tables between them and dividers separating the pairs. Each table has a lamp and a button for silent bidding. Although some lamps have missing shades, or holes eaten through the fabric. Some have been knocked over, the bulbs broken.

Deja vu.

I've done this before. Spun. Gaze wide open, mouth dry, taking in the room. I can almost smell my old fear, feel how it used to choke me. I swallow sharply, almost to prove that it's not the same.

I'm not the same.

"I found this," Reese says, motioning to the table beside him. His voice simultaneously drags me deeper into this place and lifts me out of my memories. "I called... But I didn't know what to tell them. Or how to explain."

My chest tightens, and I climb the steps to his level. A cardboard box sits on the slim table next to him, the flaps open. I creep closer and peer down at a mess of wires inside, and a small digital clock frozen at 6:23.

"I disarmed it."

"Why are you down here?" There are more questions, of course. Like *how* he disarmed it, why he's still sitting beside it, why he hasn't been sleeping, what brought him back to Sterling Falls... But because I still have a grip on my self-control, I shut my mouth after the first one.

He shrugs.

"Tem," Apollo calls out. "Get away from him."

I automatically step back, glancing over to see my brother striding toward us. His gun is inching higher—but the last thing I want is more death.

Senseless death without answers.

"The bomb is here," I tell my brother. "It's disarmed."

"Did he tell you that?"

I don't answer—he's probably thinking that it would be easy for Reese to lie. If the man sitting only a few feet from me had rigged the frozen clock, while an internal one counted down...

That would be suicide, true, but it would take out me, too.

Who knows if that's the goal?

"Artemis," Apollo snaps.

Reese meets my gaze. "You should go. I'll see you around, Artemis."

A chill sweeps down my spine. I don't think I want to see him around—I just want him and Kade to *leave*.

I hurry down the steps. As soon as I'm within reach of my brother, he grabs my arm and tows me behind him. He remains staring at Reese until I tug on him, forcing him to abandon the man from my past.

We get upstairs just as Sheriff Bradshaw arrives. The farther I get away from that hallway, that amphitheater, the more I tremble. I stand and stare at my shoes while Apollo directs the bomb squad to the right place.

"We should evacuate," the sheriff says.

"No," I say. "It's disarmed. Do your damn job and make sure it stays that way. No need to disrupt my guests."

Apollo sighs.

Doesn't take a genius to know he's judging me for believing Reese. If I'm wrong, hundreds of people could be hurt. But the strange thing is, I *do* believe him. My gaze stays on my shoes. Nathan Bradshaw's gaze lingers on me for a second, burning the side of my face, before he continues behind the geared-up men.

There are about to be a whole lot of questions for me.

And I'm not sure I can answer.

10 KADE

MY HEAD IS SLAMMING. I run my finger around the edge of the glass, glancing up at the security camera in the corner of the bar. It's tiny. Incongruous, minus the blinking red dot. It's not meant to distract from the lushness of Bow & Arrow.

And this club is lush.

Luxurious.

Like Artemis Madden herself. Golden skin, golden dress, dark hair that promises to be silky and full when I run my fingers through it. Her amber eyes burned when she looked at me through her mask, and it stopped me dead because I knew those eyes. I want to see them again.

"Can I get you another?" the pretty bartender asks.

I shake my head and toss money on the counter. I've been here almost two hours, and nothing. No amount of goading the camera—*silently*—or watching and waiting has done any good.

The bartender collects the money. Her gaze lifts over my shoulder, her eyes widening just a fraction.

And then someone slides onto the stool beside me.

Not Artemis.

I glance at him, only to find his attention already on me. Dark-tanned skin, dark eyes. His features are similar to Artemis. If I block off his head, replacing it with a deer skull mask...

"Apollo Madden." I rest my elbow on the bar and face him. The name was a guess, but if Artemis wasn't named in irony, I'd bet her brother wasn't either.

He narrows his eyes.

I, on the other hand, smile. Years of masking my true feelings have trained me how to wear a mask of my own—all the time. I want to yell at Artemis for being a coward, for not coming here herself. She must've seen me and sent her brother to deal with me.

"Kade Laurent," Apollo replies. "Age twenty-seven. Last known address, an apartment on Silver Street in Emerald Cove. Shitty little one-bedroom, from the sounds of it. Your landlord was quite eager to talk, however. Said you hadn't been around in a few months, that she let the apartment go to someone else when you stopped paying rent."

The more he talks, the straighter my spine gets.

He's done his research.

And while I've been hell-bent on finding Reese, I find myself on uneven footing.

Which means it's time to call it a night.

"I get it," I tell him. "She's sending me a message."

He raises one eyebrow. "She's not sending you anything."

I don't believe that. But still, I rise. He follows me to the exit of the club, where there's a line of people waiting to enter. I cross the street and climb into my SUV. The windows are blacked out, and once the doors are shut, I let out a long breath.

My body is still bruised from my fight two days ago. Every time I move, there's a delicious pain that hugs my rib cage.

Jumping off that fucking cliff didn't help.

I eye the doorway again. Apollo still stands there, his hands in his pockets like he's got nothing to worry about. I take the hint, though, and start the car. The engine purrs, and I shoot away from the club.

Bow & Arrow.

Getting back to my rented house takes only minutes, and I park in the driveway and hop out smoothly. The house is dark and locked up tight. The air smells like the ocean, and it would otherwise be silent if not for the crashing waves behind the house.

Artemis had a physical response to being here...

I glance around. I chose this not because it was affordable—frankly, I don't give a shit about that—but because of the glass. The realtor told me the owners recently remodeled, and they included essentially one large wall of glass facing the water.

I leave the lights off and cross through the house. I haven't brought in much furniture. There were barstools at the kitchen counter. I hauled in a cot and sleeping bag. A lamp sits on the floor upstairs beside it.

Apollo spoke the truth about my Emerald Cove apartment. It was a shithole above a 24/7 convenience store. The woman who owned the store leased the building from an out-of-state company, but the guys who collected rent were... well, I don't think they operated wholly on the right side of the law.

Emerald Cove was just another hiccup on the road to find Reese Avery.

My gut twists, his face flashing in my mind. It wasn't a leap to assume that if he went to Emerald Cove, his next stop would be Sterling Falls. The stories he told...

There's a reason he's here.

I glance at the folder on the counter. I tried to ply Artemis with it, for her to *help* me. She's known in this town as someone who fixes things. Who solves problems. The people I talked to spoke about her with reverence—but not fear.

It makes her a target.

It makes her valuable.

Reverence can be manipulated far easier than fear.

Sure, her brother and his two friends are talked about in similar regard, but I never found it easy to play nice with other men. Not when they think they own the town. That just doesn't sit right with me. Arrogance isn't to be rewarded.

Leaving the house behind, I kick off my shoes and shed my clothes. I make a beeline for the water, enjoying the push of breaking waves against my shins, then my thighs. My hips. When I'm deep enough, I dive under an oncoming wave and swim out.

I'm going to find you, Reese.

And Artemis is going to help me. Willing or not.

11 ARTEMIS

JUST DO IT.

Taking a deep breath, I peel the bandage off my shoulder.

"What the fuck?" I stare at my skin, then meet my own damn gaze in the mirror.

Because I've been duped. Tricked. I rip the last corner of the bandage off and ball it up.

There's nothing but damn red scratch marks in my skin. No ink to speak of—*nothing* except a few spots where pinpoint-fine dots of blood have welled up.

I sat through that tattoo. I *hurt* through that tattoo. I questioned what he was going to put on me, and a sad part actually was thrilled that he would want to do it. Even under the circumstances.

I grit my teeth, only pausing for a moment before lurching out of the bathroom and striding across my condo to Saint's room.

He's going to pay for this.

I hammer my fists on his closed door. Impatience takes over, and I shove it open without waiting for his reply.

And stop dead.

He's sound asleep.

It *is* a normal time for people to be sleeping, I guess—a little past one in the morning—but I'm wired for the night. The room is dark, save for the path of light that cuts across it and shines on his face.

The peaceful face of someone with no worries.

Not sleeping anyway.

The furrow between his brows that I've grown so accustomed to seeing is smooth, his lips barely parted. Earbuds play piano music that I can hear—tinny but audible. They must've easily blocked out my pounding.

Irked and caught off guard, I waver in the doorway.

When's the last time he actually slept?

Even though he's probably going to go deaf from listening to music at such a loud volume.

I heave a sigh. He did this to irritate me—to get a rise out of me. And it worked. Which means I one hundred percent cannot give him what he wants.

A reaction.

Stepping back, I slowly close his door again. Leaving him to his dreams. Or nightmares.

Instead of going to bed, I change clothes and head down to my bike. It's that or drink, and I don't want to be that person.

The city is quiet. Everyone is sleeping, even the college students. I whip past the university, heading into West Falls. This side of town was once ruled by the Titans, and now it feels unusually tense.

I don't see the truck in time.

It comes out of nowhere, headlights bursting on a second before it clips the back of my bike. The engine roars in my ears, the lights searing my eyes. The bike wobbles, but somehow I keep it upright. I coast to a stop and hop off. I'm shaking, but I ball my fists and face the truck.

What the fuck is their problem?

It could be some drunk idiot who didn't see me—but by the way it's idling in the middle of the road... a bad feeling overtakes me. I can't see past the lights who's driving. Or how many people are in the car.

Something is wrong.

The engine revs, which is the only warning I get. The vehicle shoots forward, aimed straight for me. The street we're on has houses close together, everyone has chain-link fences blocking their yards, their cars pulled under covered driveways or in garages.

Empty.

Silent.

The neighborhood is holding its breath.

I dive out of the way, managing to lift my body up and over the chain-link fence. I land hard in the grass and roll, keep rolling, until I hear the sickening *crunch* of metal.

My bike.

I dig my fingers into the grass, tempted to push myself up, but then the truck window lowers.

"This is our neighborhood," a man spits. He's bald, pale white skin, with tattoos across his forehead and under his eyes. "We see you here again, you'll get a bullet instead of a warning."

The truck reverses.

I tear my helmet off and drop it to the ground, swearing under my breath.

We knew this could happen.

In the wake of the Titans' end, it created an opening for some new gang to slip in. And try as my brother and his friends might, they weren't able to stop it.

I shiver and flex my fingers. My hands are shaking.

The Titans sucked. But with Kronos, their leader, there was familiarity. His guys regularly fought at Olympus—disguised, sure, but we knew who they were. The Hell Hounds, too, run by Wolfe's father. The lines were blurred in the neutral areas of the city, and Olympus offered an outlet.

Better than them killing each other on the streets, right?

Now, the power vacuum that my brother, Jace, and Wolfe left behind seems glaringly obvious. I use the gate to get back onto the sidewalk and touch my elbow. My fingers come away wet with blood, even through my jacket. It takes a minute for the pain to hit—my adrenaline is still soaring.

The bike has fared much worse than me, though. It's mangled past disuse.

"Are you okay?" Across the street, a woman pokes her head out of her door. A dim light spills out behind her, giving her a silhouetted appearance.

I automatically move toward her. "I'm fine."

She stiffens, like me coming closer is a bad thing. "Best be going back to your side of the Falls, dear."

"What does that mean?"

She gestures. "You're marked. One of *them*. They've made it clear that they won't tolerate..."

"Who won't tolerate...?"

"They call themselves the Cyclopes." She shudders. "Didn't you see what they did to—"

Abruptly, she cuts herself off. Her head turns, tracking another car that coasts down from the top of the street.

Patrol?

My skin prickles.

She slams the door. The scrape of her deadbolt is audible from here.

Swallowing sharply, I press myself to the shadows and watch the car. It turns down another street, headlights swinging away. As soon as it's out of sight, I jog in the direction of the university. I pat my pockets, cursing that I didn't think to bring my phone with me.

Cyclopes.

What did they do? To *who?*

I have to hide three more times before I make it to the university. The sheriff's office is nearby, and I head for it. I don't give a shit that it's the middle of the night—he has to know about this. One of his deputies can get him there faster than I could.

But when I arrive, his car is already in the parking lot.

Butterflies—the bad kind—take wing behind my rib cage. I ignore my apprehension and keep moving. Going back just isn't an option.

I get to his office and pause just beyond the open doorway. His secretary's desk is dark and unmanned, but light spills from his. Voices, too.

I peek around the corner, and my shoulders hike.

Seated across from Bradshaw's large desk is Jace King. My brother's best friend.

The urge to burst in is overwhelming until I catch what they're talking about.

"They've been missing for almost a week," Jace tells the sheriff. "It's not like them."

I bite my lip.

"They could've just left town," Nathan points out. "You run a tight ship. Maybe they wanted out. I'm not sure why you decided to storm in here in the middle of the night."

"It's not like we initiate them," Jace growls. "We *pay* them for their information. And I'm here because you've been avoiding my calls."

The informants?

Suddenly, Wolfe telling me that they went missing rings in my ears.

And the woman's ominous words about what they did to *who*.

Does Jace not know about the Cyclopes?

Does the sheriff not?

A chill sweeps down my spine, and I step back. Growing up in Sterling Falls, I knew the sheriff's office was corrupt and Jace knew everything. Wolfe, Apollo, Jace... they had their fingers on the pulse of Sterling Falls.

"How's Kora?" Nathan asks suddenly.

I shake my head in disgust. I love Kora, I do—but now's not the time to ask about her.

Not when I have a feeling something bad has just arrived in Sterling Falls... and they've decided to make it their new home.

12 ARTEMIS

I SHOW up at Antonio's house bright and early. The man barely sleeps, so the dawn arrival isn't off-putting. Even if I normally call first.

But I couldn't stomach going back to my condo. Saint would ask questions, or he'd simply look at me like he wants to peel apart my skin. *Or*, even worse, he'd be waiting for me to bring up the tattoo. Maybe he'd even goad it out of me.

Antonio sets a cup of espresso in front of me in his warm, sunshiny kitchen. Vittoria, his wife, repainted it after...

Well. *After.*

"My youngest has officially moved out," he informs me. "And I put your cake on hold, seeing as the excitement of the day got away from us."

He joins me at the table with his own little cup, although he knowingly slides me the crystal jar of sugar and a pitcher of cream.

I fix up my espresso and sip it, considering his words. They're officially empty nesters, yes. But also the fact that he is still acknowledging the birthday. The one that started with cliff jumping, reliving trauma from Terror, a fake tattoo, and ended with a bomb threat.

"Is the house too quiet?" I ask.

He makes a noncommittal noise and watches me closely. His keen eyes pick up too much. He clocks the blood on my elbow, the tenseness in my face and shoulders.

Maybe even the dark circles under my eyes.

"No more quiet than usual," he says. "Is it too quiet for you?"

Antonio is the father figure I *wish* I had growing up. I guess I did get him for half of my teen years, technically. He is an authority figure, a source of comfort and knowledge, and he does his best to keep me safe. Along with the rest of his family.

All that to say—I'm not going to drag him into it this time.

"Nope," I deny. "Everything is fine."

He grunts, muttering about bomb threats.

Vittoria comes downstairs, and she doesn't seem the least bit surprised to see me. She kisses the top of my head, her warm hand on my shoulder.

"Good to see you, Tem. Happy birthday. Belated."

My face heats. "I'm sorry I didn't stop by."

"Oh, don't you worry. We'll find a calmer time to celebrate." Her fingers squeeze my shoulder gently. "How are you?"

Antonio hops up to fix his wife an espresso. They have a fancy machine that hisses and groans, but his movements are practiced and steady. In no time, she's joining us with her own little cup.

In classic Antonio style, he seems comfortable in a dark-blue quarter-zip sweatshirt, Bow & Arrow's logo stitched on the breast, and a white dress shirt under it. His jeans are clean and free of rips, although he's currently wearing moccasins instead of his signature leather loafers.

Vittoria, by contrast, has her long dark hair loose around her shoulders, the knit sweater she has draped over a long-sleeved shirt and yoga pants giving her a warm and cozy appearance.

"I'm okay," I tell her.

"You're bleeding," she comments.

I'd been trying to ignore my elbow, but it isn't so easy when it's dripping blood.

Sighing, I peel off my jacket and examine my skin. I must've landed on a rock or something, because the cut is jagged and deep. Antonio hands me a damp cloth, which I press to the wound.

Vittoria goes for the first-aid kit.

"Are you going to tell us what happened?" he questions.

"Fell off my bike."

"Your bike isn't here..." Vittoria narrows her eyes. "What happened to it?"

"Collateral damage." I wave away her concern. "It's fine, I'm going to handle it."

She pulls my arm toward her and removes the cloth. She takes her time laying out supplies—bandages, antiseptic ointment, witch hazel—on the table.

"Did Saint crash your bike?" Antonio demands. "Or this Reese guy? I knew he was bad news—"

"No, you didn't." I roll my eyes, wincing when Vittoria dabs at the cut. "And it wasn't either of them. You sent the sheriff out on a goose chase for Reese, but he's not dangerous."

He glares at me. "Wasn't he found with a bomb below Bow & Arrow, Artemis?"

Ugh.

"He disarmed it," I point out. "He saved Bow & Arrow." *And everything under it.*

"He could've planted it for all you know. Disarmed it because he knew how he made it." He points at me. "Dangerous. After all you went through..."

His phone rings.

I look away, my face heating. Vittoria reaches forward and squeezes my arm. She's going to say something about how he is protective of me like a fourth child, one who *hasn't* left Sterling Falls. One who he rescued so long ago...

"What?" he chokes out.

I tune in to his conversation, twisting in my chair. His hand is over his mouth, and his gaze flies back to me.

"Okay. We'll be there."

"What?" I demand as soon as he hangs up.

"There are..." He winces. "There's a dead body outside of Bow & Arrow."

Well.

That's not good.

"YOU CAN'T BE HERE."

I duck under the crime scene tape, rolling my eyes at the sheriff. "Pretty sure you can't give orders like that when just a few hours ago you were telling Jace this guy left town of his own free will."

He has a better poker face than to look surprised—but he doesn't have a reply either.

I put my hands on my hips, staring up at the body. Only one, notably, even though there were two who went missing. I tuck away that piece of information. One shoe dropped—but there will be another.

Antonio downplayed the situation. It's not just *outside* of Bow & Arrow—it's been pinned to the wall over our heads. It being a bloody, bloated corpse.

One of Wolfe's informants, I'd imagine. What they need to be informed of, I have no idea. Why the murderer chose *here*, also no idea. Or how they got it up so high.

My head hurts.

Also, most importantly, he's missing an eye. In all the gore and blood coating his skin, it's almost easy to miss.

The sheriff steps in front of me, blocking my view. "Go home, Artemis."

"I'm not squeamish," I counter.

"I know that."

"I'm not sentimental."

"Obviously."

"I'm not stupid enough to dirty your crime scene."

"Naturally."

"And I'm not fragile."

He frowns.

"I'm *not*," I snap. "Whoever did this was sending a message to me. So... let me take a look, and then you can send in your goon squad."

He grunts. Considers. He's very official in his uniform, complete with the rather outlandish, round-topped hat. It's everything he hides behind when he does questionable things for other people that make me not trust him completely.

Sheriff Bradshaw has been known to follow the money when it suits him. So perhaps I'm not as forgiving as some other people when it comes to him. Why should I? He was in the Hell Hounds' pocket, and then the Titans'. Then, when it suited him, he double-crossed both.

I step around him while he's still deciding. The sun is

up. The waves crashing as the tide comes in sits in my ears like background music. Rather that than the hum of police chatter, the attention it's drawing.

I focus back in on the missing eye. The left one. There's a trickle of blood running down his cheek, dripping off his chin and onto his shirt. I don't know how he died, but he's spread-eagle on the wall. Nails through his hands and feet. A stake through his stomach.

My stomach turns, but I swallow sharply and force my attention to keep moving.

The man is barefoot. Blood droplets fall off his down-turned toes, creating a pool on the concrete beneath him.

Whether or not he was alive when they put him up will be left to the professionals. It's got to be a message of some kind—I just don't know for whom.

It's no secret that Apollo, one owner of Olympus, is my twin brother. While Olympus might've been a good staging area for a dead body, it doesn't get nearly the foot traffic Bow & Arrow does. Even now, midday in the middle of the week, there's a crowd collecting at the edges of the yellow crime scene tape.

"When is he coming down?" I ask Bradshaw.

He wrinkles his nose. "As soon as you leave and my *goon squad* can do their work."

"Fine." I head for the door. It's a good thing the body is centered on the building, and the door is off-kilter. Otherwise, I'd need a damn umbrella—and nerves of steel—to get inside.

The sheriff catches my arm. "You can't go in there."

"That's not a crime scene—the outside is."

He scowls. "A planted bomb one day, someone murdered the next? You think you should stay open?"

"Luckily, that's not your call."

I jerk out of his hold. I fumble with the lock and wrench the door open. The heavy doors are meant to block the light, especially if patrons enter before sunset. It doesn't ruin the illusion of darkness for everyone else. But it also blocks most of the noise from traveling out onto the street.

I shoulder inside and lock the door behind me.

This club is my home. I love everything about it, and I'd do anything to protect it.

But right now, I'm *exhausted*. I make a beeline for my apartment and lock myself in. After a quick shower, in which I'm careful not to get my elbow bandage wet, I towel off and head to bed. I draw the shades, pull the blankets up to my ears, and fall asleep faster than I could've imagined.

The mystery of bombs and one-eyed dead bodies can wait.

13 ARTEMIS

I WAKE to someone touching my shoulder, and I swing before I am fully conscious. My fist connects with something hard. A light pain ricochets from my knuckles up my arm, into my elbow.

My eyes snap open, and I'm faced with a looming Kade Laurent.

I wish I didn't know his last name, but my brother likes to meddle.

He's rocked back on his heels, crouched next to the bed. Even this way, at eye level, he seems bigger than life. His dark gaze burns, and his fingers probe his cheek.

"Good to know how you wake," he finally says.

I sit up and scowl at him. My brain, for all the adrenaline in the world, is slow to catch up. That he's in front of me right now. That I was, moments ago, sound asleep in my Bow & Arrow apartment alone.

But the door was locked...

"It's time to help me," he says.

My gaze goes back to his face, and I slowly push the blankets off my lap. I swing my legs over the edge of the bed. He doesn't move, but I slide out around him and head to the bathroom. My phone is still at the condo, leaving me clueless about the time until I pass the kitchen. The glowing green stove clock informs me that it's almost ten. At night, judging by the darkness pressing up to the windows.

The faintest hint of music coming through the walls.

I lock myself in the bathroom and lean against the wall.

It's time to help me.

Does he know I already found Reese? Although, if we're going on technicalities, he found me.

I brush my teeth and rebandage my arm. It's not too bad, the skin around the cut pink and shiny. It'll be healed in no time, with only a scar to serve as a memory. Once that's done, I brush out my thick hair and let it swing free. I'll braid it if he makes me get on another bike—but I'm not eager to do that.

I'm not eager for anything.

Dread fills me up, and the dead man attached to the club wall flashes in my eyes. I left Antonio to deal with Nathan Bradshaw and everyone else. I left him to open the club or keep it shut, and...

I think I should just go back to bed.

"Artemis." Kade knocks on the door. "Are you okay?"

A strangled laugh slips out. I shake my head and rummage through my makeup bag. Makeup usually helps me feel better. It's as good as my gold mask. I swipe on mascara, then concealer and foundation and bronzer that deepens my already tanned skin. Secure gold bow-and-arrow earrings in my lobes. Paint my eyelids with kohl and shimmering gold powder. A gold-hued highlighter on my cheekbones. Deep-red lipstick.

There.

No one would think I was run off my bike last night,

that I made a narrow escape through West Falls, or that I was awake for twenty-four hours before I crashed.

I look fine.

But when I open the door, Kade's brows furrow.

"I'm going to work," I inform him.

He sighs.

I go to the closet and pick out a flowing gold shirt and black leather pants. My leather boots are by the door, ready to go. Ignoring him completely, I strip off my shirt and drop it to the floor.

He's so silent, he might as well not be here. But his hulking presence isn't that concealable. Even if he's quiet, I feel him in the doorway.

Watching, waiting.

I take off the sports bra next, my back to him. I slide my arms through the straps of my new bra—tonight seems to call for underwire—and hook it behind me. Then the shirt.

"You don't have to watch me," I call over my shoulder. "I'm not going to climb out of the window."

"And miss the show?" His voice rasps.

"Didn't take you for a pervert." I tilt my head, still facing the wall. "Didn't take you for anything, really."

I change into my pants faster, then socks and my boots. He trails me out the door, into the stairwell that takes me up to the offices. Out here is louder. Not like inside the club itself, but definitely not as soundproofed. Bussers with trays of glasses use this stairwell, along with managers and bartenders. Dancers tend to stick to their dressing rooms on the lower floors.

Kade becomes my shadow, and I can feel his frustration growing.

"Maybe you should ask for something different the next

time you fight," I suggest. "Something from the guys actually offering favors."

He growls. "I just—"

"I know." I whirl around, two steps above him. It puts us at eye level. "You want to find Reese. He's been missing for two years. You were in Emerald Cove before Sterling Falls, so I can only assume you've been tracking him for some time. But you didn't say *why*, and quite frankly, you haven't offered me anything in return."

His expression... well, I can't lie about how handsome he is. He's clean-shaven now, but I feel like stubble or a beard wouldn't be out of character for him. He seems like the type to be perfectly fine surviving a year in the wilderness by himself.

Which is all the more strange that he can't find Reese by himself.

"I'm not familiar with this town," he finally says. "I had a guide in Emerald Cove—"

My eyebrows hike. "Oh, really? Who?"

He just shakes his head, eyes narrowed. "Reese is important, Artemis."

I shrug. "That tells me nothing. Go away, Kade."

I continue up the steps, to the top floor with the kitchens and offices. Less noise, less bustle—especially now, with the kitchens closed. I find Antonio's office closed and locked up tight.

Same with mine, although that's not unusual. And I do not have my keys on me.

My stomach lets out an untimely growl.

"Dinner," Kade rumbles behind me. "And I'll explain."

I consider what awaits me if I head downstairs to find Antonio. I'll be immediately slammed, pulled in eighteen different directions by employees who need something, just want to prove that they know what they're doing, or want to fucking gossip.

Just thinking about that makes me tired.

So...

Fuck it, right?

He sees the moment I decide, and before I know it, his hand is on the small of my back and he's ushering me the way we came. All the way to the exit, where I pointedly ignore the doors that go down *there*. To where my nightmares reside.

A whole world resides under this club, and I spend a majority of my time pretending it doesn't exist.

He doesn't notice my avoidance, and then we're outside. We go to the street, and I glance down at the row of people waiting to get into the club. Pride and satisfaction fill me at the want—no, the need—people have to experience Bow & Arrow. To release their inhibitions, to dance...

And then I'm in Kade's blacked-out SUV and he's climbing into the driver's seat.

He drums his fingers on the steering wheel, seeming to debate something, then shakes his head. The engine purrs to life, and he heads away from North Falls. Down the center, back toward the university and the government buildings.

But what's surprising is that I don't really know where we're going, especially when he continues into South Falls. There's one main road that takes us into the industrial district. Our view shifts from residences to warehouses.

Past it, the marina.

My brow furrows, and I glance from the road—which dead-ends into rows of docked boats—to Kade.

He parks and hops out. Circles around. Offers his hand.

I glare at him, then take it. He doesn't release me when

I'm standing, though, and instead leads me toward the locked gate that protects the boats. The air is cooler than I expect, and I shiver.

He pauses, turning to face me. Wordlessly, he pulls his sweatshirt over his head and pushes it into my chest. I can barely see him, his expression, but his teeth flash with a quick smile.

There are goosebumps on my arms, so I tug it on hurriedly. It's huge on me, falling almost to my knees, and his scent wraps around me.

Not entirely unpleasant.

No, in fact, a new hunger curls in my belly that has nothing to do with food. He stares at me for another second, then takes my hand again.

Our boots crunch on the gravel. He types in a code to the keypad, and the gate beeps quietly. It swings open under his hand.

"I'm not getting on a boat," I warn him.

He chuckles. "Of course not."

"You promised me food."

He inclines his chin.

There's a path to the right, and he steers us in that direction. It's so dark, I'm suddenly glad he's holding my hand. I can barely make out the hulking shadow of him, let alone any features. The sound of water lapping is the only noise around us.

He could do anything to me in this moment. He could force me on a boat and take me far, far away from here. Kidnap me, torture me. Rape me.

Sell me.

A shiver coasts down my spine.

Why do I put myself in these situations?

I tug on my hand, but he holds fast. My dread is cold

and sluggish, but the panic that begins to flare to life is white-hot.

"Just trust me," he murmurs, like he can sense it.

It doesn't help.

What sort of trustworthy guy says that?

And then we round a corner, and there's a boat all lit up. It's a flat houseboat decorated in string lights, torches lit around the perimeter with real fire—a true sailor's worst nightmare—and, inexplicably, the smell of cooked meat.

My mouth waters before the rest of me catches up.

"Bobby!" Kade calls. "You still open?"

A sandy-blond head pokes out of the open doorway of the houseboat, and my confusion grows.

It's not like I know everyone in Sterling Falls. That would be ridiculous. But—

"For you?" the guy answers. "Of course."

He disappears back inside.

"What is happening?"

Kade laughs under his breath. "Bobby runs a food truck of sorts."

"A food boat...?"

"Yeah." He snaps his fingers. "I took a boat out to Isle of Paradise, and he was docked over there catering to some of the workers coming off the ferry."

"You went to Isle of Paradise?" My tone is wary. There's an organization there that claims to be a trauma rehabilitation center, but they really just keep people for as long as possible. Forever, if the money doesn't dry up.

He shrugs. "Covering my bases when it comes to Reese. But Bobby and I got talking, and he said he's open late. Sometimes he's over in North Falls to catch the late-night drunks leaving your club."

I turn another, speculative eye toward the lit-up boat.

From this angle, I can barely make out a sign that proclaims *Bobby's Eats*. But it solidifies what he's saying.

And come to think of it, I have seen a crazily illuminated boat around Bow & Arrow's closing time.

"Come on," Kade murmurs. "He doesn't bite."

Sure.

He easily steps up onto the boat, swinging his other leg over the railing. Straddling it like that, he extends his hand to me.

Not a chance.

I copy him, hauling myself up and climbing over.

There's a picnic table on the big front. The house part looms over us, probably only one story but seemingly taller. Maybe one and a half. I peer in through the still-open door.

Bobby has shoulder-length blond hair tucked in a hair net. An unbuttoned floral Hawaiian shirt exposes his bare chest. Pink jean shorts and matching boat shoes.

You know what?

It's not the weirdest thing I've seen today.

If you can call a dead person weird.

"So?" I tear my attention away and find Kade. He's taken a seat at the lone table, once again watching me.

"So," he repeats.

"What's he making?"

He shrugs. "I'm not picky. Are you?"

It's a dare.

I've had enough dares from Saint to last a lifetime. But unlike Saint, this one doesn't have malice attached to it. Just curiosity.

I take a seat across from him. "Sometimes I'm picky."

"Good," he murmurs. "Standards."

"High standards," I correct. "Which leads us to why you need my help."

He inclines his chin. "Reese is important to me, and we had developed a system over the years. Even if we weren't close. But two years ago, he stopped communicating."

"So you started stalking him?" I raise my eyebrow.

Reese didn't mention Kade.

I didn't ask...

"No." He shakes his head. "He wouldn't just stop. Something is wrong. At least, I thought he was in danger, so I broke our protocol and went to his apartment. It was already a crime scene—absolutely trashed, the door blown off its hinges. A neighbor had called the police. But no body, no blood."

"No Reese."

He shakes his head. "At that point, I started my search in earnest."

Our conversation in that house comes back to me. "You said he wanted to send a message through me?"

He lifts one shoulder. "He once mentioned you. Well, he mentioned Olympus and a goddess named Artemis, and I thought he was off his rocker. It wasn't until I got to Emerald Cove that I realized it wasn't out of Greek Mythology. He was talking about Sterling Falls."

"And—"

"That photo," he continues. "Taken in the bank in Emerald Cove. He had drawn an arrow on his arm."

I scoff, but then he reaches into his back pocket and removes it. Smooths out the creases, sliding it across the table. He taps the view of the underside of his arm.

Sure enough, an arrow.

"Not exactly a scientific conclusion." But my throat is tight, and the queasiness from earlier returns. "He could've just gotten a tattoo."

He raises an eyebrow at me, and I acquiesce.

Reese Avery is not the type. And he definitely wouldn't have gotten a hipster arrow on his forearm. He's not in a boy band.

"Okay," I allow. "That led you to me."

"It led me to Bow & Arrow. And then Olympus. And then you."

"Ah."

He stares at me.

Do I tell him I've seen him?

Do I trust him?

Besides—Reese might've left town. If he was smart, he would've already. The sheriff has his picture, Antonio and my brother are up in arms about him. He was found with a bomb under my club. And while nothing bad happened, it could've.

Scary shit.

Untrustworthy shit.

Whether or not I trust Kade is beside the point, because I don't trust Reese.

"Dinner is served!" Bobby announces, striding toward us with two paper bowls. He sets one down for me, the other for Kade. From one pocket come napkins. From another—his two back pockets—come two bottles of beer.

The meal: burgers and onion rings.

My stomach growls again, and I don't bother with formalities. I've never been so fucking hungry in my life.

Kade eats slower, alternating between bites and watching me demolish mine. Bobby cracks our beers and leaves us, wandering away whistling under his breath.

Juice runs down my chin. And before I can get it, Kade swipes at my face with a napkin. Saving either my pants or shirt from stains.

"Thanks," I say after a swallow.

He makes a noise in the back of his throat. "Least I can do after your strip show earlier."

I scowl.

When my basket is empty, I eye his onion rings. My brother would never share—not that it would stop me, per se. Saint would rather stab me than offer something from his plate. But Kade wordlessly slides it into the middle of the table, still eating his burger.

Okay, fine.

Finally, the food is gone and we sit satiated. I sip the beer, swinging one leg over to get a better view of the water. Bobby has parked this mammoth on the last dock slip. The marina is more protected by natural rock formations, while the harbor on the other side is more open for larger ships.

It just means it's peaceful.

"I'm not going to help you," I say.

He doesn't reply. Doesn't try to convince me.

Because I think we both know I'm lying.

14 ARTEMIS

I SIT on the rocky cliffside at Olympus as the sun comes up. I was home long enough to grab my phone and car keys, slipping in and out before Saint could wake and register that I was back. I almost expected him to be waiting for me, but he wasn't.

Not one to let Saint get the first punch in, I left while luck was on my side.

Now I'm here, watching the sky lighten.

At first, I idly scrolled through the texts and missed calls, voicemails from Antonio. The last one concludes: *I checked the security feed and saw you go into your apartment. Sleep. We'll talk tomorrow.*

It's tomorrow, and I still don't feel like talking.

There was even a text from Saint. He wanted to know if I was alive.

I reply with a skull emoji, then turn off my phone.

"I'm starting to think you don't sleep."

I glance over my shoulder. Jace climbs the hill in my direction.

"Did Apollo send you?" My voice, like my body, is stiff.

He stops beside me, but he doesn't sit. "Nah, I was coming to water the flower wall."

I smile.

That wall in the atrium—the first big room when you walk into Olympus—was built as a declaration of love for Kora. Olympus needed a bit of an overhaul after the war, taking its own fair share of hits, and that's what they decided to do to it.

"You okay?" he asks in a low voice.

I laugh. "Me? I'm fine."

He sighs.

"You?" I crane my head back. "I mean, your informant is dead. Nailed to my club wall, in fact."

"Did Apollo tell you who he was?"

I smile, but I don't confirm. It's more impressive to just know things than admit how I found them out. Telling him I know because I was eavesdropping on his conversation with the sheriff seems... shitty.

"Saint was worried when you went offline for a day," he adds.

"Bullshit."

"He called me."

"Did you have to talk him out of throwing himself off the roof?"

I scratch at my arm through Kade's sweatshirt. My nail gets close to the edge of the bandage protecting my elbow. My skin always gets irritated by adhesive, and this is no different. But I can't take it off and bleed on his sweatshirt, that would just be rude.

"You still think he's suicidal?" Jace eyes the top of my head.

What a terrible angle. At least he can't see up my nostrils.

But then I truly consider it. He asked me if Saint could move in, but it was never really a choice for Saint. After what he went through—what we all went through—it seemed natural for Jace to want to help him.

And I was the only one available.

I should've said no. Daniel could've roomed with him, but...

Well. Daniel moved away shortly after helping us end the war raging in the streets of Sterling Falls. He's a master tech, knows his way around computers—including hacking. He saved our asses on more than one occasion.

Understandable that he'd want to leave.

If I had a choice...

No. I'd still be right here.

But has Saint healed any in the year since he lost the love of his life?

I think of his fingers digging into my skin. The insults he slung at me like mud while he fucked me. The way he dragged an orgasm from me even though that made me feel dirtier than anything else he could've done.

Do I think Saint is moving on? Thinking more about living than dying?

Absolutely not.

When I don't answer, Jace sighs.

"I can't babysit him forever." I push myself up, dusting off the bits of rock and dirt that stick to my pants. "It's not fair to me. Or him."

He nods, but his expression tells me he doesn't agree.

I motion for him to go away. "Water your plant wall and leave me be."

I came here to be alone.

And yet, no sooner has he returned to Olympus does a motorcycle turn onto the long driveway.

I recognize Saint immediately, and my hackles rise.

By the time he reaches me, I'm ready for a fight.

He's pissed, too. He takes one look at me, at the sweat-shirt that drowns my frame, and he doesn't just stop at me. He grabs me. One hand on my throat, the other on my hip, and propels us over the cliff.

I can't say I'm even surprised. The freefall isn't unpleas-ant. It's like my mind detaches and lengthens the time it takes us to hit the water. I note that I'm still wearing my boots—*that's the worst*—and Kade's sweatshirt. It won't smell like him anymore.

But wasn't it just the other day that I did this with him? On my birthday. At sunrise.

It feels like an eon ago.

Saint falls faster than me. He's heavier by quite a bit, although he doesn't release me. I cling to his wrist, clawing my nails into his skin. I take a breath and keep my eyes on him until the very last second.

We hit the water hard, plunging down, and catch a wave at the wrong time. It sends us toward the rocks, our bodies twisting. It's no match for the speed at which we descend, though.

Neither of us let go.

My feet hit the bottom, and my old habit of lingering almost sticks. But Saint still has me in his grip, his one hand around my throat—so loose, though, it barely feels like anything other than pure possession—and the other fisted in the fabric at my hip.

He drags me upward.

A wave crests over our heads, and we pop up a second later.

He yanks me into him, until I grasp at his shoulders. We

both kick to keep ourselves afloat. My knee grazes his groin, and his eyes narrow.

"You aren't allowed to disappear on me," he says harshly.

"Careful, Saint, or else I might start to think you care."

He shakes his head, and his fingers tighten on my throat. Maybe he's considering throttling me.

His white t-shirt is soaked, plastered to his skin and nearly translucent. The branded hourglass in the center of his chest is still a little raised, and I put my palm against it.

"I'm fine," I tell him.

His heart beats wildly under my hand.

His fingers twitch.

Another wave rolls over us, and it's easier to go under than get caught on top of it. When we break the surface again, I push my soaked hair out of my face. Wipe my eyes. My makeup is smeared, I'm sure of it.

What gives him the right to possess me?

I kick harder, drifting closer, and his gaze flicks to my lips.

Not that he would ever kiss me in a million years.

Saint Hart?

More like Saint Heartless.

"Stop," I whisper. "Just... *stop.*"

"I'm not doing anything."

I scoff. "Okay. Then why do you care?"

He pulls at the sweatshirt, his fist still tangled in it. Why? Why is he still holding on to me?

The movement sloshes the water between us, splashing it up into my face. His face.

"I don't." His voice is rough.

He's *lying.*

The relief that loosens my chest surprises me. I cannot —no, I will not—face the truth. Not this morning, not from him.

"Then let go of me." Another challenge. My brow lowering, my glare not subtle.

He does, and I push away from him hard. I kick for the ladder, ignoring my pounding pulse. Unlike when Kade and I climbed it, Saint gives me space. He waits until I'm a few rungs above him to start. My muscles ache when I'm halfway up. The sweatshirt weighs a million pounds, and water pours off me.

I hope it hits Saint in the face.

As usual, when I get to the top, I flop onto my side, then roll onto my back.

Saint climbs up a second later, pausing with his knees digging into the rocks like he's paying a penance to some demon.

Or Nyx.

The thought twists my gut, and I force myself to my feet.

I came here for peace, not to be shoved off the cliff.

And sure enough, Jace is waiting for us at Olympus with a scowl fixed firmly in place.

"Jace," Saint greets him. His tone and expression are both far away. "Didn't see you."

Jace grunts. His blue eyes flick to mine, and there's a softness there that usually is reserved for his family.

Which, recently, hasn't really included me.

Look—don't get me wrong. I love him as much as I love Apollo and Wolfe. They're all my brothers, in a way, but they've all been caught in the throes of *love*. I respect that enough to take a step back, even if I don't understand it completely. Doesn't mean they don't care, it just means they're preoccupied.

And maybe that's how the Cyclopes slipped into Sterling Falls.

I bite my lip against that accusation. It's a guess anyway.

It makes me think he's suddenly reevaluating my relationship with Saint. He can't know about the hate-fuck. If Saint said anything, he would've been in worse-off shape than Kade left him, and that would've just been from my brother.

Never mind what Jace and Wolfe would do.

I glance at Saint, who still isn't fucking tuning in.

And just as Jace opens his mouth to decree his judgment, his phone rings.

He takes one look at the screen and swipes to answer it. Already turning away, already dismissing us without follow-through.

I roll my eyes and head to my car. There's a towel in the trunk, and I shed the sopping-wet sweatshirt along with my shirt, wringing both out the best I can. I put the shirt back on, then slip off the bra and toss it into the trunk. I use the towel to blot the water from my hair, then wrap it around my waist.

My leather pants are shucked next, along with my boots and socks.

Saint leans against the bumper of my car.

Watching.

Judging.

"What?" I finally snap.

He lifts one shoulder. "Your secret boyfriend is safe with me."

There's an unspoken part of that sentence: for now. As in, as long as I keep his secret, he'll keep mine. I don't have a secret boyfriend, but I have secrets that I seem to be collecting.

I already told Jace that Saint wasn't self-destructing. Who fucking knows, though, right?

"Don't push me off a fucking cliff," I retort.

"I won't if you answer your damn phone."

"It was in the condo," I hiss.

"I know. I found it when I thought you had been kidnapped or something."

My heart picks up speed. It's that weird feeling again, the creeping dread. My heart is trying to outrun it. It hits a little too close to home... But Saint doesn't know that.

No one knows that.

Forcing a bravado, I ask, "Do you know how ridiculous you sound?"

He eyes me, then snorts. "Whatever."

"Bye, Saint." I slam the trunk and drop into the driver's seat, hitting the lock button before he can try to get in and pester me more.

He pushes away from the hood, still staring. Even as I drive away.

Staring and staring and staring.

15 ARTEMIS

I SLIDE into the dark booth, eyeing the man who definitely shouldn't be anywhere near Bow & Arrow. "Pretty sure my brother warned you away."

Kade smirks. "He tell you about our little conversation?"

"He mentioned having a chat with you."

Tonight, he's dressed in all black. Silky black dress shirt —buttoned a respectable way up his chest—and black slacks. Black shoes and socks. Well, okay, I'm assuming. His legs are under the table, but I would assume it's all matching. Imagine if he was wearing neon-yellow socks?

I tilt to the side and glance under the table.

Nope, black.

Whew.

"What are you doing?"

Something else catches my eye, but I sit up straighter and shake my head. "Just making sure things are in top order for our VIP guests. How did you get into this lounge anyway?"

"I paid." He flashes the sleek black bracelet that denotes our *very important patrons*.

I suppress my irritation that he waltzed in. Somehow.

"You're blacklisted," I inform him.

He braces his forearms on the table and leans in. "I have a fake ID." His voice is low, conveying the secrecy, but the words somehow coasts across the distance to me.

My lips part, and then I'm scowling and holding out my hand. To his credit, he retrieves his wallet from his pocket and places it in my palm. I flip it open and tug out the ID on top.

Thomas Atwater.

Great.

I examine it closer, trying to spot something that will give it away—but there's nothing. Either I suck at this or it's a really stellar fake. Which I hope is the latter because otherwise I'll be firing my bouncer.

There's no sign of his real ID in the wallet. He has a credit card in the name Atwater, too.

"Are you sure your real name is Kade?"

He smiles.

"Fine," I relent, handing it back. "Are you here to try and cajole me into finding Reese?" *Again.*

"Nah." He catches the attention of a waitress.

When she arrives at the table, she casts a confused glance in my direction.

Probably doesn't help that I've been playing hooky from working for the past twenty-four hours. I followed up with Antonio, and he gave me slack. Said he had it covered, that it would be understandable for me to take some time off.

Most of my life is spent in this place... and here I am, supposedly taking personal days, right back here again.

"Artemis," she says. "Do you want your usual?"

I smile and nod. It's not her I'm annoyed with anyway. It's the guy sitting across from me, who seems to enjoy getting around my security measures.

Reese does, too.

I should find him. Not for Kade, but because he very well might've had something to do with that bomb. The bomb he disarmed. He was gone before the sheriff found the amphitheater, which leads me to question *why*.

Why is he in Sterling Falls?

Why did he seek out *that place?*

What good is any of this doing?

"Put it on my tab," Kade says, sliding a black credit card across the table to the waitress. "And I'll have another."

Her eyes round. "Artemis drinks for free—"

"So charge him double," I order, leaning back and crossing my arms. To him, I say, "This isn't impressing me."

"What do you drink?"

Answering him, giving him any information at all, seems dangerous. My gaze drops to the highball glass in front of him. It's got a sip left in it, the liquid looking slightly tinted. Maybe whiskey, diluted with ice...

"It's a Manhattan."

"I didn't ask," I reply.

He lifts a shoulder.

"So if you're not here to get me to find Reese, then why?"

His gaze roves from my face down... *down.* I swallow. My *assets*, for lack of a better term, are more of a hinderance than anything. Or an insecurity, I guess. I wear clothing that shows off my breasts and hips, I don't make an attempt to hide it, and yet I hate when it gains me unwanted attention.

"Can't I just want to talk to a pretty girl?"

"No," I blurt out. "Not when you're here under suspicious circumstances."

He snorts. "Okay, Tem."

"You can't call me that."

"You're right. We're going to be more than friends."

I shake my head. Of all the things I should be doing, sitting here entertaining this is low on my list of priorities. And yet, I find that I don't want to leave. I'm curious about him, and he's being forthcoming for once.

Of all the mysteries right now, this one seems the easiest to pick apart.

"You find that funny?"

"I find it funny that you're trying to hit on me."

And yet...

My face slowly heats the longer he stares at me. Because it isn't probing or inquisitive, it's hot. A smolder like none other I've encountered, and irrational fucking butterflies flutter in my chest.

He's handsome. I noted as much before, his roguish charm helping him out in that regard. It's the confidence, too. He doesn't give a shit if I reject him—it just makes him try harder.

It's not fair.

"Where's your guard dog today?" His voice is pitched low.

Saint.

I wince, all the heat falling away from me, the walls around me stacking back up again. He almost had me for a minute there.

"My brother was a Hell Hound." I keep my tone mild.

"And?"

"The new recruits were all so curious about him and his friends. Guess who they came to for information?" I meet his dark gaze. "They'd flirt. They'd make me think the conversation was about me. And then they'd reveal their intentions."

His lips flatten. Just for a second. Then, "Let's dance."

I don't want to dance with him.

I don't want to dance with anyone.

He stands and holds out his hand. Waits. Wiggles his fingers, and there it is again. A silent dare. Standing at the edge of a dock. Standing at the edge of a cliff. Standing at the edge of a dance floor.

I take it.

He keeps my hand trapped in his, his long fingers threading through mine. He leads us out of the VIP lounge and into the madness below. The main DJ has taken the stage against the far wall, and the dance floor is packed. It throbs with the beat of the music.

My body throbs, too. Just in a different way.

Don't be attracted to him.

His wide shoulders help carve a path through the dancers. Where I can slip between, he's got the energy—and the audacity—that tells people to get the fuck out of his way.

It's kind of funny—he and Reese both have similar statures, but they *feel* different. Reese is more careful. He seems well versed in being invisible. He'd slip through the crowd without an incident, without touching anyone else.

Kade hasn't been invisible a day in his life.

We find a spot, whatever spot seems satisfying to him, and he faces me.

I tip my head back to look up at him.

He takes our joined hands and drags me a step closer. One palm touches my hip, the heat seeping through my gold shirt. Something flutters again.

I shouldn't like it.

But it's been a while since someone touched me like this. Not the bruising grip of Saint, disdain coating his expression. It's more gentle than that. Softer. My body reacts with a pulse. An embarrassing pulse that travels right between my legs...

I touch Kade's chest, sliding my hand up his silky shirt. To his shoulder, then the back of his neck. He is quite a bit taller than me, but he's graceful. Like a fighter, sure, but also like something wild.

"Why Atlas?" I blurt out. I don't know if he can hear me over the music. I can barely hear myself. The beat thunders and begs me to move.

My fingers drift through the short hairs at his nape, and he cocks his head. He doesn't answer except to guide my other hand to his shoulder, then cup my waist.

Around us, people dance with abandon.

But Kade pulls me close, and I close my eyes.

"Dance, Artemis," he says right in my ear.

I wish I had stuck around for the drink, but it's too late now.

Like fighting, my body picks up his cues. Where he wants me to go by the gentle pressure, the way his arms are relaxed and loose on my hips. He follows when I sway them, slowly at first and then picking up speed. I find the rhythm of the music, and he follows me.

His knee nudges between my legs. My nails dig into the back of his neck.

This is more sensual than any dance...

He leans down, and I cock my head to the side. Giving him access to my ear, because he seems like he wants to say something.

His lips land on my throat.

A quiet annihilation of my coyness.

I gasp. My hips roll, both to the music and to the way his lips drift toward the corner of my jaw. His teeth scrape my skin, and my knees go weak.

Not that it matters, because he holds me up just fine.

This is really wrong.

And yet—

Stop it.

One of his hands slides from my hip to the small of my back. Then higher. His fingers tangle with my hair, and he *tugs.*

Jesus.

New kink unlocked.

He tilts my head farther and bites my neck, and a moan slips out of me. He shouldn't be able to hear it, but his ear is practically even with my mouth.

So when he draws back and smirks at me, I just stare at him.

He still has my hair in his fist, his leg wedged between mine. We're still dancing, somehow, so slow while the rest of the room seems to be double time.

Even the music isn't loud anymore.

And I'm fucking sober.

Any minute now, Kade will ruin it. He'll ask about Reese, he'll bring up my brother. He'll talk about Olympus, or fighting again.

And when he doesn't, when he just smirks and continues to dance against me like he's got all the time in the world, dread edges closer. The longer this game goes, the worse it'll be.

"Kade—"

"You're the most beautiful woman I've had the pleasure of dancing with," he says in my ear. No, *rumbles* it.

I never understood that. Or growling men. But I have a feeling Kade could do both and win awards while doing it.

My expression closes off in preparation for the *but*.

It doesn't come, and that's worse.

"I've got to go," I say, using my palm on his chest to put some distance between us. Any sort of distance, so I can breathe and not think about what my brain and heart are arguing over.

"Artemis—"

"Stop," I interrupt.

He releases my hair.

My hip.

And that abrupt loss is all I need to break the last hold he had on me. I spin around, find a slim opening in the crowd, and use the dancing bodies to disappear.

16 ARTEMIS

SAINT TEXTS that he's staying at Starlight tonight, which suits me perfectly fine. That cot in his shop must be uncomfortable and small, but I can't imagine going home to *his* energy. Especially when I check my neck in the rearview mirror in my car and find red hickeys. They're just the beginning, and I'm sure Kade did it on purpose.

Bastard.

I drive home slowly, mindful of the sheriff's deputies staked out along the way. He's upped patrol since the informant's body made an appearance. I haven't inquired about his investigation.

Honestly? Not my problem.

There's no evidence that it was a pointed threat in my direction. It could've just been a nice blank wall for whoever murdered him. Jace, Wolfe, and Apollo are on it anyway.

Besides, there's one more missing informant.

When will he turn up?

And in what manner?

Police lights flash behind me. I grip my steering wheel

tighter and groan through my teeth, then pull off to the shoulder. A small part of me hoped they'd fly past, but I've got no such luck.

It follows, stopping a good distance away, and I squint into the rearview mirror to see which asshole on Bradshaw's force it is.

Their uniforms are green, and they wear ostentatious dark-green hats with a narrow, rounded brim. Apparently they're not allowed to be outside without the hats, which makes it all the funnier.

Yet it slightly disguises the deputy as he approaches my car, the flashing lights behind him silhouetting his body.

I roll down my window, and the sheriff himself leans down into the opening.

"Artemis," he greets me.

Great.

"Brad," I respond.

Nathan Bradshaw has had more of a *Brad* attitude lately,

His smile widens. "Aw, don't be like that. I just wanted to talk to you."

"You could've called." I drum my fingers on the car door. "I'm exhausted. Can I not go home?"

He sighs. "I just wanted to warn you that we're getting outside pressure to take the investigation into Bow & Arrow."

I rear back. "What? Why?"

"Because the body was attached to your building, Tem. It took four of our guys to get him down." He stares at me. "You're not taking this seriously."

"Jesus. I'm just not jumping to conclusions. Am I supposed to run around afraid? We just spent a year doing that, Nathan."

"Nathan," he repeats quietly. "Now I'm Nathan."

"You're annoying," I snap. "I wasn't speeding. Unless you have anything else to say, I'm going home."

He sighs. "The warrant is coming. I can't stop it."

"Thanks for the warning." I restart my car.

He steps back, and I hit the gas.

Outside pressure from *whom*?

There's the city council, of course. They've undergone some changes recently, but it's all been in our favor. I can't see them turning on me. The Hell Hounds are now led by Malik, and while we don't exactly see eye to eye, he's not a bad guy.

These Cyclopes that are digging their way into West Falls... do they have enough momentum to pressure the sheriff?

I'm still puzzling it over when I get home. I park in the garage and take the elevator straight up, definitely more distracted than normal when I unlock my condo's door. I get inside and shed my jacket, drop my phone and wallet on the entryway table, and kick off my shoes.

What I said to Bradshaw wasn't a lie—I'm fucking exhausted.

If only I could sleep.

My gaze is drawn to the kitchen, then Saint's bedroom. I make a regular habit of dumping out his alcohol, if only to spite him. But he's surely restocked...

"Artemis."

I scream.

Shit. Fuck.

I'm not a screamer, but—

Reese steps out of the shadows by the window. He blended in over there. I wouldn't have even glanced in that direction, bypassing the living room to find alcohol in the dark and then retreating to bed.

He switches on a lamp.

His blond hair looks slightly damp, the strands darker than the last time I saw him. He runs his fingers through it, dragging the longer top pieces back. They flop right back into his eyes, and I hate that it gives him a devil-may-care appearance.

"Reese." It comes out hoarse. "What are you doing here?"

"I wanted to talk to you."

What is it with guys these days?

"You could've called," I point out. "Does no one here have a phone anymore?"

I throw my hands up and change direction for the kitchen. With him showing up, I *definitely* need a drink.

Reese's gaze is on my back as I rifle through the cabinets without luck. Halfway through the second one, it occurs to me that Saint is 1) an asshole and 2) tall. So he probably shoved it in the back corner of the top shelf, out of my line of sight.

I climb up onto the counter, knocking travel mugs out of the way. I spot the red wax of a whiskey bottle, stretch, wiggle my fingers, and finally grasp it.

The next thing I know, I'm back with my feet on the floor and Reese taking the bottle from me.

Close.

He's so close.

I catch his scent, cedar and smoke. The good kind, like a campfire.

Even so, I sidle away to put some distance between us. If I could get a damn minute to breathe, maybe I could figure out what I want to do. Or how I feel. But right now, everything is jumbled and I'm confused and I think I'm on the verge of a panic attack.

Yep.

A weight presses down on my chest. I struggle to keep my breathing even, but my muscles tighten so much it's impossible to draw in more air. I stumble back farther, gripping the counter, and the room tilts.

I close my eyes, then open them again just as fast.

Reese's back is to me. He doesn't notice my struggle as I inch around the island and put more distance between us. I can't tell if I want him to leave or tell me what he wants or hurry up and pass that bottle over.

When he faces me, his brows pinch together. "Jesus, Artemis. Sit down."

I... I don't think I can. I don't want to follow his orders.

Between him sneaking in here—*sneaking or breaking?*—and Kade waking me up in my Bow & Arrow apartment, and Saint living here while hating me...

I can't get a grip.

I can't catch a fucking *break.*

"Okay, okay." Reese pulls at my wrists, carefully untangling my hair from my fingers.

I hadn't realized I had done that, but my scalp aches. He keeps ahold of my wrists and directs me backward, until my calves hit the couch and my knees automatically bend. He lowers himself in front of me.

His gaze locks on the red marks on my neck. "Who gave you those?"

"Please just leave me alone," I plead.

His green eyes search my face. "You know I can't."

"I don't know that. I don't know why you're in Sterling Falls, or even why you went down to Terror. I don't know why Kade—" I cut myself off.

His brows raise. "Kade Laurent?"

Shit.

Fuck.

"Uh..."

He glances around like the man might be hiding in my apartment. Comical, seeing as how he was that culprit tonight.

"He's in Sterling Falls?" Reese's gaze swings back to me, the intensity of it catching me off guard.

"Y-yeah, he's been looking for you."

"Did he—?" He squeezes his eyes shut for a second, and then he's up and moving. He goes to the window, peering down at the street far below.

"Reese."

"I'm leaving," he murmurs. "I'm going. I wanted to talk to you, Artemis, but I thought we had time."

"He doesn't know—"

"You cannot tell me that." He shakes his head. "Just... stay safe. Please."

My brows furrow.

He wants me to be safe?

What the fuck does that mean?

I don't get the chance to find out, because before I can ask, he slips out the door.

And he's gone.

"WHAT'S a girl like you doing in a place like this?" A man leans an elbow on the bar beside me. He's at least fifteen years older than me, judging by the gray at his temples and the fine wrinkles around his eyes. Still handsome, but not my type.

I scowl. "The bottomless mimosas, obviously."

We're in what used to be Descend, a bar that was run by the Titans in West Falls. It fell into a bit of disrepair—okay, a lot of disrepair—but a few months ago, someone bought the shell of a building and sent in a crew to fix it up.

And now, it's *Madness*. Because whoever now owns it seems to have a sense of fucking humor. Get it? Descend into madness? That's where I'm going anyway, the way I've been spiraling lately.

Just to be clear—there are no bottomless mimosas here. They probably don't even have orange juice in stock, let alone Prosecco. Descend was never that type of bar, and the new owners apparently decided to keep up the same motto.

It's dark, the atmosphere mostly dim string lights, lamps, or fake candles, with splashes of neon around. Like the one that says, *fall down the rabbit hole* behind the bar, casting all the liquor bottles in red.

The guy doesn't seem to know what to do with me, especially as the bartender reappears in front of me with a glass of whiskey.

Getting a clear liquor in this place is about as likely as a fucking mimosa.

I toss it back and wipe the back of my mouth.

"Do you want to get out of here?"

I swivel to face the man, making a show of looking him up and down. He's wearing a leather jacket over a flannel, jeans, work boots. And yet, he doesn't strike me as someone who's ever had a hard day's work.

It's just a costume.

I wrinkle my nose. "I'm good."

"You're drinking, and it's nine o'clock in the morning," he points out.

"This place opens early." And it seemed better to come here instead of drink alone in my apartment.

After Reese's abrupt exit, I kept expecting Kade to storm in. I waited on my couch for an hour, then another, without moving. Finally, when the sky began to lighten, I showered and changed and headed out.

I walked here, but I wouldn't say Madness was my destination.

I'm not *crazy*. Or an alcoholic.

I just am not coping well with life.

"You're here, too," I add to the man who's still judging me.

He raises both hands in surrender, and I face the bartender again. I motion for another, silently cutting myself off after this. This will be my third, and I still need to function for the rest of the day.

My phone buzzes in my pocket. I retrieve it and scan the screen, and for some reason, I flush.

"Hey." I clear my throat. Shift on my seat.

The bartender arrives with my drink, and I swallow it just as fast as the last.

"Where are you?" Malik asks.

I roll my eyes. "None of your business."

"Uh-huh. Well, I thought you might want to know that our search was successful."

It takes me a minute to work out what the Hell Hounds' leader is talking about. It feels like eons ago since I asked him to find Reese for me.

But he has?

Too late—I found him first.

A giggle slips out, and I smack my palm over my mouth.

"You don't sound right," Malik says. "How did you find him?"

Did I say that out loud?

"Yeah, you're talking out loud," he says. "Where are you?"

"Descend." I roll my eyes. "Okay, Madness. Same thing."

He sighs. "Stay there. I'm on my way."

"Watch out for the one-eyed monsters," I whisper.

Did I mention those drinks were doubles?

I hang up on Malik and sag on the stool.

Reese was in my apartment only hours ago, and I haven't slept a wink in... I don't know how long. Every time I blink, the sandpaper feeling in my eyes intensifies.

If I have to then deal with Malik? I'm one hundred percent not doing it sober.

17 REESE

KADE LAURENT STRIDES from the marina parking lot toward the docks. I track him through the scope of my rifle, focused on keeping my breathing even. Steady. It's the only thing holding back a vague, creeping sense of panic.

How did he find me?

My former best friend types a code into the locked gate, makes sure it is shut firmly behind him, and heads down the walkway. He turns onto one of the narrower docks, pausing at the slip of a small speedboat. Its name is obstructed. He steps on board and disappears from view. I wait another minute, then climb down from my position.

My finger was nowhere near the trigger—the asshole was safe from me this time—but I still double-check the safety as I exit the roof and hurry back toward my apartment.

Once inside, I lean the firearm against the wall.

Kade didn't actually find me. He's about four blocks off, currently, but he's still *here*. In Sterling Falls. The last place I want anyone I care about to be.

I strip off my shirt and exchange it for a clean one. The

studio apartment was cheap to rent, the landlord accepted cash, and he didn't ask a ton of questions. It's also one of the taller buildings in the industrial district that has apartments. It's just on the edge of South and East Falls, where the warehouses give way to housing. Most of the people who live in this building work at the harbor, on the ships, or in factories dotted around South Falls.

As a result, they're relatively quiet, and a lot of them live alone. It's an eat-sleep-work mentality during the week, which is fine by me.

The roar of a motorcycle below reaches my ears. I automatically stiffen, but it continues on. I stay still until it fades, then hurriedly finish getting dressed. The Hell Hounds' compound is a fifteen-minute drive from here, which means motorcycles aren't out of the norm. Especially on nice days, when it seems like the whole club goes out for a ride.

Still, the sound reminds me of things better left in the past.

Going to Artemis once was foolish.

Seeing her a second time was dumb.

And seeking her out a third time was... *problematic.* Stupid seems too light a word, but I regret it. I regret it even as I remember the feel of her skin on mine. I regret it even though I cause her panic attacks.

She's lucky she didn't pass out last night.

Guilt strikes me. And a second emotion is quick to follow: *jealousy.* That someone left hickeys on her neck. That she moved on from Terror while I seem trapped in the past.

It's my fault she has this reaction to me. My fault my parents brought me to Terror and forced me to...

Pounding at my door jars away my thoughts.

I grab the rifle and creep to the apartment door, peeking through the peephole.

A man in a leather cut stands waiting, his hands in his pockets.

"What do you want?" I call, standing off to the side of the door. My fingers tighten around the rifle.

"Artemis Madden," the guy replies. "She wants to have a word."

I pause.

Debate.

"Come on out," the guy continues. "Just a conversation."

I'm curious, so I relent. I unlock the door and crack it, keeping my foot braced so he can't shove it inward.

"Who are you?" I bite out.

The man appraises me. "Malikai Barlow."

I glare at him, but he just shrugs. Like none of this bothers him. Knocking on a stranger's door, sending a very particular kind of message... There's a knife in a very visible holster at his hip. The handle alone looks wicked—the blade has to be seven, maybe eight inches long.

It means he'd rather maim than kill. Or he prefers his enemies to suffer a slow death.

When I don't reply, he adds, "She's downstairs."

With that, he turns and leaves me standing there like an idiot.

Do I want to talk to Artemis again?

Is she in any state after I walked out on her?

I sigh and set the rifle aside, checking that my handgun is still in the holster in the small of my back. It is. I meet him at the end of the hall, where the green *exit* sign flickers ever so subtly.

Tall as it is, there's no elevator in this building.

We take the stairs to the ground level. Around and around we go, until my knee protests and I grit my teeth to stop from complaining.

My knee is always the first thing to ache. The first to alert me to incoming storms, even. A weird trick, but true enough. And it's helped me avoid the rain on more than one occasion. The reason for the ache isn't positive, but whipping out the party trick to impress the random person beside me at the bar gives me a dose of levity.

We exit into a small lobby. There's a row of mailboxes along the left wall. Some packages are collecting dust on the floor. One of the fluorescent tubes in the ceiling light is out.

Malikai Barlow spares none of that a glance. The back of his cut says *Hell Hounds MC*, and I bite the inside of my cheek. I should've noticed it before I followed him down eight flights of stairs.

Bad enough still that I left the rifle, but this? Willingly following a member of a motorcycle club—one who could've easily lied about who awaits me at the exit.

Unprepared.

Sloppy.

This could be a trap. A clever one. No one knows—no one *really* knows—my relationship to Artemis Madden. But he said her name easily, as if he'd said it a thousand times before.

—the golden girl is up next—

I blink hard, erasing the hazy image that floated up out of nowhere, the echoing words that followed.

We get outside, my muscles tensing for the attack.

But no—here she is.

She fiddles with a helmet in her lap, half sitting on a motorcycle. There are three other guys surrounding her, taking up most of the street.

Not that anyone gives a fuck.

Her half-lidded eyes stick on my shoes, and she giggles to herself.

"Drunk," Malikai mutters. "At nine-fucking-thirty in the morning."

I scan the street. Besides Malikai's three club members, and the bike Artemis uses to keep herself upright, there's nothing. No movement, no sounds. A block away, in the opposite direction of the docks, floats the sound of construction.

A decimated warehouse is being rebuilt.

"Well?" Malikai demands.

I straighten. His words are for her, not me, but they rake down my spine all the same.

"Don't talk to her like that," I snap.

The Hound eyes me. "Oh, really?"

I keep my expression even and don't reply. I haven't dealt with him before. I've barely got the lay of the land. But I do know that guys like him respect confidence. If I show fear, I'm done.

I'm *not* afraid, though. Not of him.

"S'okay, Mal." Artemis shoves off the bike and weaves toward us. She pats his chest, tipping her head back to see him clearly.

She's in a black cropped top and ripped, light-washed jeans. Her dark hair is long and flowing around her shoulders, not in its usual braid. Her eyes are bloodshot, but her makeup is perfectly in place. Black powder on her lids, mascara lengthening her lashes. She has layered necklaces that almost conceal her cleavage. Conceal or accentuate, I can't decide.

Her tanned skin is almost glowing bronze in the morning sunlight.

She focuses on me, and her breathing hitches.

Malikai grips her forearm in response.

I smirk at him.

"I found him," Malikai says slowly, his gaze not leaving mine. "Now I want my favor."

Her expression changes. Drops into nothing, like liquid glass being set back in the fire. Her lips twitch, the slightest inclination of a frown flickering. Then back to smooth glass.

"Your favor," she repeats. "Okay, then. What is it?"

"I want you to stay away from him." He gestures to me.

My eyebrows hike.

She laughs.

I don't get the joke.

Her laughter fades when he doesn't smile.

He's serious?

She's considering it?

"He lives on the top floor," Malikai continues. "Apartment 8F."

"Gee, thanks," I mutter.

He ignores me. "Tem. Are you going to pay me my favor?"

She studies him.

Then me.

Then back to him.

I don't like this. I don't like that she's thinking about doing what he says, because I don't know how to avoid her. I'm drawn back to her, time and again, and it isn't just because of how stunning she is. It's because of our past. And a bit of our future, too.

We're woven together whether she wants to be or not.

"You need me," I finally say, like I can help my case any more. Push myself a bit farther. "You don't know what's coming, Artemis. But I do. And you're going to need my help to stop it."

To stop *him*.

It's too late, though. My words have little effect, as she nods to herself and seems to make a decision. She slides the helmet on and flips the visor down, blocking my view of her eyes.

She's drunk—he said so himself.

She can't decide to cut me out while inebriated.

But they're all moving, the verdict heard even though she didn't fucking say anything. She climbs on the bike. Malikai swings his leg over, sliding into the position in front of her.

Artemis doesn't wrap her arms around him, just grips the two handles on either side of her ass. She stays leaned back enough that she doesn't even touch him, although she sways when he kick-starts the engine.

I grimace.

The others are on their bikes, too. The roar of four motorcycles in front of me rings in my ears, and they all take off. I'm left on the sidewalk alone, with my heart oddly in my throat.

No one even looks back.

But especially not Artemis.

18 ARTEMIS

COLD WATER HITS MY FACE.

I flinch and swing, although the culprit is too fast. By the time my eyes crack open, he's taken several steps back.

The pitcher he used is tucked under his arm.

I growl through my teeth.

"Easy, wildcat," he says, fighting a smug smile. "You were snoring."

I glance around, slowly wiping water from my face. The front of my hair is soaked, as is my face and chest. I'm on the couch, which is... weird.

I don't remember getting home.

"Who sleeps at five o'clock anyway?" he continues.

My first real sleep in what feels like a week—interrupted by this bag of dicks? I open and close my mouth, trying to come up with some witty comeback, but...

I've got nothing.

I push myself up off the couch, and he steps back farther. Expecting retaliation? If only I wasn't so bone-tired. The good news is, the couch is wet—not my bed. I go straight to my room and kick the door shut behind me. I strip off my necklaces and wet shirt, unhook my bra. I'm halfway out of my pants when the door creaks open.

"Artemis—"

Silence.

I press my lips together, reversing my motion and yanking my pants back up. Covering my breasts with one arm, I whirl around to face him.

He's standing in the doorway, his gaze locked on... my chest.

Naturally.

"Get out," I seethe. "Is living here not enough? You need to invade *my* privacy, too?"

I drop my arm.

"There. Take a picture, for all the fucks I give."

His brow furrows. "Your nipples are pierced?"

Lord help me.

I cross to the dresser, yanking out one of my favorite t-shirts. I hurry to get it on and don't breathe until the fabric hides my chest.

The memory of my right nipple being pierced comes back to me, the old pain hauntingly sharp. I pierced the other one two years later, reliving that day in a different way. I wanted to rewrite it, but it just added to my complex feelings about the subject. Simply removing the one didn't feel like enough. I had to take ownership of it.

And... well, Saint didn't seem inclined to touch my breasts when he was mauling me.

He seems to be waiting for confirmation.

I do the crazy thing and lift my shirt, exposing a breast. I flick the gold bar and make a face. "Yep, seems to be a pierc-ing. Not some figment of your imagination."

He stares at me.

"Oh my God, Saint. Get out of my room." I march forward and shove at him.

He must still be in shock over seeing my tits, because the big man *stumbles*. Just a step or two back, but it's enough for me to slam my door in his face. And lock it, for good measure.

Yes, my nipples are pierced.

One was consensual. One wasn't.

But if I told him that, I don't think he'd believe me. I hardly believe it myself.

Sometimes, Terror feels like a distant dream. Something my subconscious made up, and I slowly forgot about it over time. I didn't want to remember, and yet, standing in my bedroom all alone, the memories surge from where I've locked them away.

And all at once, I'm drowning in it.

19 ARTEMIS

Terror - nearly ten years ago

I SIT IN A DARK CELL, my back to the wall. My breast aches and burns where the silver hoop they shoved through my right nipple touches the loose t-shirt. A spot of blood has formed on the white fabric, just barely visible in the dim overhead light.

A single bulb that buzzes and flickers.

There's a wide window over my head, but it's only a few inches tall. Thick bars ensure detainment. That and the metal door that remains locked at all times.

I am alone at all times.

Until the guards come anyway. They shuffle girls into the hall like cattle, prodding at us, directing us into showers. Where the filth of our cells is scrubbed from our skin, new outfits are presented. Rough hands grip our chins and paint rouge on our lips and cheeks, breathing fake life into our appearances.

I was fifteen the first time I was raped.

Fifteen and naïve.

Fifteen and devastated. Confused. Scared.

Fifteen and innocent—until, suddenly, I wasn't.

I've been here for weeks, if not months. Pushed onto a stage, one girl after another, the bidding and judgment silent and loud all at once. It's all the same, every time I am prodded through the dark curtains. Every time the lights blind me, and what feels like seconds later I'm swept away to a private room.

To be someone's plaything.

But this time...

This time, when I'm shuffled into one of the private, fancy rooms, there isn't just a man waiting for me. Or even just a man and a woman.

There's a boy, too.

A boy with sea-glass-green eyes and blond hair combed back, slick and secured with gel. He can't be much older than me, and he's the one who tentatively steps forward.

Who holds out his hand like I am a feral animal.

I haven't been allowed to be feral. There's a constant threat of going downstairs, where there are no rules. Nothing to protect us from the dark pleasures of men.

"This is the golden girl?" the woman behind him questions. "She looks frightened."

"Just the new environment, ma'am," a man says in a low voice. "She's not used to boys her age."

The woman sniffs.

A single sound that carries a lot of weight.

If I wasn't hollow, my cheeks would burn.

They back off, though. Put space between themselves and the boy.

I don't want this.

It isn't the first time I've thought that. As soon as I step back, though, hands grab at me. They stab a needle into my left upper arm, and a hot sensation spreads across the muscle. And then... worse.

The heat goes straight between my legs, my whole body tingling.

I gasp.

"New cocktail," the man behind me, another guard, says.

Not to me, though. To the couple. And the boy.

"Enhances desire."

I shift. Squeeze my legs together. The words register, and then it makes sense.

The boy is eyeing me curiously now. They all are.

I can't.

I won't.

My body is on fire. Ants crawl across my skin, and white spots flicker. My throat closes, making it hard to draw in a ragged breath. It comes in on a wheeze, exhales as a rattle. It's then that I realize something is wrong.

I can't breathe.

The first panic attack of many to come.

That won't protect you, a small, snide voice in my head whispers.

The white spots take over my vision, and my hearing goes out. I'm still conscious. I'm still functioning. But my brain just... *stops.* The urge to be touched, to feel something —*anything*—overtakes my thoughts.

Something breaks in my mind, because I hold myself on the razor's edge of giving in. Even as the boy inches forward and my fist snaps out, catching him in the nose. Even when my gaze stays cutting, but my body has another motive.

The first time is the worst, they said. The pain between my legs, the blood.

But this, arguably, surpasses that. Because the ability to separate pain and pleasure—*there's never been pleasure before*—crumbles, leaving me only wanting touch. Wanting something I cannot voice, which the boy slowly finds.

And that's when I lose the last of my real innocence.

20 ARTEMIS

Present

"THERE YOU ARE." Apollo strides across the rooftop restaurant, looking irritatingly put together. His hair is damp, and his t-shirt, dark-blue board shorts, and sandals are really not suited for the cool autumn morning.

I, on the other hand, am bundled in Kade's sweatshirt, gray sweatpants, and moccasins with fuzzy insides. About as comfortable as I can be when my mind is *not*.

Antonio and I are set to have our regular employee meeting in a few hours, but I came in early to do some reports. And the kitchen here is much more stocked than mine. A half-eaten omelet sits next to my elbow. My coffee was just replenished, and my laptop is open in front of me.

We're in Distraction Mode. *Hard.* Because I don't want to have to think about the memories that assaulted me last night. I stayed in my room until it sounded like Saint had left, the *bang* of the door shutting hard giving me a modicum of peace. And then, when I couldn't resist anymore, I tried to sleep.

Nightmares.

I think I'm more tired today than yesterday—and that's saying something.

Apollo drops into the chair across from me, grabbing the plate with the omelet. He smirks at me, but I just wave for him to help himself. He digs in, not quite as much as a heathen as one of his friends. Wolfe, actually, is the worst of them.

Watching him when he's hungry is like watching an actual starving wolf.

"What brings you here?" I ask, bracing my chin on my hand. My eyes ache from staring at the screen. And probably not sleeping, too. That's more of a plausible culprit, on second thought. I absently rub at one. Normally I wouldn't, but today I ran out of the house without an ounce of makeup.

Strange of me.

"Saint said you were out of sorts."

I narrow my eyes. "Oh, did he?"

"Are you?" His brows pinch. "Out of sorts?"

"No—"

"Because if it's that Reese guy, or Kade—"

"I'm fine." I close my laptop. "I'm one hundred percent fine."

Lies.

I'm just as bad as Saint, pretending I'm fine and hiding my wounds so I can lick them in private. But then he goes and rats me out to my brother?

"You know he still thinks about joining Nyx," I tell him.

My brother swears.

"So maybe you shouldn't believe what he says, because he's just trying to get out of my life. If only Jace would let him..."

He gives me a weird look but doesn't comment on it. Maybe he doesn't know that Jace asked Saint to move in with me?

Maybe he thinks it was *my* idea?

Gross.

I wrinkle my nose and gulp the rest of my coffee. As soon as he finishes the omelet, I collect the plate with my mug and take them to the kitchen. It's even cooler in here without the stoves and ovens on for the day. The prep cooks will come in soon, and then the waitstaff for our meeting will get fed lunch. A perk of coming in early... or a bribe so everyone shows up.

Even Antonio isn't here yet.

The doors swing inward, and Apollo crosses the threshold. He comes right up to where I'm washing the dish and leans a hip on the sink counter.

"Are you trying to hide from me?"

I scowl. "No."

"Okay, then talk to me. Please, Tem."

"I'm fine." I eye him. "I don't know what you want me to say. There's a lot of shit going on, but it's not all directly correlated to me."

He sighs. Pinches the bridge of his nose. "The sheriff wants to get a warrant and search this place."

"He already made that perfectly clear, thank you."

"He—"

"I do not want to talk about Nathan Bradshaw and warrants and dead bodies," I snap. "I just want to do my work and prepare for this meeting and then go home."

It never works out that way, though.

Apollo raises his hands in surrender, but that never means what I think it means. And true enough, he takes a seat at the bar and fiddles on his phone in silence. Seemingly convinced that I'm not well enough to leave unattended, watching me out of the corner of his eye.

Eventually, the prep cooks come in, and slowly the rest of the staff arrive, too. Antonio joins me at our table, a stack of papers in his hands.

"Inventory," he says. "And the schedule."

"Perfect." I take the pages and flip through, scanning the numbers. It seems in order, and also in line with the end of the tourist season.

"Nice sweatshirt," he comments.

I glance down.

It's clean, washed, and unfortunately back to the scent of laundry detergent. After Saint pushed me off the cliff, I couldn't very well leave it salty. There's an embroidered emblem on the breast, an eye with a snake poised to strike behind and over it.

I hadn't given it much thought, to be honest.

But now I frown, because...

I don't know.

I'm not taking it off, though.

"I wanted to be comfortable," I murmur, tapping the sheaf of papers on the table. "Do you have a problem with that?"

"Not in the slightest." He raises an eyebrow. "I wasn't judging, Tem."

"Uh-huh." I stand, and our staff goes quiet.

I'm glad I don't have to yell for them to shut up.

"Good morning," I call. "Better to get the work over with so you guys can have a good lunch, right?"

They voice their assent, and my gaze flicks to Apollo. He's watching me a little closer now. I push my shoulders back and lift my chin. It doesn't matter what he thinks—I'll prove that I'm fine.

Nightmares, dead bodies, and new gangs or not.

NATHAN BRADSHAW'S house is small, tidy, and tucked into a bustling neighborhood of East Falls. It's close to the Financial District and downtown, where his offices are, and I think he came to some sort of agreement with the Hell Hounds to leave his particular block alone.

Not that they mess with anyone, really.

Okay, they totally do. But not on Nathan Bradshaw's street.

I leave my car at the corner and stroll down the sidewalk, my hands in my pockets. He *should* be at work, which is why I'm choosing broad daylight to make my move.

The street is quiet, most people still working at this time of day. When I'm two houses away from his, I cut down a driveway and into a backyard. People in this neighborhood don't fence their yards, which has always felt strange to me.

West Falls is totally different. But here, there's the *slightest* bit more breathing room between the houses, and the yards all seem to mesh into one another. It makes crossing them to get to his back door easier anyway.

I climb the steps to his back porch and crouch, flipping the mat up. The sheriff is too fucking predictable, and a key gleams at me. I unlock the door, then pocket it.

Silence.

There's no beeping alarm, no scuffle of claws on the floor.

Nothing.

I've been here twice before, but always with others. And never on the assumption of Nathan Bradshaw's guilt.

There's a little stack of dishes in the sink, and unopened

mail on the counter. I take back the *tidy* part of my description. It doesn't matter, though, because catching him with dirty dishes isn't my goal.

I'm here looking for evidence of corruption.

Nathan Bradshaw has been known to take a bribe or two in his day. In fact, just a few years ago he would've been labeled a *bad guy* by some. My brother, for one.

I draw my knife from my ankle and clear the house, making sure no one's going to leap out at me from the closet or from behind a door.

He has an office-slash-guest room, his room, and one bathroom in the hall. Living room, laundry room, kitchen.

That's it.

And besides the kitchen, it's relatively clean.

I start with his mail, flipping through it for anything that can catch my eye. There's nothing except some overdue bills, magazine subscriptions, and a letter from Nadine.

His sister.

There are a few envelopes with the local funeral home listed as the return address, and I pause. I set those down carefully. It sucks to lose a parent, and Nathan Bradshaw's dad... Well, I met him once, too. He was nice, as far as I could tell.

Moving into his home office, I first try my luck with the filing cabinets.

They're locked.

Naturally. Even someone who hides a key in the most obvious place would lock up their sensitive documents. My curiosity burns, but I can't waste valuable time trying to pick the lock. Not if I expect to search the whole house... but the locked cabinet certainly draws my attention.

Desk is next.

There's not a lot in there, however. Printed phone records—which I scan, but the name of the person isn't on the sheet, and none of the numbers jump out at me at first glance. Two are highlighted, though.

I frown and take a picture of it.

He has a safe in the bottom drawer. Maybe for his gun?

I reach for the last drawer, a large one on the opposite side, just as a car door shuts—too close.

I peek out the window and immediately duck.

Nathan Bradshaw is home.

Fuck.

I dart for the closet. Since it's a guest bedroom, it still has one. And lucky for me, it's relatively empty. I pull the door shut softly, and the front door creaks open a split second later.

Not good.

I glance down at myself. Did I leave anything on the counter? Did I leave the back door open?

The key is still in my pocket, but I'm fairly sure I flipped the mat back down. If not... I'm about to have a gun shoved in my face. I just know it.

The sheriff moves around his house. He's talking to someone, although I didn't hear a second person enter.

And it's a one-sided conversation.

"Yes, I have it." His voice drifts closer. "I told you I would get it. I have it here."

Pause.

"No, you absolutely cannot come to my house. I'll meet you. Tonight."

Pause.

"Yes, that's fine." He's in the room now, opening a drawer and closing it again. The rustle of papers. "No, six o'clock—because when I get out of work, I'm leaving my badge at home. I'm not meeting you in my fucking uniform."

I hold perfectly still, but my line of sight through the crack in the door allows me to see him holding the highlighted paper. He unlocks the top drawer of the filing cabinet, and he...

He puts that in there.

Locks it.

"I hear you," he says.

My heart stops.

"I understand your concern," he continues, still on the phone. "But I'm doing my job, and I expect to be fucking compensated."

His voice drifts farther away, and I release a slow breath when his cruiser's engine starts. I wait another minute, then slowly creep out of the closet.

I go straight to the filing cabinet and yank uselessly at the top drawer.

Whatever it is, someone wants that.

And it was pure luck that I found it in the first place.

I pull up the photo and again scour the page. The two highlighted numbers aren't marked, but they are different. One call is logged from two weeks ago, and it lasted thirty seconds. The other number called a month ago, and it lasted three minutes and four seconds.

There hasn't been much activity on whoever's account this is since then.

Before I can think it through, I dial the older number. I add the digits to the beginning that will block my number.

It doesn't even ring. Just a robot voice saying, "This number is no longer in service."

I try the next one, expecting the same. But I almost drop my phone when it *does* ring through—and then again when it picks up.

"Who is this?" a familiar voice demands.

I hang up.

21 ARTEMIS

FOLLOWING the sheriff is a really bad idea.

And yet...

At five thirty-two p.m., I am parked down the street from the sheriff's house. He has to get here soon if he's going to be meeting someone at six. And sure enough, just a few minutes later, he arrives. He gets out of the cruiser and heads inside, reemerging minutes later in civilian clothes.

His gun is still on his hip, however.

He wastes no time climbing into his personal car, a sporty white SUV, and backs out of the driveway. Tucked between cars the way I am, I doubt he sees me.

I start the engine of Apollo's bike—*borrowed, not stolen*—and head out behind the sheriff. His car's engine is loud. It's flashy, and it strikes me as a splurge purchase. I should've known he was on the take, because he drives way too nice a vehicle for someone on a cop's salary.

I stay well back from him, even taking a different route and running parallel to him for a while. Motorcycles aren't known for their stealth, so I have to stay creative.

Creative-ish.

Eventually, I have to get back on the same road and just keep about a block behind him. The smart move would've been pilfering some tracking equipment and planting it, letting him get well and truly ahead of me.

But I didn't let anyone know where I was going, and getting that sort of equipment probably would've required advanced notice. So... here I am.

My phone vibrates, and I hit the button on my helmet. It's the only thing I managed to save from my bike's violent death.

Don't think about violent death.

"Where is my bike?" Apollo's voice comes through the Bluetooth in the helmet.

I smirk. "Where did you leave it?"

"Outside of Olympus—but your car is here and my bike isn't."

"Oops."

"Artemis—"

"*Ooh*, you're full-naming me. What next, my middle name?" I grin.

"I can literally hear you riding—"

"Good point, I shouldn't drive and chat at the same time." I hit the button to hang up the call. I'm sure he's got this thing tricked out with GPS and whatever else. He could be tracking me right this second and come find me within minutes.

Since the sheriff is heading through West Falls, maybe I have more than minutes. Apollo would be coming from the opposite end of the city, especially if he's only just leaving Olympus now.

A prickle of unease slides down my spine at being in West Falls. It's not nighttime, which means I *should* be relatively safe. I don't know if this bike is marked the same way mine was.

They didn't really elaborate on that.

Well, actually, she said that *I* was marked.

I check my mirrors. There are a lot of cars out and about, people coming home from work or heading downtown for dinner. Still, the hair on the back of my neck rises.

We're working our way toward... the reservoir?

Once we're out of the tightly packed neighborhoods, I let the distance between us grow. And sure enough, he heads toward the reservoir. It's a huge lake that supplies the town water. It sits up high, and one of its waterfalls is a frequent destination.

There are also more unsavory things hiding in the woods up here.

I round a corner and cut the engine. The bike rolls silently now, coasting on my momentum, toward the parking lot for the waterfall. There's a hike here, too.

My phone buzzes with an incoming call.

The number I dialed in the sheriff's house... I thought I made my number private, though. Unless I did it wrong?

Unless I only did it for the first number?

My throat goes all tight, but I answer it anyway. "Hello?"

A surprised inhale. "Artemis?"

"The one and only." Around another corner, and I squeeze the hand brake.

The sheriff's vehicle is *right there*. I manage to steer down a little hill and behind a giant tree. Branches snag at my clothes and Apollo's bike, leaving a scratch in the paint.

Whoops.

"What are you doing? How did you get this number?"

"Quick question," I say. "Did you have another burner phone?"

Reese doesn't reply, which essentially confirms it.

Who would he have called? And not once, but twice? It's a shame the logs were blacked out... it would've saved a lot of this trouble.

I drag Apollo's bike farther off the path and leave it in the trees. Once I'm sure it's out of sight, I head around toward where Nathan is now climbing out of his vehicle. He walks to the fence and braces his arms on the top rail.

Waiting.

I check the time on my phone. It's 5:49 p.m., which means we're essentially going to be waiting for eleven minutes. Or longer. Bad guys are never on time—and the sheriff being early isn't a shock either. He's still got a cop's brain, which means getting the lay of the land. Surveillance. No surprises.

"What are you doing, Artemis?" His voice comes through my helmet.

"I'm digging into the mystery of Reese Avery."

I'm funny, because that's exactly who I'm talking to.

"I—"

"Save it, Reese." I shake my head. "Who did you call?"

"I—"

"*Reese.*"

Another car is coming.

"Goddamn it," he mutters. "My mother."

I flinch.

"And what's up with Kade?" I peek out to see the newest vehicle.

"He and I were..."

If I were with him, I think he'd shrug at me. But now, he

just trails off like he doesn't know how to classify what he and Kade were.

"Lovers?" I ask.

He chokes. "God, no. Kade might not care about what his partner has between their legs, but I like women. I'm only attracted to women."

Interesting. Another detail filed away for later.

"And why does he want to find you so badly? Have you been leaving him clues?"

The new vehicle is blacked out, the windows tinted so strongly I can't see the driver. But I recognize it, none-theless. After all—I was in it not too long ago.

I press my lips together, suddenly sick.

Kade climbs out, and the sheriff meets him halfway. I flip my visor up in an attempt to hear them better.

"Artemis..." Reese's voice is low in my ear. "Don't."

"You're running from someone," I whisper. "Is it Kade?"

The sheriff holds something out to him. The papers.

"I expected you to just email it," Kade rumbles, taking it from him. He towers over Nathan. "You went old school. Paper."

"This was cleaner," the sheriff snaps. "Take it or leave it."

Kade sneers. "I'll take it. But I'm not leaving."

"Where are you?" Reese suddenly asks in my ear.

"Shh," I whisper to him.

He swears.

Too bad.

I take my helmet off and set it on the ground next to me. Getting closer would be stupid—but so would letting Reese distract me from their conversation.

"You're disrupting my city," Nathan says with a

grimace. "The deal was, I give you this and you leave Sterling Falls."

Kade inclines his chin. "I came here looking for something, and I haven't found it yet. This is just a puzzle piece slotting into place."

The sheriff is going to make the fucking connection. Any second now. But instead, he sticks his hands in his jeans, seemingly passive. Considering, sure, but he's not upset about it. He's giving Kade phone records to Reese's mother. Reese Avery, who Apollo *and* Antonio have raged about in his office.

Is this the sheriff's method of getting Reese out of Sterling Falls? He hopes Kade will take him and go?

This can't be legal.

No, dumbass, it's definitely not.

Kade pulls an envelope from his back pocket and tosses it to the sheriff. It's thick, and Nathan catches it against his chest. He takes his time opening it, thumbing through what I can only assume is cash. He nods, and they go their separate ways.

The sheriff back to the railing, overlooking the waterfall, and Kade to his vehicle.

I stay where I am until it makes a swift three-point turn and disappears back down the road. The sheriff doesn't move, but I sense his attention shifting toward me.

"Come out, come out," he calls softly. "You make an awful tail, Artemis."

I stiffen. I grab my helmet and hang up on Reese, then pick my way out of the brush and up to the road.

"How'd you know it was me?" I fold my arms over my chest.

"Your brother doesn't have breasts."

A flush heats my face.

"Besides, you were parked at the top of my street earlier today. And again when I got out of work." His lips quirk.

I open and close my mouth, but I've got nothing.

I thought I was so smooth getting in and out—all for nothing.

Stupid.

What can I say? I'm not on my A game.

Months of sneaking into a Hell-Hound-controlled Olympus, making not a whisper of noise, being *perfect*, has transitioned to this?

Sloppy.

"It's okay," he says carefully. "He has you searching for something, too, doesn't he?"

"Not a *thing*," I hedge.

I don't bother telling him I've roped the Hell Hounds into it, too. Maybe that's for the best—our appearance could've scared Reese away from that place. Moving to a new location, getting a new burner phone, all those things will help keep Kade off Reese's trail a little longer.

Wait.

Whose side am I on?

"Do you trust him?" I ask Nathan.

"No." He narrows his eyes. "Who's he looking for?"

"You highlighted the numbers on the phone records. I think you know more than you're saying, Nathan. Like... you know those are burner phones belonging to Reese Avery. Maybe you even tracked them. How long do you think it will take Kade to realize you can find him that way, and come back for more favors?"

His expression darkens. "I was highlighting numbers I couldn't trace. That's all."

I snort. "Jesus, Brad, you're not a good investigator. You

want Kade and Reese to leave Sterling Falls? Try actually having a moral backbone."

I leave him standing there. It takes a lot of muscle to get the stupid bike back up onto flat ground, and I'm sweating by the time I do. I peel off Kade's sweatshirt and tie it around my waist, and in no time I'm zooming away. It's a miracle I was able to hear everything over the sound of the waterfall. My sweatshirt—*Kade's sweatshirt*—is speckled with fine mist from being up close to it.

On some level, the sheriff knew I was going to follow him. It doesn't matter if he spotted my vehicle before or after the meeting was set—he could've easily called Kade back and changed the time. He could've driven like a bat out of hell and lost me, or confronted me outside of his offices.

He didn't.

Which means what?

Was I supposed to follow him, or was the sheriff simply banking on my curiosity to help *him*?

He also seemed unafraid of the idea that Kade would return and ask more questions. That leads me to believe Kade doesn't need the sheriff to find Reese. Whether by leveraging Reese's dear old mom for information, threatening her to get him out of hiding, or something worse.

This is a mess. One I should warn Reese about, at the very least.

It's not like I owe him anything, but I don't know if I could live with myself if I just sat and watched Kade put his plan into motion.

I get back into West Falls, heading home at a good speed. I could take this road all the way south and swing by the apartment building to check and see if Reese is still there.

Or... not.

I could call him, fill him in.

Or... *not*.

Maybe the sheriff is right, and once Kade finds Reese, they'll both leave. Can I leave that up to chance?

The decision is still unmade when something on the road catches my attention.

And the people. Too many men, crowding both sides of the sidewalk. Only one watches me, his dark gaze full of loathing. I instinctively hit the throttle.

But then the line across the road is pulled tight, lifted in the air, and it catches my bike just below the handlebars.

I never stood a chance.

22 SAINT

I ENTER the house in West Falls. My chest is full of an old pain that pulses with every heartbeat. I can never get rid of that reminder. Like the hourglass branded on my chest, or the scars that mar some of the tattoos on my lower torso.

That torture was inflicted as punishment, and I remember it to punish myself, too. It's why I return to this house, why I now sit on the floor and throw my head back against the wall. I do it until I'm dizzy, until the spots in front of my eyes don't immediately go away.

Sometimes I think about concussing myself badly enough that my memory leaves me completely. I'd be a blank slate. Wouldn't that be nice?

Slam.

Elora's face floats in front of me.

Slam.

Artemis lifting her shirt, exposing her breast.

Slam.

Tattooing Elora, her pale white skin soft under my gloved hand.

Slam.

Going through the motions of tattooing Artemis, even though I have no ink. I'm just doing it to fuck with her. But she hasn't mentioned it at all.

Slam.

Shoving her dress up, feeling irrationally angry that my body was reacting to hers.

Slam.

Nothing.

I breathe out raggedly, the pain from my chest now transferred to the back of my skull. I sag down the wall, nearly falling over. I catch myself on my forearm, then crawl toward the bathroom. I barely manage to get there before my stomach cramps, and the little I ate for breakfast comes back up.

From outside comes shouts, jeers.

Cheering.

Not the nice kind.

I drag myself to my feet and crash into the wall. *Fuck, that hurt.* I keep going to the front window, splitting the blinds to see the street.

Someone is being carried.

My brow furrows, and I lean forward more. The sun has mostly set, giving everything a twilight hue. It's hard to pick out details, but I do see long brown hair caught up in a fist.

I yank open the door and stumble down the front steps, barely keeping myself upright.

Too many hits.

I somehow stay on my feet and push the gate open, calling to them, "Where's the party, fellas?"

There are five of them. No, six.

One turns back to me. "Go home, bro."

Anger stokes in my chest, and I glare at him. "Bro?

We're buddies now? I just want to know what kind of fun you're having."

"You're drunk," he says.

A brush-off.

He gives me his back, and I follow him. My head throbs, but it's my own fucking doing. I hurry. My stride is uneven, the pitch of the sidewalk definitely not helping. And yet, I can't let them take some girl with them—

I reach out and clamp my hand down on the guy's shoulder. The one who stopped to talk to me, who's at the back of the pack.

They're shit talking. Saying what a good catch they found.

An Olympus bitch.

I drag him backward, and it opens up my line of sight to the girl in their grip.

Artemis.

She's not conscious, not as far as I can tell. Her feet drag on the concrete. They've got her by her arms, although one just holds on to her hair, keeping her head yanked back.

Eyes shut.

Limp.

I don't think—I just react. The first punch sends blessed fire through my knuckles, and the guy's eyes roll back. They haven't noticed me yet, somehow, and I catch the guy before he makes noise collapsing to the ground.

"Fuck her up and leave her at their altar." The one with his hand in her hair laughs.

They agree.

"Good idea." My tone is cold, and the red that had been creeping across my vision engulfs me completely.

They jump. Turn. But I've got the drop on them. The first two take my punches and stumble away, clutching bloody faces. Fire sings through my body. The third gets a hit in, but he goes for my stomach. My abs tense, absorbing the hit, and I strike back harder.

I move like a dancer, until there's just one left.

He has an arm under Artemis's breasts, holding her back to his front.

A knife at her throat.

We stare at each other, and he edges backward.

She looks innocent like this. The way she judges me, the hostility in her gaze any time she so much as catches a glimpse of me, isn't there. Of course, I don't get the warmth of her brown eyes either.

"Let her go," I order.

He sneers.

I want to ask more. Like *why?* And *who are you?* And *how fucking dare you?* But I don't. I keep my mouth shut, waiting for him to make a decision.

His gaze ticks from me to his fallen buddies, and then my bloody knuckles.

I think they're bloody. They feel wet, although the pain isn't there. The pain in my head is gone, too. Blasted away by adrenaline, only to surge back later tonight. I'm sure of that much.

He shoves her toward me. Still fully unconscious, her body falls forward. I dive for her, managing to save her from breaking her face.

He turns and strides away. Not even fucking scared—like he knows I won't go after him.

What the fuck is wrong with people?

I lift Artemis into my arms and carry her back to Elora's house. She feels solid in my arms—unlike living with the memory of Elora. Her skin is warm, her head lolls against my shoulder. Her hair spills down my arm.

Stop it.

There's a sweatshirt tied around her hips, but otherwise she wears a plain black t-shirt and gray sweatpants. The t-shirt is cropped, exposing a slice of her golden abdomen.

I get Artemis up the stairs and into the house, kicking the door shut behind me.

We had Elora's funeral here, but there were a lot of other memories, too. Now, it's up to me to keep everything maintained. Her parents never came back to Sterling Falls, which is fine. I mow the lawn once a week, planted wildflowers in the raised beds out front. Repaired a broken window from some stupid kid. Installed a security system.

It's not enough, but it gives me the slightest bit of peace. Like she might actually be okay with how I'm handling this.

She wouldn't judge me. No, she loved me. We talked about everything, we were in everything together. Together or nothing.

And now I'm nothing.

I stand in the living room for a second, blinking back tears. It takes me a minute to focus, to remember what I was doing in the first place.

I lay Artemis on the couch, making sure her head ends up on a pillow. There's blood on the backs of her forearms and elbows, her sweatpants are ripped down the fronts of her thighs, her skin dirty and scraped up. Even her shirt is messed up, with bits of rocks stuck into the cuts on her chest.

What the fuck happened to her?

I fumble with the blinds, shutting everything before I switch on the lamp.

Almost immediately, there's a knock at the door. Before I answer it, I grab a knife from the kitchen and return, peering out the little side window.

It's a woman.

A neighbor?

I open it roughly, and she starts.

"What?" I snap.

She fiddles with the front of her coat. "I told her not to come back," she whispers. "I warned her that she was marked. The Cyclopes are serious about it. Is she okay?"

Cyclopes?

"She's fine—"

"You should get out of here. It's not safe for her."

I'm experiencing some weird form of déjà vu, I swear to God. The woman seems... *normal.* Mid-forties, maybe older. Maybe younger. Curly hair. The kind of makeup style that makes me think she might be a grandmother.

That's kind of mean, isn't it?

It's definitely mean.

"Okay," I tell her, although I'm not sure I fully understand what's going on. "Thank you."

"Hurry," she says. "Just—"

She spins on her heel and rushes away. I track her down the sidewalk, where she crosses the street and disappears into a house. No light comes from it.

Is she paranoid?

Or...

I shut and lock the door, then arm the security system.

At least I didn't wave the knife in that lady's face. It was in the hand braced against the door. I toss it on the counter and hunt for the first-aid kit. I locate it under the kitchen sink, which I never understood. My mom always kept hers in the bathroom. Under *that* sink, but still. It's different. Kitchen sinks are for cleaning supplies and dishwasher tablets.

The adrenaline is fading. By the time I drop down next

to Artemis's hip on the couch, my headache is creeping back at an alarming rate. I clean the wounds I can reach on her arms. There's a gash on her face, too, that I pinch shut and tape gauze across.

All the while, she doesn't so much as fucking stir.

I should remove her sweatpants. They need to be thrown away, with the state that they're in. But some sort of moral... I don't know, high ground, keeps me from doing it. So I just clean the skin that I can reach, shift her legs over my lap so I can sit more comfortably on the couch, and lean back.

My eyes close.

It's not too late to forget everything, a little voice in my head whispers.

The same voice that tells me to hurt myself.

I need to get us out of here, another voice says. The rational one.

Instead, I pass out.

23 ARTEMIS

EVERYTHING HURTS.

There's a glow of warm light coming from over my head, and it takes several long minutes to work up the courage to open both eyes at once. And longer still to piece together what happened right before I lost consciousness.

The bike... riding through West Falls... the wire across the road.

Apollo's motorcycle was caught up easily in the trap, and I flew over the handlebars. My head—thankfully in a helmet—slammed into the asphalt, and I slid on the road. Everything hurt, and I cursed myself for not wearing my leather gear.

An outfit I always wore when I was riding on *my* bike—but taking Apollo's was a spur-of-the-moment thing. It felt like fate that my helmet was in the backseat of my car.

Those guys grabbed me. Yanked my cracked helmet off, pulled at my hair and my clothes. I tried to fight, and someone swung something at my head.

I touch my forehead gingerly, wincing at the resulting pain. But my fingertips brush a bandage instead of blood.

Also, I'm inside, not left forgotten and bleeding on the side of the road.

I shift, and something warm lands on my shin. I freeze and slowly lift my head.

My legs are on Saint's lap.

His hand is on my leg.

I glance around, unfortunately immediately recognizing where we are.

Nyx's old place. She grew up here until she moved in with Saint, and her parents moved out of Sterling Falls... She let the guys use this house.

I must've driven through the neighborhood, although I don't think I was on this road.

So how did I end up here?

His head is tipped back against the couch, his mouth open as he breathes deeply.

Carefully, I lift my legs and put my feet on the floor. He didn't take my shoes off, which is good of him. I sit up and immediately have a wave of vertigo.

I squeeze my eyes shut and count to five.

Doesn't help.

Instead of standing, I slide off the couch and sit on the floor. Breathing doesn't help either. I mean, breathing keeps me alive, but it still feels a bit like I'm standing on the bow of a ship at sea.

In a storm.

Stop the ride, I want to get off.

My stomach turns, and I force my eyes open. I'm going to puke in approximately thirty seconds. Without thinking, I scramble for the bathroom and throw my body in. I don't even get a chance to flip the light switch.

Vomit is probably my least favorite thing on the planet.

The way my whole body tenses up, the headache immediately worsens. I clutch at the edges of the toilet.

The door opens behind me.

Saint, obviously.

I brace myself for another wave, my stomach cramping hard, but also brace for his snide comment. Something about how I ended up in whatever position he found me.

Instead, he silently gathers my hair back. He holds it with one hand and rummages in the drawer of the sink vanity with the other.

I close my eyes and throw up again.

Could this get any worse?

Today has *sucked*.

Something lightly scrapes at my scalp, and then Saint is sighing and moving away.

My hair stays in place.

I touch the plastic clip.

He flushes the toilet and holds out his hand. I carefully take it, letting him pull me to my feet. We eye each other for a minute. His eyes are bloodshot, and there are dark circles under them. He probably doesn't get much sleep nowadays either.

"I don't remember—"

"It's okay," he interrupts. "You don't want to know."

My attention drops to his hand, which keeps flexing into a fist and releasing. His knuckles are busted, the cuts not yet scabbed over. It seems like they've barely stopped bleeding.

"What did you do?"

He stares at me. "I think you should sit back down."

I roll my eyes.

Bad idea. My body immediately flushes hot, and my knees buckle.

Saint grabs me.

Saint stops me from hitting the floor.

Saint practically carries me back to the couch.

I think I'm in *The Twilight Zone*. Because what the fuck is happening here? When I'm seated, I finally appraise myself. The hoodie is gone—and good riddance—but my shirt is ripped and bloody, my sweatpants have massive tears in the thighs, all the way down to my knees. Like the soft fabric was flayed open.

Plus the head wound, and my arms...

"I look worse than I feel," I lie.

But honestly? How I look is a great indication of how I feel, which is to say, thoroughly chewed up and regurgitated.

The fear of that trap comes back to me, and I hold my breath. Like taking a dive, I use it to cut my panic short.

I've spent too fucking long panicking this week.

This month.

"Just stay there." He points at me, then disappears around the corner into the kitchen. From behind the wall separating the two rooms comes the sound of drawers opening and closing, and then running water. Shortly after, he comes back with two glasses of water and a bottle of pills. "Take these."

I shake out some of the painkillers and pop them in my mouth, accepting the water next. He does the same, and I eye him.

"What's up with you?"

He stiffens. "What's that supposed to mean?"

Asshole.

"It means you don't normally..." I gesture. "Something is wrong, isn't it?"

He's *here*. In Nyx's old family home.

Of course something is wrong.

He grunts and sits back down. There's no television, no entertainment of any kind. Just us facing a picture window with the blinds and curtains drawn. It's fully dark outside, and the lamp on the side table is the only light source.

"Did you find my phone?"

He shakes his head.

I sigh, imagining it flew loose in the crash.

Can I call it a crash? What else would I call it?

Stop it.

He pulls his from his pocket and hands it to me. "You should call your brother. We're going to need..." He makes a face. "Some sort of extraction."

I shiver. "Because of...?"

"Some lady warned me that you had a target on your back."

"And what makes you think my brother would be any different?"

He frowns. Considers. Then drops his phone to his thigh. He runs his hand down his face, exhaling noisily. "Well, I don't know what the fuck to do. We can't leave."

"How did *you* get here?"

He blinks at me. "I walked."

"You walked." I twist to face him, ignoring the twinges of pain. "You walked from my condo?"

"No, from Mars." He glowers at me. "Where else would I come from?"

If I didn't know how much it hurts to roll my eyes, I'd do it at him. Walking is the worst. Running at least serves a purpose... kind of. If you tell me to run around the block, I'd just scoff. But if you tell me to run for my life, sure. I'm on board with that.

But *walking* is akin to *trudging*, and I do not trudge.

I like fast.

"I don't have anyone to call," Saint says, crossing his arms. "I'm not calling Jace."

It clicks, and I smirk. "You don't want the almighty Jace King to know you were hanging out at your..." I don't know what to call Nyx to him, so I skip over it. I skip over calling her *dead*, too, which is how I do often describe her. Because she is, even if he acts like she's still alive. So I end, rather lamely, with, "Nyx's house."

His brow lowers.

"It's fine." I snatch his phone. "I'll call Malik."

He grabs the phone right back. "Are you fucking crazy? He wouldn't come into West Falls unless he wants to start a war."

"With...?"

"The Cyclopes," he says under his breath. "I thought you were supposed to be the smart one."

Oh, I hate him.

"Where did you hear that name?" I demand.

"The woman who came to warn me that you were *marked*." He rolls his eyes perfectly fine. "She seemed convinced, and come on. What else inspires fear quite like a new gang in Sterling Falls? After what this town just went through, it's probably the only thing that can scare them."

I hate him. And the woman. She's probably the one who slammed the door in my face last time.

Then, though, was a warning.

This was... more. Although I don't know what they did after they tried to grab me. I open my mouth to ask, then think better of it. Some things are better left unknown.

"Okay, so not a Hell Hound, not my brother or Jace or Wolfe..." I pause. "I only know one other person."

Two, really.

But one, I'm not fucking calling.

He eyes me.

"You're not going to like this," I warn.

And then I dial a number that I seem to have accidentally memorized.

24 ARTEMIS

I WAS RIGHT.

Saint *doesn't* like this.

He doesn't like it when I dial a number by heart that isn't a close friend's, doesn't like when the gruff voice on the other end of the line is a man.

Too bad. He said he didn't know anyone.

"I thought you'd call the sheriff," Saint says in a low voice. He's at one window, peering out through the slats of the blinds.

I'm at the other end of the house, angling to get a view up the street.

The lamp is off, and it's been quiet. But not good quiet, I'm talking unusual quiet. No cars, no people walking their dogs before bed, *nothing*.

The plan is to leave out the back, cut through the yard, and exit through the gate that opens onto an access road.

And that's where Reese Avery will be waiting. He's coming from the other road, though, so there's no good way to see him coming. He's going to text Saint's phone when he's here, and our job is to wait until then. But since Saint and I are equally bad at waiting, we've taken turns trading barbs and staring out at the road.

He pointed out the woman's house, and I nod to myself. That night, I hadn't even realized I was so close to this one. Not that I would ever willingly come here.

In fact, I'm looking forward to leaving it. And not because I know what Saint's dick feels like, and this is very much a Nyx-and-Saint place. But because it seems like he's trying to keep her memory alive by coming here, and that...

He's going backward.

I suppress my concern. "They have patrol cars, you know. They could just be... hiding."

"Hiding?" He snorts. "Hiding where, in the access road?"

The hairs on the back of my neck rise. "Yeah, Saint, *maybe.*"

He considers, then swears. I hate that I like how it sounds when curses come out of his mouth, especially when they're not directed at me. Or maybe even then. He lets the blinds fall shut and goes to the back door. It creaks as it opens, and he leaves me alone.

"Sorry, Nyx," I say to the air. "Feel free to fight me when I join you."

My throat closes, and I hurry after him. I just touch the door handle when it swings inward, nearly cracking me in the face.

He pauses. "What are you doing?"

"I—"

"It's clear. For now anyway. I didn't see anyone." His teeth score his lower lip. "You've run into them before, then?"

Oh. "I was out riding, and they hit my bike."

He stops. "What?"

I shrug. If he didn't notice my bike has been out of commission, that's his problem.

His phone chimes, temporarily pausing his questioning. He scans it, then looks over his shoulder. I crane around him, spotting the top of a truck moving down the row.

I grab Saint's arm, ready to tow him back into the house, but he's immobile.

"It's your friend," he says when the truck stops near the gate. "Let's go."

He brushes past me back into the house. I watch him for a second, then leave him there. He might want to say goodbye to Nyx in private, or... I don't know, check that the front door is locked?

I lever open the gate and slip out, heading for the passenger side of the truck. It's an older model, with a single row in the cab. Which will mean a tight fit between the two men and me. The window is rolled down, so there's no disguising who waits for us.

"Thanks," I breathe, climbing into the truck.

Reese stares at me. "What the fuck happened?"

I open my mouth, but then Saint is here a second later. The gate is closed and locked, and he urges me none too gently farther into the truck. I slide in close to Reese. He stares at me. The bandage on my head, the open wounds everywhere else.

I stare back.

Reese is in a white t-shirt and jeans, and a backward cap keeps his hair out of his eyes. My gaze drinks him in, noting the holstered gun barely visible on his left hip. I have a knife in my shoe. Saint probably has some sort of something on him.

It seems like everyone in this town is armed.

"Reese," he introduces. He stretches his muscled arm past me.

Saint eyes him, then shakes his hand.

"That's Saint," I say. "He doesn't have any manners."

Reese smiles. His teeth flash in the darkness. A low chuckle fills the cab.

Not Reese.

Not me.

Since when does Saint chuckle?

"You're one to talk," Saint says to me.

I glower.

"Artemis," Reese says. "You have an address for where I'm going?"

"I'll give you directions." I grew up in this town. There's only a rare street that I haven't traveled down. And from here, I can easily pick my way back home.

Except...

Roadblocks.

The first is two blocks down. Three trucks are parked across the road, and guys loiter around beside them. Only one remains behind one's wheel, clearly meant to back out of the way to let *approved* traffic pass.

We turn.

Another one, this with concrete lane dividers dragged into the street. Two men with guns stand in the only opening to pass through.

We turn.

It's clear for a while, but then there's another. Reese swears. Saint closes his eyes. My arms are crossed over my stomach, the painkillers not doing much against the growing tension in the cab. The more opposition we hit, the more claustrophobic I feel.

How does the sheriff not know about this?

Reese's hand touches my wrist.

I glance at him out of the corner of my eye and slowly release my hand from where it's clutching my upper arm. His fingers run along the bone of my wrist, down to my pinky.

I let him unwind my arm and take my hand. He drives one-handed and changes directions again. Avoiding *again*. I don't know if these guys see us coming, since we can spot their lit-up checkpoints from blocks away.

But we hit the main road that connects with the one that exits Sterling Falls. The only road that can be considered a highway. He takes a right, and we head up toward the reservoir. If we keep going and don't turn toward the body of water, we'll end up in North Falls.

We'll pass right by Kade's rented mansion.

My fingers tighten on his, and he glances at me. A question in his gaze.

I release his hand and curl in on myself.

We follow that road with no incident. Approaching Kade's place, I nudge Reese with my elbow and lift my chin.

He takes in the mansion with a quick, disconcerting eye.

Saint glares at it, too, for an entirely different reason.

"Is that asshole still in town?" he questions.

Okay, maybe not.

Reese's eyebrows hike. "He knows Kade?"

"*You* know Kade?" Saint asks. "Who the fuck is this guy, Artemis?"

"I'm not answering that." I sink lower. "Can we just get back to my condo, please?"

Reese presses his lips together. I can't even fucking *look* at Saint, because I have a feeling he'd make some connections he shouldn't make.

Like how Reese and I know each other.

I close my eyes. At first, it's just a ruse to get out of talking. But then real heaviness takes over, and I slump.

I wake up on Reese's shoulder. A cool wind lifts my hair, and I slowly sit up straight. The passenger door is closed, but the window is open and Saint is gone.

My face heats. I wipe at my mouth and take note of where we are.

Parked in front of one of the late-night diners near Sterling Falls University.

"What...?"

Reese touches the corner of my lip. "Saint went in to get us food."

"Us?"

"I may have spun it to be payment for saving your asses." His green eyes soften. "But really, I just wanted an excuse to be invited up to your condo again."

Oh.

My mouth is dry, and I should have a witty comeback. But the only thing I can muster is, "I like pizza."

He smirks. "Who doesn't?"

"Psychopaths." I smile. "Saint probably doesn't like pizza."

"Is he a psychopath?"

"Pretty close to one."

He laughs. But he doesn't know the full story, so I just sit back and try to blink away the sleep. Now that he mentioned Saint being inside, I can see the back of Saint's head inside at the counter. He collects boxes and exits, rounding the hood of the truck with three pizzas.

My stomach growls loud enough for both of them to hear.

Reese cracks a smile. Saint remains straight-faced, although he looks for a moment like he's about to put the boxes on my lap. And then he sees my skin and thinks better of it.

At least he has some sense.

Reese backs out of the space, and I lean into Saint. I ignore the way he tenses and crack open the top box.

Cheese, pepperoni, and spinach. I don't know who remembers my favorite pizza, but I don't question it. I take a slice.

Saint scowls. "Wait—"

"Can't," I interrupt, shoving the tip into my mouth. It's hot, but I chew and swallow quickly. And then blow on the cheesy goodness before I try that again.

I can almost forget that I'm sandwiched between two guys I don't particularly like.

Pizza makes everything better.

By the time my slice is finished, Reese has pulled his truck into my building's parking garage and killed the engine.

Saint hops out with the boxes.

Reese glances at me, raising his eyebrows. I take my time licking my fingers, and he groans under his breath.

Huh.

I mirror his expression.

"You'll be the death of me." He shakes his head and chuckles. "You coming?"

I take his offered hand with my clean one, and he helps me down.

Let's just be clear about something, though. I don't *need* help getting out of a truck. But it's nice to not be left in the dust. *Cough, Saint, cough.* To have someone actually care.

But it is weird that it's Reese Avery.

"I'm glad you called," he says in a low voice.

Saint is already at the elevator, waiting with his back to us.

"I didn't know who else to ask." I squeeze his fingers and then release. My fear-slash-nausea at being in close proximity to Reese has abated... for now. But not knowing who else to ask isn't exactly a compliment.

It just means there were literally no other takers.

I lead the way to Saint. The elevator chimes right as we approach, the doors sliding smoothly open. Once we're in, I realize that this might be worse than the car.

They're eyeing each other now, with nothing like *driving* or *evading capture* to distract.

It's a miracle we made it here in one piece.

"So." Reese hits the button for my floor without prompting. "How do you know Kade Laurent, Saint?"

Saint frowns. "He won our fight at Olympus. Apollo shared his name."

Reese's gaze cuts to me. "Apollo, your brother."

"That's the one."

"He won a fight at... where?"

Oh, boy.

"Where have you been?" Saint's tone is incredulous.

It's a bit warranted. Stay in Sterling Falls for any amount of time, and you're bound to hear about Olympus. The fighting, the masquerades. Hell, even the cliffs.

"Living under a rock," Reese says. "What is Olympus?"

Saint and I trade a look.

This weekend... I mean, what could be the harm?

Doesn't really matter that Kade *and* the sheriff are now searching for Reese. Or that I was supposed to find him for Kade. I seem to have switched sides.

The sheriff is acting weird, and Kade pulling some sort of scheme...

"I don't trust him," Saint says under his breath.

"Who?"

"Kade." He pushes his shoulders back. "He shouldn't be staying in that house."

That, again.

"And he was too presumptuous with Artemis."

I open and close my mouth.

But... *maybe that's fair?*

Reese frowns. He's about to retort when the elevators open, and we're saved from further questioning. I make a beeline for my door, then register that I don't even have my keys on me. Reese takes the pizza boxes from Saint, who unlocks the door.

And then we're in.

I am in desperate need of new clothes. I grab stuff from my room and lock myself in the bathroom, slowly stripping out of my ruined shirt. I toe off my shoes and undo the ankle strap that holds the sheathed knife, but I don't know how to get the sweatpants off easily.

There are scrapes across my upper chest and stomach, the backs of my forearms and elbows are torn to shit. Everything hurts. I wet a washcloth and try to dab at the cuts, tackling those before my legs. Blood is soaked into the shredded edges of my sweatpants, down past my knees even. It takes a long time to peel them down, and I kick the ruined fabric into the corner.

Ten minutes later, *ish*, I've doused myself in antiseptic, wrapped what I could in bandages, and slipped into new clothes. Unable to delay any longer, and partially driven by the smell of pizza, I slowly limp out of the bathroom.

Reese sits on a barstool. Saint leans against the counter across from him. They both have beers, but they're not talking.

This is weird, right?

It's *weird*.

Them together... At least they're not spilling secrets.

"You live here?" Reese asks Saint.

"Yep."

I help myself to a slice, going the same route as before and shoving it into my mouth as fast as possible. It feels like an eternity since I've eaten anything of substance. Not that pizza is the be-all and end-all of foods. Well, it is in terms of deliciousness. But not health-wise.

"Do you hate pizza, Saint?" Reese asks.

I choke.

Saint has a single slice on a paper plate like a true gentleman, and he's taken maybe two bites. He scowls at me —for my reaction, I'd bet—and shakes his head. "I don't mind it."

"But it's not a top-ten favorite food?"

Saint narrows his eyes. "Why?"

"Only psychopaths don't like pizza." Reese smirks and takes a big bite.

Proving a point?

Some would say that Reese is the biggest psychopath of them all.

At that thought, I shiver. My analysis of Reese could be entirely wrong. Especially if he was forced into the situation by his parents.

My stomach turns, and I touch the bandage on my head. Maybe I was concussed, because I don't feel right. I blink, and the room shifts. Not a tilt or a spin, just... a little wobble. Barely noticeable.

Besides that, I'm thinking rationally about Reese. Since when does that happen?

"Are... okay?" Reese's voice goes in and out.

"What?" I drop my pizza crust and grab the counter.

"...she's..."

I shake my head, trying to clear the cotton suddenly filling my ears.

"...was fine..."

"I am fine," I mutter.

I'm not.

Hands grab at me.

"Not the couch," Saint says. "...damp."

Ugh, yeah. *Asshole.*

"...shouldn't have slept..."

Hands touch my cheek. "Stay awake, Tem."

Neither of them call me that. I drag my eyes open, but I'm fighting an uphill battle. My lids are so heavy. After a long minute, I give up.

But then something occurs to me. Something I should've told Reese a while ago...

"Don't go home." *Kade can probably find you.*

That's the last thing I remember.

25 KADE

THE CLUB THUNDERS AROUND ME, but there's something missing.

Some*one* missing.

It's evident in the way this place is run. Not in a bad way—just different. The staff here do an exceptional job with or without Artemis Madden in the building. But there's a spark that isn't here, and I tie that to her.

After my drink, I hail a waitress and ask for Artemis.

Her lips flatten for a split second, then a practiced smile takes over. "Sorry, she's unavailable. I can pass along a message? Or if it's a manager you need, Antonio is here tonight."

Antonio. Has Artemis mentioned him before?

I find myself nodding anyway. I order a new drink, as well, and she leaves. I sit back in the booth. I was hoping she would see me on the cameras and come to me. Short of breaking into her house, I haven't seen her in a while.

Not since dancing with her at Bow & Arrow almost a week ago.

Her club is sexy. Dark. *Hot.* There's an allure that

draws people back, no matter how many times they walk these halls.

I peer down to the dance floor two floors below. There are caged dancers illuminated, their platforms hovering out of the second- and third-floor levels. Has Artemis ever danced in one of those? Some of the bars are neon, with lights that throb with the beat both above and below their bodies.

They wear paint that glows under those lights, too. But those dancers only come out after midnight. There's a subtle shift, then. It's like the club takes a step deeper into the dark. Sexier. More primal.

I'm hungry in a way I haven't been in a long, long time.

Finding Reese has been my goal.

Finding *Artemis* just seemed to happen.

Now, I have to actively consider why I want to see her. And that's not to get an update on her search for Reese. I've taken it into my own hands, too, well on my way to tracking down those numbers. Not just the ones the sheriff highlighted, but the rest, too. No stone left unturned.

But with limited resources in this town...

Reese has to call his mother, and those two highlighted lines are my best bet. He loves her as much as he hates her, and I'd bet anything that she's the only tie he keeps to his past.

Too bad both numbers have since been disconnected.

Back to Artemis—she's who I keep seeking out. I almost don't want to do it, almost wish she had been uglier or younger, something to convince me that she's absolutely not worth chasing.

Wrong.

She's fucking beautiful. She can dance. I bet she can

fight, too, because her body is corded with muscle. Even though she's soft, she's strong.

What a fucking dichotomy.

It's been six days, and she's been off the radar.

Similarly, Reese has been a ghost, too.

"You asked to see me?" A short Italian man stands at the edge of my table. His dark hair is flecked with silver, especially at his temples. His uniform—I'm assuming of his own choosing—is a white dress shirt and vest, slacks, Italian loafers. His style is at odds with the rest of Bow & Arrow.

Everything about him screams *in charge,* but also, that he already doesn't like me.

Interesting.

His trimmed goatee is more silver than what's on top of his head. His hands are in his pockets, and other than the subtle sharpness in his expression, he appears relaxed.

This is his element, clearly.

"Are you Antonio?" I lean back in the booth, very nearly kicking my feet out and crossing my ankles. But with the table in the way, it wouldn't have the desired effect.

"I am."

"Nice to meet you, Mr....?"

"Antonio Greco," he supplies. "And you are?"

"Kade Laurent."

He inclines his chin. "What can I help you with, Mr. Laurent?"

"I need to get a message to Artemis."

His brows furrow. "I'm afraid that's not possible."

"Why?"

"Because Ms. Madden was in an accident." His expression turns severe. "She's indisposed until she recovers."

My annoyance flares. "An accident. Indisposed. Pretty

little cover-up words to disguise wherever she actually is. If she doesn't want to see me—"

"Rest assured, she doesn't," Antonio snaps. "Now, Mr. *Laurent*, our waitstaff have been serving you under a different name. I do believe you've been banned from our establishment."

He steps back and motions. From the edge of the room come two bulky security. They wouldn't be a match against me, not if I wanted to put up a fight.

But finding Artemis... well, I want to find her. Need to find her.

An accident implies she's been injured. Antonio didn't back away from that claim, didn't fold and tell me she was just in a stupid meeting with investors or whatever the fuck she does to keep this place afloat.

Every other time I've been here, she's sought me out.

Or her brother has.

Something has distracted them—and her being hurt strikes a chord in my chest.

Worry.

Reese can wait.

I get up and let the security escort me out. I glance up at one of the cameras, hoping that she'll know I was here. But even then, she'll misinterpret it.

She'll think I wanted to follow up on Reese again.

I do.

I did.

Now...

Now, it's not the only thing I want from her.

26 ARTEMIS

I HAVE A NEW HOUSE GUEST. His name is Reese Avery, and I'm pretty sure he and Saint are either going to become best friends or kill each other. He's made himself at home on the couch, which I guess has dried to an acceptable level.

I slept for over twenty-four hours. When I stumbled out in search of something to eat, my stomach growling, Reese was passed out on the couch.

Shocking, 'til I remembered telling him to stay here.

And Saint didn't object?

Anyway, I found cheese and crackers, sat on the counter chewing slowly, then made it back to bed. I was asleep in minutes.

Now it's Saturday, and there's a fight at Olympus tonight. I'm just mustering the energy to get out of bed when a soft tap comes on my door.

"Come in," I call.

Reese enters. He pauses at the foot of my bed, his gaze drinking me in.

This is really the first time we've been awake at the same time. I had a whispered conversation with Saint the other morning, but it was so early, Reese was asleep.

Or pretending to be.

"How are you feeling?"

I lift one shoulder. "About as well as I can, I guess."

"Headache?"

"Mostly gone." I draw my knees up. "Want to sit?"

He nods, but he closes the door before he ventures closer. Just that small action sends my heart into overdrive, and my chest tightens. He gives me space, sitting out of reach. His hair is messed up, the waves flopping down on his forehead and nearly getting in his eyes. Even as I watch, he rakes his hand through it and offers me a glimmer of a smile.

The fact that he's attractive isn't even fair.

"Saint was telling me about how he found you." His gaze shutters. "The guys who... had it out for you."

"The Cyclopes." I make a face. "We still don't know anything about them. I really need to tell my brother—"

"I know them."

I stop. "What?"

He shifts. "Um, I know them. Knew them, really. In Emerald Cove. They weren't established there by any means, but they were getting organized. There just wasn't space for them, but then rumors about the war between gangs in Sterling Falls caught wind."

"And they decided to come here," I finish. "Who are they?"

"Their leader is a mystery. No one speaks about him, and there are layers of leaders before you get to the top." He rubs at his eyes. "I was involved with them. A little."

"No." My throat closes.

"I needed money off the record, Tem."

I can't believe I'm letting him call me Tem. It feels closer than I want him, but at the same time, heat curls in my belly.

He's being honest.

And if *I'm* honest, I've been judging him on our past. But there's almost a decade of the unknown between then and now.

"Why?" I wave my hand. "Don't feel like you have to answer that. God knows I've done my fair share of fucked-up stuff."

He smiles. "I want to hear about that."

"Are they... Are the Cyclopes here to stay?"

His smile fades. "Unless something is done about it, yeah. That's why I'm here."

"You're here because you want to stop them," I repeat.

Reese sighs. "Something like that. Sometimes it feels like they're the oncoming tide. They've got the numbers, and their momentum is impossible to stop."

I don't love the sound of that.

"But then I found you. And what you've done..." He meets my gaze. "Bow & Arrow is beautiful, Artemis. Sincerely."

My face heats. "Thank you."

"I went down to confront my own demons, and then I found the bomb."

Right. That.

"And you disabled it?"

"I'm a former Marine." He sighs. "I worked with bombs overseas. It wasn't... it was in my wheelhouse, I guess you can say, to examine it and stop it."

"You were deployed? And you just so happened to find a bomb that you could disarm."

I lean back against my headboard, considering his words. That it was just a coincidence he was down there? That he has demons of his own—as I started to suspect. It doesn't mean it's easy information to swallow.

"The bomb had dust on it," he says in a low voice. "Someone set it up and then left it. They had to get back down there to trigger the timer... or not. It could've had an hour, a day, two weeks set on the timer. There's no telling what it started at. But *I'm* telling you, in my opinion, this wasn't just some spur-of-the-moment thing to incite fear."

"Why call the sheriff?" I reach for him.

He takes my hand automatically, without even thinking about it. Like *my* touch doesn't freak him out. Not like how I thought I'd react to his touch.

But his calloused fingers are warm and dry, and it grounds me.

—hand reaching out for mine—

I jerk back.

He just looks at me.

I suddenly feel the need to apologize, but he cuts off my attempt.

"I wanted someone to know about it, so I reported the bomb," he says. "It wasn't my intention to make you go down there again, but I waited to see if you would. And you did."

That headache I thought was going away? It's back. I thought, out of everything, *Reese* would be the thorn in my side. From the moment he arrived, from the panic attacks, everything screamed that he would be my enemy.

But he's not. It's Kade.

"If you're lying to me, I will find out," I warn.

He softens. "I know what it's like to be lied to. I won't do that to you." He rises. But instead of leaving, he steps closer. Leans over me.

His lips touch the top of my head, and my traitorous heart fucking skips.

And then he's gone.

"ARE you sure you're up for this?"

I glare at Saint. His bruises have all healed from his fight with Kade, and with it he has apparently suffered a memory lapse. Unlike me, because I still look like I got in a fight with an ogre.

"Of course I'm up for this." I scoff. "Why wouldn't I be?"

"You just spent the week in bed," he replies. "It's common fucking sense."

"She's okay." Reese comes out of the bathroom. He's been wearing his own clothes, which means at some point during this week, he snuck back to his place. There's a black canvas duffel bag tucked against the wall I can only assume is his.

I adjust the necklaces hanging down my chest. I layered them extra thick today, intending to cover the scabs and bruises, but it's still uncomfortable. My shirt is a silky gold halter top, and I added elbow-length gloves to cover my forearms. Brown leather pants.

"I made you both masks," Saint says, retrieving boxes from the counter. "Don't read into it, I just don't want to stand next to cheap generic shit."

I take the box and roll my eyes. Reese takes his, but he doesn't open it until I've flipped the lid on mine.

The mask is gold and brown, a perfect complement to my chosen outfit. It catches the light. I examine it, and it dawns on me that he used real arrowheads. Gold ones. The brown is soft, like velvet.

Deer fur.

A wicked combination that seems to tell a story in and of itself.

A hunter and the hunted.

"Thank you. This is beautiful."

Not to mention, it'll hide the healing cut on my forehead.

The back of the mask, which will sit against my skin, is a creamy silk. The ties to secure it are suede cords, not unlike the ones that hang from Apollo's mask. I hold it to my chest, not really sure what else to do.

Saint dips his head in acknowledgement.

"We talked about who you would pick," he says to Reese. "And I kind of jumped off of that."

I'm intrigued.

Reese's clothing doesn't give away who he intends to go as—but I'm glad Saint explained the masquerade portion. More than I did, which was not at all.

He removes the lid and stares down at the mask.

I creep closer and peer in. "Wow."

"I..." Reese licks his lips. "This is stunning, Saint."

I smile.

He knocked it out of the park. And judging from the satisfied smile on *his* face, he's happy with how we accepted them.

"Who are you?" I ask Reese.

He lifts the mask of fire from the silk bed, setting the box aside. Truly, I don't know how Saint managed to make it look like actual *fire*. It gleams in the light, a million pieces of slender, delicate stained glass that form flames.

Reese holds it up to his face, and his green eyes meet mine. A grin curves his lips.

"I chose Prometheus."

The titan who gave humans fire.

I wonder if that says more about him than he's letting on.

27 ARTEMIS

IT'S ACTUALLY KIND OF fun watching Reese's face as
we drive up to Olympus. And then again, even behind our
masks, as we are waved through the huge doors by boar-
masked employees and step into the large atrium.

We're at the tail end of the admittance window, which
means most of the guests are already present. So many
different masks, people of varying ages and genders.
They're all a blur of a crowd and individual in their own
right.

I'm on Reese's arm, mine threaded through his and my
hand on his forearm. As if this was a Victorian era instead of
Ancient Greece—or modern society.

Saint follows like a shadow. His mask is made of bronze
wings. Hermes, the messenger god. When he hosts, he has a
staff of a similar make.

Saint has designed all the masks for Jace as Hades,
Wolfe as Ares, and Apollo. As himself. He designed a litany
of masks for Kora, too, especially when the guys were
getting to know her. It was fun to see how different they

could spin the theme of Persephone to match their own gods.

He designed one singular mask for me, back when Olympus was surging in popularity. He said something similar about not wanting me to have a generic mask, but I suspected it was Nyx's doing. Now, I'm not so sure.

He designed many masks, including hers. He was right there with her for the first Olympus fight night.

He's been here longer than anyone...

I shiver, and Reese tucks me closer against him. It seems automatic, and a part of my brain seriously balks. I shouldn't be letting him get this close to me.

"All these people pay to get in," Reese marvels. "To watch... fighting?"

I nod.

My brother appears at the top of the stairs on the left. The left and right sides meet at the center landing. He comes down with his staff, with his bare, gold-painted chest, his mask of horns and bone.

"Welcome to Olympus," he booms. "I'm Apollo, your host for the evening."

Pause.

His gaze sweeps through the room and lands on me. Then Reese.

His fingers flex on the staff, and it's his only tell that he's upset. Or annoyed. Or angry. Maybe a combination of all three? Either way, I'm going to hear about it later.

"We have an unusual predicament tonight, ladies and gentlemen," he continues. He isn't shouting, and yet his voice carries. "One of our fighters is ill. His opponent is requesting we find a suitable replacement."

I suck in a breath and reach back for Saint. I grip his wrist, willing him to *not* volunteer.

He doesn't move. Doesn't try to shake me off either.

"What are the odds it's Kade?" Saint says in my ear. "Not the sick one—the one who wants a replacement?"

Reese twitches.

Fuck.

"Anyone?" Apollo drawls. "Our requirements are not normally so... lax. As I said: unusual circumstances."

"I will." Reese's voice rings out from beside me.

I close my eyes, then force them open. I stare up at him, daring him to take it back.

But you can't unring a bell.

Saint moves closer, prying my hand away from Reese. Freeing him enough for him to slip out of my grasp and move through the crowd. They part for him—but why wouldn't they? He's a hulking guy in a mask of fire.

Of course they would rush to clear a path.

Apollo meets him at the bottom step. They talk for a moment, and I turn to glare at Saint.

"You wanted him to volunteer," I accuse.

He shrugs. His blue eyes are dark tonight, but the burn in his gaze is no less potent. "I think he should prove himself before you go falling all over him."

Oh, for fuck's sake. "You think that's what this is?"

He goes back to watching Apollo, who has shooed off Reese toward the fighter's corridor with a boar-masked employee, and he has retaken his position on the stairs.

"It's not," I tell him. "Reese and I have history, and it's not the good kind."

Saint ignores me.

I ignore him back, shaking off his hand from my wrist and moving backward. I shift behind a couple, then another. By the time he turns to check for me, I'm well and truly out of sight.

Apollo finishes his speech and slams his staff into the floor. Smoke rises around him, and he's gone when it clears. I give Saint a bubble and head for the stairs. I squeeze around people, hurrying to one of the balcony boxes. I plant myself in the corner of one and look across to where Hades, Ares, and Persephone—better known as Jace, Wolfe, and Kora—are taking their seats.

Wolfe pulls Kora down on his lap, his hands settling at her hip and thigh. Her mask is back to springtime flowers, a mix of pink carnations and white roses. Her dress is baby pink, and it would be demure if not for the cut of it. It stops at her upper thigh, exposing her pale legs.

"Can I join you?" someone asks.

I glance over my shoulder and squint.

The voice should've been my first clue.

"Malik," I greet him. "What brings you here?"

He leans on the wide marble railing, staring down at the people who prefer to be on the ground level. Usually that's me, wanting to be right up close to the action.

Tonight, I think I need the railing to hold me up.

"Antonio asked me to check on you."

I cough. "No, he didn't."

The old man does not like Malik. Never warmed up to him, barely musters the energy to be polite. It's kind of funny, really. There are only a few people living that stay on Antonio's shit list no matter what they do, and the Hell Hounds' leader is one of them.

"No, he didn't," Malik agrees with a smile. "But he did ask me who Kade Laurent is."

That, I would believe. You don't have to like someone to know when they have information.

"Can I get any peace?" I groan.

The answer is no.

Antonio should not be going to the freaking Hell Hounds. Reese shouldn't be fighting. Kade shouldn't be sneaking around behind my back. Saint shouldn't be... well, I don't know what Saint is doing or not doing, just that I don't really like it.

Or maybe I do like it, and I won't admit it.

Nope—I don't like it.

End of fucking story.

"Reese Avery."

I cringe. "What about him?"

"He didn't leave town."

"No, of course not. He's not the type to be bullied by a few bikers." I peek at Malik. "Using your favor against me like that is poor taste."

His mask is emerald green, but I can't think of a single Greek god who corresponds to that color. It's more akin to the fighting masks—fabric instead of plastic, so it doesn't cut when you're getting punched in the face—instead of the finer ones the guests wear.

Knowing him, he didn't actually pick it with the intention of emulating a god.

"But he's not at his apartment anymore. Landlord said it's been emptied out."

I hum.

Am I keeping a fugitive?

"You seem awfully interested, seeing as how I asked you to find him and you fulfilled your promise."

He scoffs. "You said you'd stay away from him."

"And I did." *Until I didn't.*

"Okay, Artemis." His tone even says he doesn't believe me.

I focus across the opening to the other balcony.

There is Saint, staring at me and Malikai.

I heave a sigh. "Go away, would you?"

Malik chuckles. "Anything you want."

Thankfully, he goes. Right in time for Apollo to get through the introductions and the first pair of fighters to walk out. I missed their names, but it doesn't really matter. It's not Reese.

Or Kade.

I watch the fight with an analytical eye. The two guys dive right into it, and soon the platform is sprayed with a mist of blood.

"What did *he* want?" Saint asks, stepping up beside me.

"Oh, you're speaking to me again?"

"Artemis."

"Saint." I wish he had a longer version of his name. Something better than *Saint*. Did his mother know she had birthed a demon? Is that why she named him that? It's a sick form of irony, really.

"You tell me, or I tell your brother what happened."

My scowl is lost on him behind the mask. "I need to tell him, regardless."

"Uh-huh."

Jace is an expert at dealing with shit. And the emergence of a new gang is the epitome of *shit*.

"How have they not gone into West Falls? You'd think they would be attacked, too." His words are nearly lost by a groaning reaction of the crowd. "But they attack you twice, and someone says you're marked..."

"I wasn't even riding my bike the second time," I add. Just my helmet, and that's nondescript. "So it's not just me. It could be any of us."

"Reese got in and out."

"You did, too. *Walking*, no less."

"I got in, but that doesn't mean I would've made it out."

That's fair. I hold up my hand. "Me and Apollo, then, for sure." I tick two fingers. "Do we assume Jace and Wolfe? You?"

"I don't know."

Not helpful. I'm distracted, though, by a falling body.

Not unconscious—the guy falls *off* the platform. He hits the floor with a crack, the crowd leaping away to avoid him. He scrambles to his feet, but suddenly Apollo is there. He uses the staff to separate them.

"Fighter, you lose by forfeit. Exiting the platform is immediate disqualification."

The crowd boos.

It was an intense fight, and I think the other literally roundhouse kicked him in the chest. That's hard to absorb without going flying.

"Do you think Reese found Kade back there?"

I glance at Saint. "You care?"

"I'm curious. I didn't meet Kade, except for those brief moments. But I didn't like him."

"You don't like anyone."

He dips his head. "I'm a good judge of character, Artemis. Most people are just full of shit."

Ugh.

"What about Reese?"

"He stepped up to the plate, so..." He seems to debate. "We'll see how he handles this little reunion. Did he say how he knew Kade?"

"That's the one thing he didn't elaborate on."

Saint grunts.

There's another pair of fighters next. Two women. One wears all white. She comes with her husband, I think. I like her style, which is more aggressive than mine. She comes out on top, her opponent dazed and staring blankly at the ceiling from the floor.

"This is it." Saint straightens.

Apollo retakes the platform, and his gaze finds mine. When he announces Prometheus as our late entry, the crowd erupts. Turns out, they like someone who impulsively decides to fight. Just another Saturday night in Sterling Falls.

He strides out in just his pants. Shirt gone. Mask exchanged for a plain black one.

My mouth drops open of its own accord.

Reese is *ripped.* His muscles flex with every step, from his veiny biceps and traps to his tight abdomen, even his freaking chest. I stare with a new appreciation, because with a shirt on he doesn't really look like this.

Granted, I don't think I've seen him in short sleeves. Those muscles definitely would've been a red flag.

Green flag?

I swear, I'm not drooling. Although I run my thumb under my bottom lip just to make sure.

He circles the platform, gazing at the crowd on his level. Searching. Then it lifts, and he finds Saint and me in record time. He winks, but I don't have it in me to gesture back.

Like... what if Kade beats the shit out of him?

"It could *not* be Kade," Saint says. "We could be wrong."

I roll my eyes. "Naturally, that's your conclusion. That this is all for nothing, and you goaded him into a fight with a stranger."

"I didn't say that," he mutters. "It's just an option."

"Back from last month," Apollo's voice rings out, "please welcome... Atlas!"

Also known as: Kade Laurent.

I glare at my brother.

Then Saint, who's in the process of eating his words.

Fucker.

KADE EMERGES. Reese's back is to him, so maybe he doesn't recognize him just yet.

My heart is in my damn throat waiting for Reese to turn around. Waiting for recognition to dawn.

It doesn't.

They step up beside each other, and while Kade watches Apollo, Reese stares down his former friend. Seeing the two beside each other is kind of nuts. They're both tall and broad-shouldered, but Reese has a more tapered waist. He's an inch or two shorter than Kade, too. Not much, but enough that it could cost him the difference. Where Kade is tanned skin and dark hair, and his facial features more sharp, Reese's dirty-blond hair makes his pale skin seem almost translucent. His square jaw and gleaming, sea-glass-green eyes scour his opponent.

It's kind of clear, at least from here, that Kade is not aware of Reese's identity. Reese knows, though. He stares across the platform, his lips pressed in a flat line. He's *acting* indifferent, but he knows.

He can't not know.

Apollo waves them on and hops down, and Kade's stoicism drops away. The two circle, and I grip the railing hard.

Kade is fast. I know that from watching him fight Saint. But I don't think he expects Reese, who immediately attacks. He gets in two punches before Kade can even move a step, and then Reese dances away.

Kade grimaces and wipes blood from his lip.

It seems like his mind is clicking into place and lands on: *challenge accepted.*

They could kill each other.

I instinctively grab Saint's hand.

The two trade blows, but Reese is clearly the faster of the two. And Kade is stronger.

"I can't watch this." I use my other hand to block my eyes. I just go off the sounds of the crowds, wincing with each yell and jeer.

"Reese just took one on the mouth," Saint narrates. "Glancing blow, it won't damage his teeth."

"Shut up."

"Kade just tried to kick him. Like the roundhouse kick that guy did in the first fight, which is a little cheap if you ask me. But Reese grabbed his foot—" Saint laughs. "Damn, I think he dislocated Kade's knee. He's down. He's staring at Reese. Oh, shit."

I peek.

Kade is staring up at Reese—who's bleeding from his nose—with a mixture of fury and hope. He hops up and continues to stare, and then just fucking stands there as Reese punches him in the face.

Lights out.

Certain hits will do that, and it's not surprising that Reese nails it. Kade's expression flickers, and I squeeze

Saint's hand as the man tumbles to the platform. Unconscious.

With Reese as the winner.

"What do you think this asshole is going to ask for?" Saint shakes loose my hand and leans one elbow on the railing to face me. "A date with you?"

"I highly doubt it."

He shrugs. "Did you tell him about the favors?"

"No." I squint. "Did you?"

"Nope."

We both look down at Reese, whose arm Apollo has captured and lifted over his head.

Reese and Kade are both taller than my brother. Probably the same height as Wolfe and Jace, actually.

Reese meets my gaze and smiles.

"So he just knocked out his ex-best friend for the hell of it," Saint muses.

I shake my head.

We watch the last fight in silence. It's the show the crowd has waited for—one of the female fighters pitted against Hercules. A big asshole like Minos, but worse. I've fought him a few times, too. He hits hard no matter who he's fighting and rarely shifts his style to match his opponent.

And tonight, his sheer strength prevails.

I sigh. "Well, let's go eavesdrop on what Reese asks for."

Saint perks up, and he easily follows me out and down the hall. I find one of the alcoves and trigger the hidden door to open, and we take the cramped stairs down to the first floor. They meet in the back room once the fighters have a chance to clean up and the crowd disperses.

"What were you going to ask for?"

Saint side-eyes me.

"Come on." I stop short and plant my hands on my hips. "What were you going to ask for if you won?"

"Nothing." He rolls his eyes and continues. "We're going to miss them."

I scoff. "Yeah, right. *Nothing*, my ass."

My words fall on deaf ears. Saint leaves me behind. I hurry to catch up, mindful of the twinge of pain in my side. I'm not a hundred percent—not even close. My head still hurts, although now it's manageable with painkillers.

In short? Still a mess.

"Saint."

"Artemis."

I really hate him. "Would you have asked to move out? To be done with this?"

By *this* I mean *us*. There isn't even an *us* to consider, to register, but Saint has been with me for almost a full year.

He's hated every second of it, as have I. But... I think I'd hate it more if I was alone in that place.

Typical Saint, though—he ignores my questions and enters the back room. There are columns here along the walls, providing excellent shadowy places to linger. He doesn't, though. He just walks right out into the open and down the long room toward where my brother and his friends are gathered.

I scowl at all of them, now well and truly left in the dust.

"Tem!" Kora enters through a side door and meets me in the center. She throws her arms around me, hugging me tightly. "God, I've heard what's been going on with you. Are you okay?"

I extract myself with a small grimace. "I'm... I'm fine, Kora. Really."

Her eyes narrow.

"Okay," I allow. "There's some shit going on, but I'm handling it. I promise."

She accepts that and brushes her dark-red hair off her shoulder. I've always secretly wondered if she dyes it, but Apollo said it was natural. And then the asshole made some comments about the carpet matching the drapes, and I decked him before he could finish his sentence.

Because *ew*.

I do not need that visual of my friend. Although I'm thinking about it now... But that's just in an effort to distract me from Saint's low chatter with the guys.

As I watch them, Wolfe watches Kora. His eyes are red tonight, still in performance mode. He holds out his hand, and Kora takes it. She curls into his side, resting her head on his upper arm.

I'm not jealous.

I'm not.

I'm definitely not lonely.

"Reese Avery," Apollo grits out, turning everyone's attention to me. "You were with him tonight?"

"And you goaded him into fighting the one guy searching for him." I exchange a look with Saint. "Then we left them alone together?"

My brother rolls his eyes. "Are you kidding me? Kade was unconscious."

"How long do you think it takes someone to regain consciousness, idiot?" I snap.

"Okay," Saint interrupts. "He's not going to kidnap him from Olympus."

Well... it's possible.

The door at the far end, which we entered through, opens. One of their employees pokes his head in, and Jace gives the man a sharp nod. Jace is Hades, and Hades is truly one of the scarier gods. His mask is a skull without the lower jaw, bleached bone-white, with metal horns extending out of the temples. They twist up high over his head, the points glinting even in the low lighting.

His black body paint is smeared across his chest in a familiar, dainty handprint, and I have no doubt they have Kora decorate their flesh before every appearance.

I'm not jealous.

Not of her, but... of having someone who wants to be touched.

Saint extracting his hand from mine flashes in my mind, and I turn away from all of them. I don't need Saint. If he wants to fight and prove that he can be on his own, *fine.* If he wants to be an idiot and suffer in silence, *fine.* If he can't move on, if he just wants to linger in Nyx's shadow, *fine.* I can't stop him.

I won't stop him.

Reese is the first to enter, flame mask and outfit he arrived in back in place. I lean against one of the columns, and my heart does this weird extra little flutter. He glances around, clearly confused.

So no one explained it.

Hades, Ares, and Apollo stand in various power poses. It's intimidating for those who don't know them. Kora, in her flower mask, is still pressed to Ares' side. Saint drifts back to me, although he doesn't say anything.

Doesn't dare to interrupt.

Some things—like this—are better run on ceremony.

"As the winner, you receive a favor," Ares says.

Reese glances his way, then mine.

"You cannot ask for anything to do with my sister," Apollo adds.

I sigh.

"You can't blame him," Saint says under his breath. Just for my ears. "After what happened with Kade…"

That was a disaster. On my birthday, no less.

"You came after me." I look at him. "I didn't say thank you for that, did I?"

He grunts. "I was ordered to."

"We lost you. You didn't have to—"

"Artemis." He meets my gaze. "Just drop it."

My lips flatten, but whatever. I can drop it. I will. No, I *do*. I vow to never bring it up again, and then I refocus on Reese.

I thought he might just ask for a favor, but instead, he's questioning them.

"…all powerful?"

Oops, should've tuned in sooner.

They stare at him. "We have power in this city," Hades finally says. "More power than you can imagine."

Reese laughs. "More than I can imagine? I know what power looks like, *Jace King*."

I stiffen.

Everyone does.

Their identities are known to us, of course, but Jace and Wolfe have strived to keep their names out of the public eye. Normal people do not know them.

"If you aren't going to ask for something, Reese Avery," Jace shoots back, "then get out."

Reese smiles wider. He resembles the Cheshire Cat.

"Prometheus was a trickster," Saint says in my ear.

I shoot him a look.

"My favor?" Reese pauses, glancing at me. I'm already off-limits, that much was made clear. But he's not checking in with me, he seems to be internally debating something. "I have a friend who needs help in Emerald Cove. They're suffering under the weight of a gang, and I don't have the resources to extract them."

Huh?

Jace inclines his chin. "Give us the details, and we'll help him."

"I want this to be you," Reese says. "Not you sending some half-assed mercenary or *employee* to fix it."

"Done."

Reese nods. He withdraws an envelope from his pocket and holds it out on offer to them.

After a minute, Apollo steps forward to take it.

"Before the end of the month," Reese says. "Swear it."

"We swear." Jace glares at him. "Now get out."

He doesn't. He comes straight to me, his hand fluttering over my shoulder without so much as a whisper of a touch.

"You okay?" I ask.

He tilts his head. "I was going to ask you."

"I'm not the one who got punched by a former bestie." I narrow my eyes at him. "Did you know this was going to happen? Did he recognize you?"

"At the end, he did." His palm finally makes contact with my arm, sliding down over my elbow, my forearm, fingers probing at my wrist before he takes my hand. "They're all staring daggers at me, aren't they?"

"Yes," Saint says. "It's quite remarkable."

Reese chuckles. "What is?"

"How you make enemies everywhere you go."

"Ah." Reese squeezes my hand. "Time to go, then."

Absolutely. We just have to make sure we don't run into an angry Kade Laurent on the way out.

29 ARTEMIS

REESE, Saint, and I arrive back at my condo, and I'm struck by how *weird* it is. I know I've said that before, but it bears repeating. Saint and Reese don't really hate each other, although they argue. And Saint hasn't tried to get me to kick Reese out...

It's probably just because Reese came to our rescue and saved us.

And Saint saved me.

Who have I saved, lately?

A big, fat *no one*.

But I'm not going to dwell on that.

I saved my brother and Wolfe plenty of times, and then the vigilante shit kind of dissipated as we moved out of the gang war and into peacetime.

This is peace, isn't it? The gang leaders were dispatched —*a nice way to say killed*—and Jace, Wolfe, and Apollo reestablished themselves as in charge. The Hell Hounds got Malik, who plays nice with my brother and his friends.

Well... it *was* peace.

Now, I'm not so sure. I have been so caught up in my

own shit, I haven't stopped to actually feel the vibe of the city. Even Bow & Arrow is usually a good barometer for what's happening, and I've been absent from there.

Removed from everything.

I've been off. I've said it for weeks, maybe months now. Saint to Reese are both just... existing. They take off their shoes, put their masks away. Reese grabs a frozen bag of veggies and presses it to his face.

"Did you tell them about the Cyclopes?" I ask Saint, setting my mask back in its box on the counter. To be worn another day. "When I was talking to Kora?"

He frowns. "No. I thought you were going to."

"I—"

Reese glances between us. "So, the so-called rulers of the Sterling Falls underground world don't know about the gang that's moved into West Falls?"

"That's what it sounds like," I admit. "My brother hasn't mentioned anything."

"Then it's up to us," Reese declares.

"Up to us to what?" Saint counters. "Kill them all? Negotiate for our city back?"

Reese doesn't reply, which typically means the worse of the two options. And that would definitely be *kill them all*.

I plant my hands on my hips. "We are not going out and murdering people."

"I didn't say that," Reese counters.

Saint grumbles something under his breath and heads for his room.

I stare at Reese. "Who needs help in Emerald Cove?"

"An old friend." He gives me a weird little smile. It seems a bit sad. "They've been stuck for a while, but maybe your brother and his friends can help."

Uh-huh.

"Most people ask for favors for themselves," I tease. "And you go and ask for an old friend? You had it all written up just in case?"

He shakes his head and approaches me. I force myself to hold still. The instinct is still to step away, to avoid his space. But he doesn't have any trouble stepping right into mine.

"One of the other fighters mentioned it when we were waiting." He raises his hand like he wants to touch my face, but he drops it just as fast.

No.

God, I'm so starved for touch, I want *him* to touch me. The ache is right there, thrumming under my skin.

I grab his wrist before he can withdraw further, and I put his hand on the side of my neck. My heart is going to burst out of my chest, but I can't stop it. I just—I want contact.

Not the hateful kind, like what Saint offers. If I wanted something quick and dirty and mentally destructive, I know exactly who to go to. But right now, I just want to burn hot... without the degradation.

His gaze intensifies, and his tongue sweeps out, wetting his lower lip.

I damn near groan.

"Do you want me to kiss you, Artemis?"

I like how he says my name. I shouldn't, but I do.

I also like that he asks. It means he's not the same. It means he's changed for the better, and my heart skips.

Slowly, I nod.

His thumb sweeps across my jaw, and he slides his fingers into my hair. The touch sends tingles down the back of my neck and raises goosebumps along my arms. I find myself leaning in, rising on my toes.

When his lips brush mine, my eyes flutter closed.

I don't think I've ever really been kissed.

Isn't that sad?

My mind flips back, trying to pinpoint a *kiss*, but none come up. None in Terror—I did everything I could to avoid it, and the guys didn't really care if I twisted away from their mouth. As long as *my* mouth did other things... And then after, when I learned how to get over this sexual trauma, it was never about the kiss.

But now he's kissing me, his lips moving softly against mine, and my brain is finally quiet.

He breaks away and looks down at me, gauging my dazed expression. and then kisses me again. Harder. The pressure builds up, our lips dance together in a way I instinctively know. His tongue drags across the seam of my mouth, and I open.

His tongue is another level. I hold on to his forearms, trying to ground myself. Otherwise this sensation flooding through me might make me float away.

"What the fuck?"

Saint may as well have dumped ice water over our heads. I leap back, hitting my hip on the counter. My hair falls through Reese's fingers, although his hand remains outstretched. My grip on his forearms loosens until my arms drop.

We were *right there*. Our bodies a hair's breadth away. It was just our lips and hands, and the moment is seared into my brain. No matter what Saint says next.

I touch my lips.

He storms up and shoves Reese. I barely register that Saint has given me his back, that he's put himself between us. I don't know why he's doing that.

"Stop." My voice is weak. "Saint, stop."

He just keeps shoving, until Reese is back against the windows and Saint has him pinned by the throat.

"Please stop." The counter ends up saving me from hitting the floor. I touch my lips again, half in shock and... I want more. "He asked." *Louder*. "He asked if I wanted it, Saint. I—"

"You were afraid of him," Saint accuses. "And now you kiss him?"

I don't know.

I don't know anything anymore.

My fight-or-flight instinct seems to be wired to *flight* these days, because before I know it, I'm in motion. Grabbing the keys to Reese's truck, my phone, my small bag. I didn't even get a chance to take off my shoes, and small miracles for that.

I bolt. It's late—I should be at Bow & Arrow anyway. When I get into Reese's truck, I don't pause to find out if someone has followed me.

Reese or Saint.

Are they fighting? Or laughing? Or...

I put the truck in gear and get the fuck out of the garage. The drive to Bow & Arrow is as easy as breathing, and I arrive in the blink of an eye.

No thought required. I park in the back and hop out, locking it. Once I'm in the stairwell, I pause. Instead of going up to my office, I go down.

Down to the old, blocked-off hallways with desecrated rooms. Where nightmares still linger and memories threaten to assault me.

Where the past is very much still alive.

I go to Terror to visit old ghosts.

There's something wrong with me, and I need to fix it before it's too late.

30 ARTEMIS

I'M A LIAR.

I can't go into Terror. I barely make it all the way down the stairs, and a creaking noise has me *running*. I get to my office and slam the door shut behind me. I lean against it, my chest aching. I frantically try to catch my breath.

What is *wrong* with me?

A knock reverberates through my back. I shift to the side and crack the door, peeking over my shoulder to see who it is.

Antonio.

He takes in my expression, whatever it holds, and the sternness fades from his eyes. Understanding replaces it.

How can he understand?

"Come," he says, stepping back.

I turn and open the door the rest of the way. He goes into his office, and I drop into the seat across from him. I've done this many times, but this feels different.

"You went downstairs."

My breath hitches.

"I had cameras installed after the bomb incident," he says. "My notifications go off if they detect movement…"

"I went down there already. I was fine."

He snorts. He pulls an electric kettle from a drawer in his desk and quickly sets it up. He pours water in, and while it boils he retrieves mugs. Tea bags. Honey. Miniature spoons. He sets everything up with calm efficiency, giving me the space to sit with those words.

The ones where I insist I was *fine*.

"You've been living above Terror," he says. "And for a decade, you've avoided it."

I pinch the bridge of my nose. "Isn't it time to face those demons?"

"Maybe," he allows. "Maybe not. It depends on if you're ready for the fight."

Am I?

I don't think I have a choice.

"Reese is…" I cannot tell him I kissed Reese. I still feel his lips against mine, and heat surges to my face.

And between my legs.

God, not now.

I shove the memory away and focus on the mugs. He fixes my tea the way I like it, and I grip it with both hands. I don't know what to do. Not with Terror, or Reese, or Saint, or Kade, or the Cyclopes, or—

"Reese is what?"

"He's not strictly the enemy." I look away. Antonio knows quite a bit of my history, but I didn't ever have to get into the nitty gritty. He was there, in a way. He saw what Terror did to people. "I don't know what I want to do."

"Okay." He leans back. His chair creaks a little, and he crosses his ankles. "Okay, so what do you *not* want to do?"

I smile. I think he used to do that with his kids, too,

when they were struggling. Can't think of chores you want to do? Cross the least favorite off the list. Go from there.

"Did you find out anything from the sheriff about that body?"

He frowns. "No. Nothing new. There were no defensive wounds, no DNA that could tie it back to someone specific. He's labeling it a gang member death."

I bristle. "It was an informant, and he *knew* that before they even discovered it."

"Doesn't change the fact that..."

Something catches his attention on his computer. It's at an angle that I can't quite see, and I'm tempted to get up and circle around to satisfy my own curiosity. Before I can, he swivels it to show me.

The sheriff has just arrived in front of the club.

On a Saturday night, at our peak hour.

It's not just him, though. It seems like most of the force is behind him, the whole screen filled with blue-and-red flashing lights, cruisers, deputies.

He holds up a paper to the bouncer, then moves past.

Everyone moves past.

"Warrant," I breathe. "I need to get down there."

Antonio grabs my wrist. "No. You should leave while you still can."

I reach over and click to a separate view. One that shows all the cameras. They're already in the stairwell that leads up here.

"Do we have anything to hide?"

He makes a face. "Everything is above board."

"Okay, then..." I take a deep breath. "We let them search. We don't have a choice."

"We'll have to shut down for the night."

I scowl.

The club is packed. Saturday nights are always high-adrenaline as we catch the run-off from Olympus. Those who aren't ready to call it a night come here, and a lot are still wearing their masks. But even as we watch the security footage, our guests slowly stop dancing. More and more flood out.

And then the sheriff is in the doorway, watching us watch his people fuck up my club.

I look over my shoulder at him and sip my tea.

It's piping hot, but it's a comfort nonetheless. He's dressed like the dickhead he is, hat firmly in place, uniform perfect. It's annoying how put together he seems compared to how *not* I feel.

Would it kill him to have a stain somewhere?

"Antonio," he greets my business partner. "Artemis."

I scowl.

He presents us with the warrant, but I don't move. Antonio is the one who reaches out and takes it, scanning the pages.

I keep my gaze on the sheriff—which is how I miss our security feeds going out one by one.

Antonio makes a noise, and I whirl around to catch the last one darkening.

I shoot out of my chair and face the sheriff. "Kora would be disappointed in you."

He doesn't even flinch. "She couldn't stop this any more than you could. Just let us do our jobs."

"Fine." Antonio beats me to the punch.

"Let's step out." Nathan Bradshaw has the good grace to look a little sorry, shifting out of the way and motioning for us to leave the office.

"This isn't fair," I hiss to Antonio.

My steadfast friend takes my hand. We go into the hall,

and I jolt at the realization that there are more officers with Bradshaw. They file into the office and begin to take apart Antonio's computer system.

There are already people in mine.

"The computers, Nathan?" Antonio questions. "Really?"

I let out a sigh and shake my head. "It's not worth it. We need to find our staff."

"They're downstairs," the sheriff says.

Antonio and I find them all gathered in the middle of the now-empty dance floor. The DJ cut the music, although even they still linger.

There's a dozen of us, and most of the staff seem dejected, confused, or just stressed.

Not on my watch.

I put on my brightest smile and clap my hands. "Anyone hungry?"

That's how we end up at Antonio's. Not to be confused with Antonio's house, or Bow & Arrow, which Antonio runs with me. No, this is a restaurant owned by Jace that Antonio helped him build up, and he still pops in to manage the quality. It's quite the fancy place, with even a baby grand piano in the center of the room to serenade guests.

Antonio used to live above the restaurant before he and his wife outgrew the small apartment, and then they converted it into a sort of safe house.

But at this hour, the restaurant is closed, and everyone gathers around the tables in the commercial kitchen. Antonio pulls out supplies, and before I can even process what's happening, he has everyone making personal pizzas. His low voice, carrying instructions on how to stretch out the dough, the best way to spread sauce, buzzes in my ears.

It's soothing. Maybe not to me in this moment, but for everyone else.

I know everyone here.

Helped everyone here in some way.

I pause on my manager, Sam. She's been with us the longest, having come from... well, from the same sort of situation I did.

She meets my gaze and raises an eyebrow.

I tip my head. She breaks away and follows me out into the dining room, and I fiddle with a lock of my hair.

"Not like you to look nervous," she comments. "You okay?"

I shake my head slowly. "I think something bad is coming."

Her expression blanks.

"Like..." I can't say it.

She says it for me. "Like Terror."

"I don't know, it's just a hunch, but if it does? I want you to get everyone well away from here. Take them to Emerald Cove—"

"We don't have the kind of money to relocate everyone," she interjects gently.

"I do." I stare at her. "I do, Sam. When you're ready, you take it and them and you run."

She hugs me. I'm not expecting it, but being swallowed up in her grip is actually nice. Comforting.

"Thank you," she whispers. "I know you try to do so much for us, but you go above and beyond."

My throat closes.

It isn't just Sam. It's everyone who works for me.

Which is why Mel frustrates me. I haven't forgotten that she shared information with Malik. That she hangs out with the Hell Hounds, trying to be someone's old lady.

Trust me, I went through *that* phase, too. Luckily my brother didn't let anyone get that close.

And I haven't fired her yet, either. Even though I said I would, I haven't managed to pull the trigger.

Sam and I separate, and we return to make pizzas. Sam, Jackie, Ginger, Mel, Cassandra, Lisa, Tess, Mitch, Paul, and Barry. Antonio. Me. Bartenders and managers and security and waitresses. It doesn't really matter what title they hold at the end of the day.

Antonio directs Tess to the beers, and she passes them out to all of us.

I raise mine. "To the best crew I've had the pleasure of working with."

Antonio smiles softly.

"Hear, hear," he says.

"Hear, hear," they echo.

Glasses clink.

My heart doesn't feel quite so lost at the moment.

31 REESE

SAINT HART and I are getting to know each other.

While drinking. It's honestly the only way to do it. I hold my cards close to my chest—literally and figuratively—and wait for him to make a move. It came down to gin or chess, so here we are. Not a freaking chessboard in sight.

We're trading questions for shots. And playing cards, because it's better to not just stare at each other all night. God, that would be weird.

I dealt, he poured, and now he's examining his cards. He's got the first question, I'm sure, so I lean back in the chair and wait.

He finally discards and throws back his shot, smiling wickedly at me. He doesn't grimace, but I think he's been numb for a while. Liquor isn't going to change that.

"Tell me how you met Tem."

I've noticed that he calls her Tem when she's not around, and Artemis to her face. It must be some sort of tactic to keep her thinking she doesn't mean anything to him, but I can see through it.

Transparent fucker.

"I met her through my parents," I say. "When we were teenagers."

He narrows his eyes. "Where—"

"Take another shot if you want to pepper me with questions," I interrupt.

He curses.

I take the card he discarded, debate for a second, and discard something else. I lift my shot glass and swallow the liquid. The whiskey burns on the way down, but I fight back the urge to cough.

"Why do you live with her?" I ask.

He frowns.

Picks up a card.

"I have to," he says.

I growl.

His gaze rises to mine, and he grimaces. "I was on an unofficial suicide watch, and Artemis got the short straw."

"How long?"

He tsks and refills both our glasses.

I sigh.

Discard. Shot. Question.

He pulls his punch, though. "Did you have any pets growing up?"

I blink in surprise. "Um... no. Well, actually, I had some crows."

He chokes. "Excuse me?"

I frown and pick a card, slotting it where it goes. "If you offer crows gifts, they'll do the same. They're quite good with faces, actually. I didn't have a ton of close friends as a kid, so I befriended a murder of crows."

Saint doesn't seem to know whether or not he can believe me. "A murder of crows."

"They'd follow me to school and back." I shrug. "'Til Dad shot some of them."

Most of them.

The image of a yard full of dead black birds flits behind my eyes. I reach for the bottle again.

"Who's your favorite superhero?"

"The Joker," Saint says.

I snort. "He's a villain, not a superhero. Not even in the Justice League."

"Fine. Captain America, because he transformed and stood for his beliefs through everything."

"That makes sense." I shake my head and toss my card.

He smirks and takes it from the discard pile. For a second, I think he might win and end the game. I *hate* losing. But he just takes his time, then the shot, and considers me.

"Burning building, and Kade and Tem are both trapped inside. Who are you rescuing?"

I stare at him.

Back to the hard questions, then. If I say Kade, he might kick my ass on principal.

If I say Artemis... That's a whole new can of worms that I'm not ready to talk about with him.

"I can't answer," I mumble.

He shakes his head and plucks a card from his hand. He places it down gently, although everything else about him is tense.

When he removes his hand, I groan. The card is facedown.

I lose.

"Now you're definitely answering," Saint says with a hard smile.

"Kade and I have a..." My attention goes to the window.

We're so high up, the only things at our eye level are other buildings in the financial district. And beyond, North Falls just over the hill, the main street in that neighborhood creating a faint, distant glow. "An interesting relationship."

"So he's who you'd pick?"

"I'm not saying that." I meet his gaze. "I'm saying I just don't fucking know. It's complicated."

"This isn't a Facebook relationship status question," Saint snaps.

I laugh. "Okay, asshole. Artemis or Apollo?"

I down the shot waiting for me.

Saint glowers at me. "Artemis. Apollo would simply murder me if I didn't save his baby sister."

"They're twins," I point out.

"But he's a few minutes older." Saint shrugs. "I'd save Artemis."

"Great. You save her, I'll save Kade, and then we'd be square."

He mutters something I don't catch.

I gather the cards and shuffle, then deal again. He pours more liquid into my glass.

We haven't taken that many shots, and yet the pull of alcohol is strong. I haven't eaten enough today—or, fuck, the last two months—to be drinking this heavily.

I get up and grab the leftover pizza from the fridge, dropping it to the table next to us, and my thoughts inevitably turn to Artemis.

She went to Bow & Arrow after I kissed her.

You were afraid of him, and now you kiss him?

I guess I can't blame Saint's cutting question. I was the cause of her panic attacks. I broke in here and scared her, but it wasn't *me*, it was our past.

The way we met, and... interacted.

I touch the side of my nose. You'd never know she broke it when she was fifteen, because I was whisked to an elite private doctor who set it and assured my parents the break would heal straight.

It did, but the memory—and the residual pain—still lingers.

After everything else I signed up for, the last decade of my life, nothing has come close to breaking my nose. Not the bar fights, or when I graduated to cage fights. Not when I was deployed and forced into close-quarter combat.

"You fought Kade," Saint says. "Did he recognize you?"

I sigh. I knew the questions would circle back to him. I point to the shot glass, and Saint dutifully takes it. He puts his hand flat on the table, steadying himself, and grins.

We're going to be blasted by the time either of us quit.

"He did after we started, but then it was too late. He likes a fight too much to pull out."

Saint snickers. "That's what she said."

I eye him. "You ever fuck Artemis?"

He goes still.

Got you, fucker.

"Once," he admits. "You?"

"Once," I echo. I don't want to say it, but the single word just slips out.

It's a lie, though.

It was more than once.

I stand, brushing off my thighs. "I need air."

He nods and leans back in his seat, his eyes already drooping. "Good. Any more alcohol and I'd need my stomach pumped."

"Eat the pizza," I advise. I take a slice for myself. It'll be gone before I hit the elevator.

"Yes, sir," Saint mumbles.

Sarcastic fucker.

My legs aren't quite steady. I can't stop thinking about the last time I was in Sterling Falls. The last time I was here *haunts* me, and coming back was a fucking test.

"YOU'LL LIKE THE CITY," *my mother said, brushing back my hair. "It's different."*

My mouth was dry, my excitement buzzing. She sat next to me this whole trip, stroking my hair while the train sped toward Emerald Cove.

Not our final destination, it would turn out. From there, we boarded a ferry to Sterling Falls. I hadn't been on a boat like that before, so wide and high. We'd taken little charter boats before, where I could lean over and dip my fingers into the freezing ocean water. Or kayaks on the lake.

The ferry was awe-inspiring, but I was confused.

Confused about the trip, about why we didn't pack a lot.

Confused about my father, who seemed to be imperson-ating a statue. He typed on his phone, answered work calls, but otherwise didn't move.

A black SUV awaited us at the top of the pier in Sterling Falls. The driver stood to the side with a printed sign. It was Avery in block letters, and I glanced worriedly at my mother.

While we could—and did—afford certain luxuries, she made it seem like this was a spur-of-the-moment trip.

And yet, there was a driver.

A plan set in place that I knew nothing about.

"Where are we going?" I asked again.

She looped her arm through mine and held me close. In recent months, my body had sprouted. I grew six inches in three months. My joints and muscles pulled tight, my limbs still held an ache. Like being out in the cold for too long and plunging into a warm bath. But I towered over her now, the top of her head becoming my new constant viewpoint.

Not my father, though. He still had an inch on me, and muscles, too.

"This is a rite of passage." He tucks his phone in his pocket.

He chose the front seat, letting the driver open and close the door for us in the back, instead. Me first, sliding across the black leather, then my mother. There were water bottles in the doors, soft classical music playing over the speakers.

"What is?"

He twisted around and gave me a look.

One that said to stop talking, to be quiet. To just wait.

I hated waiting.

The sun set sometime while we were on the ferry, and it was completely dark by the time we reached a nondescript building. My parents led the way in. People opened doors for us, someone offered champagne. Even to me.

I was sixteen and definitely not allowed to be drinking, but nerves got the better of me.

I took the glass and swallowed all of it down before they could take it away. I set the empty glass back on the tray and continued, my nerves compounded by the fizz in my belly.

We entered a theater and walked down an aisle, having come out on a particular row. We couldn't see who was in the other booths, each U-shaped and high-backed. They faced away from us, and there were privacy screens on the row above us that blocked them out, too.

If anyone was even in the room with us.

We sat, me on one end, my father on the other. Mom perched in the middle, seeming torn about who to sidle up to.

"Are we watching a play?" I asked her in a low voice.

She shook her head and gave me a small, secret smile. "Just tell us who you like, darling. All right?"

The lights dimmed, and my attention was dragged to the now-illuminated stage below. It was dark when we entered, but the spotlight shone in the center. Waiting for its star.

The whole theater, from what I could tell, was dark velvets. The paneled walls, the booths. It screamed luxury. Gold fastenings and accents.

There was a small table in front of us with a lamp and a box with a button. It turned on at the same time as the spotlight, glowing red.

It switched to green just as a curtain down at the opposite end of the stage rustled, and a girl appeared.

Tall. Blonde. She wore a bikini and heels, and she walked to the center of the stage. Turned in a slow circle. Her bikini bottoms didn't cover any of her ass.

I...

What?

"Do you like her?" Mom inches closer. "She's pretty, but you could do better. It's all about the spark of attraction."

I tried to lick my lips, but my mouth was too dry. My heart was beating too fast.

"I don't understand."

She touched my knee. "You will."

I SLAM my fist into the wall, cutting off the memory before it can drown me.

I'm not that person.

I will not go down that road again.

Something moves in my peripheral vision. I whirl toward it, but I'm too slow. The shadow becomes a beast, which becomes a person. A person with a pipe in their hand.

They swing it at my head, and I am too slow to react. The alcohol in my system thoroughly fucks up my timing.

It smashes into my temple, and that's it.

Lights out.

32 ARTEMIS

SAINT IS SNORING on the couch when I get home. It's almost dawn, the sky lightening the tiniest amount. I stayed up way too late just talking and drinking with the Bow & Arrow crew. That's something that we don't normally get to have, but finally Antonio clapped his hands and sent everyone home.

Tomorrow, we will clean up the mess that the sheriff's department made.

Tomorrow is really today—but I'm not counting that.

I drop my stuff on the table and glance around.

There's no sign of Reese.

There are cards on the table, two shot glasses, a mostly empty bottle of whiskey. I go over and nudge Saint's leg with my foot, and he doesn't move. For fuck's sake.

And then an idea occurs to me.

A little payback.

I fill up a pitcher with water and ice and carry it back. I'm exhausted, but I'm also... kind of in the mood for a fight?

So I toss it on his head.

He comes awake with a roar, fists swinging, and I laugh.

His gaze jerks around, head swinging wildly. I imagine I looked something like that, too.

Why do we wake up so violently?

Oh, that's right: because we're traumatized.

Except he doesn't just spot me and glower, which is what I expect. He gets up off the couch and lunges at me.

He collides with me, tackling me to the floor. The pitcher—luckily plastic—goes clattering away. He collects my wrists, stopping my fight in my tracks, and pins my hips with his.

It does something to me.

Something it shouldn't.

"What the fuck, Artemis?" His face hovers over mine, dripping water on my cheeks.

"Where is Reese?"

He groans. Or growls. I can't quite tell—all I know is that he moves his hips, driving a suddenly very hard erection between my legs.

If we weren't wearing pants...

"I don't give a shit about Reese," he says. "And I fucking hate your guts."

"Well, I hate yours right back." My legs open.

He groans and lowers his head to my neck. I think, for a second, that he means to just hide his gaze from me. But then his teeth score my skin, and he *bites*. Hard.

A throb goes through me. My arms jerk, but he holds fast to my wrists. He pushes them above my head, holding with one hand and yanking my pants down with the other. He has to shift out of the way, and my cheeks burn.

"Leather pants," he mutters. "So fucking hot. But why are they so difficult?"

Jesus. "You think I'm hot?"

"I think your ass looks good in these pants," he counters.

He gets them and my panties to my ankles and shoves my legs wide again. He kneels between them, extended over me. "Are you wet for me?"

Before I can answer, he runs his finger down my center.

I arch at the contact.

"Wet," he says, and he makes it sound like a bad thing. He touches his finger to my lips, smearing arousal across them, before returning his hand to my core. He pumps one, then two fingers in and out, twisting, thrusting. Watching my face.

I glare at him.

He pauses to shove his sweatpants down. He's already hard. He notches at my entrance and pauses, gaze roving my face.

"This doesn't change anything."

"Spontaneous sex," I breathe. "Of course it doesn't change anything."

He nods, then pistons forward. His cock spreads me. The fullness is almost overwhelming. I meet his eyes, my lips parted. He stays there, seeming to search for something in my face.

Maybe he's waiting to make sure I don't fall in love with him?

"Get on with it," I growl.

He tsks and pushes up my shirt. He locks on to my nipples, and before I can open my mouth, he lowers his head. He takes one in his mouth. His tongue flicks at the piercing and the flesh around it. Then his teeth are on it. Tugging.

I groan.

"You like that?" He eyes me, then does it again. "Yeah. You're a whore for my cock."

"Move," I moan. "I need—"

"I know what you need." He licks my nipple, then shifts higher.

He bites my breast, and I clench around him. I make another noise. God, how did we end up here? I lift my hips, trying to get some friction. He hisses through his teeth and bites me harder, chasing the pain with his tongue.

And then he moves. He plays with the jewelry in my nipple with his tongue and teeth, sucking, nipping, and his hips jack forward. Back. *Again.* I bring my legs up higher, trapping his hips with my thighs.

"Do I make you feel dirty?" he asks. "Like how you make me feel?"

I shouldn't be at the edge of an orgasm so fast, but I cry out when he hits just the right spot. Over and over. It's too much, between his mouth and his cock.

I unravel, coming with a whimper of pleasure. It holds me hostage, burning bright through my body.

"I'm going to need an exorcism after this," he mutters. "Fuck me. You're so wet. Every fucking insult makes you clench around me."

I know. I'm going to need an exorcism, too. But that doesn't mean either of us are going to stop this madness.

"Tell me you hate me," he orders.

He releases my wrists and hooks his arm under my knee. He spreads me and leans up, his attention focused on where we're joined.

"I'd sacrifice you to save literally anyone else," I pant. "I hate the way you feel—"

"Liar," he groans.

"There's not a word for how much I despise you."

His eyes bore into mine. "Nice little whore. Spreading yourself for me. Your cunt is drooling for more."

His pace quickens, until I feel every hit like a bolt of

lightning through me. I dig my nails into the floor to try and stop from sliding.

"Break for me." He rubs my clit hard, his gaze impassive. Watching. "Prove to me you're a little slut for this."

He drags another orgasm out of me, and I spasm around his dick. He's stopped, just watching me writhe around him. Under him. And then, before it abates, he starts again. Faster. Chasing his own release, while I do my best to catch my breath.

Saint pulls out of me fast, finishing himself off with his fist. His tattooed knuckles wrapped around his tattooed dick does something to me. Another clench, a thrill chasing down my spine. He comes across my pussy and stomach. His chest rises and falls hard, and it takes him another moment to come back to his senses. Blinking away the lust and crashing back to reality.

I'm already there.

It's not as horrific the second time around, but I still crawl backward and scramble to my feet.

He glances at the empty couch. I try not to figure out what's inked into his flesh. The tattoos are everywhere, not stopping mid-thigh like I once theorized. A collection of small pieces all slotted together like a puzzle.

"Reese went for a walk," he says roughly, like he's just realizing we're alone. "He should be back soon."

My gaze moves to the window. "When?"

He follows my gaze. The sun has begun its assent, staining the sky in pinks and oranges.

"I..." He pauses, then swears. "I fell asleep."

"So...?"

He goes to the window and gives me a view of his ass. Surprisingly, the tattoos stop just at the curve, leaving the cheeks startlingly bare. But that's all I get a glimpse of. He pulls his sweatpants back into position. Doesn't seem to bother him that his dick is still wet. Maybe he'll take care of that in a second, because my concern grows the longer he takes to decide *when* Reese left.

An hour ago?

Two?

More?

I grab my cell and call the burner, but it's disconnected. It doesn't even ring through. I find my pants and rush into the bathroom. After the world's fastest sponge bath, I reemerge.

Who needs sleep?

"We need to find him," I say to Saint.

He grimaces, then nods. He takes his turn in the bathroom, while I put on a sweatshirt and comb my hair. I braid it quickly and wait.

Saint comes out, jams his feet into shoes, and nods to me.

Okay.

"Let's go," he urges. "I don't like the fucker, but I don't want anything to have happened to him on my conscience."

Uh-huh. I glance at Saint, who studiously ignores me. We stride down the hall to the elevator. I can't help but think he might be lying.

33 SAINT

WHY DO I keep thinking about Tem's cunt?

Hot and tight and squeezing. She's so fucking responsive to every little thing, and those damn nipple piercings threw me for a loop.

So what if my dreams have shifted from nightmares to erotica about *those*? Biting them, tugging them, twisting them with my fingers. Watching her face go from pleasure to pain and back again without reprieve.

The real thing was better than waking up with a stiff dick and only my hand to take care of it.

"His car is down there still," Tem says, exiting onto the street.

I shine my flashlight at the sidewalk. It's not really dark enough to require one, but it's not yet light enough to trust I won't miss something small. Sure enough, there's a glint of reflected light.

I pause, crouching, and touch the wet spot. My finger comes away red.

"What the fuck?" Tem breathes. She's right over my

shoulder, so close I can feel the heat of her body. "Is that blood?"

I rise and swing the light around in a wider arc. "We don't know it's his."

She hisses out a breath. "And if it is?"

Then...

"I don't know." My voice is hoarse. "I guess we'll need to ask for help, Artemis."

She bristles. "No shit, Sherlock."

I eye her. She seems genuinely worried. The cool air—and the bottle of water I guzzled while Tem got dressed—helps abate some of my drunkenness. I slept off a good portion, too. Still probably not enough to drive, but enough to think clearer.

"I shouldn't have fallen asleep," I tell her.

Tem sighs. "It's not your fault."

It is.

I meant what I said about him being on my conscience. If he's missing—and all signs point to *yes*—then we have a late start because I passed out as soon as he left.

"Stop staring," she mumbles.

The words register, and I scowl. I force my gaze away from her face and turn to the building. She picked this condo when she wanted security—when the town was literally going to shit and she was a target. Which means she chose one with locking front doors and security cameras.

"Come on." I unlock the front door and usher her into the lobby.

It's not just the doors that are monitored—the elevators have cameras, and above the third floor require fobs to activate the lifts. But the important part is the guy who sits behind the desk around the corner. He wears a *Security* jacket, black with silver light-reflecting patches on the arms and thick stitching.

"Hey, man."

He whirls around, eyeing me up and down. His limbs tense, like he's about to jump to his feet and fucking square off with me. But then recognition takes hold, and his posture eases a fraction.

"Some lady is screaming on the fifth floor. We tried calling down but it wasn't going through. It sounded kind of... violent."

He swears. "What unit?"

I make a face. "I don't know. Maybe 505? Hard to say for sure."

He jots something down, then grabs keys and leaps up. I guide Tem out of the way, keeping her behind me as the guard bolts back down the hall. The door swings shut, and I stick my foot in to keep it from fully closing.

As soon as he's around the corner, we slip inside.

"Nicely done," she murmurs. "But he'll be back as soon as he realizes you made that up."

I shrug. "He's still probably going to check on everyone up there."

I take a seat at the monitors. Admittedly, I'm not very high tech, but I can navigate my way around an old desktop computer. He didn't even shut it down. I glance at Tem, who still hovers at my shoulder, and figure out how to rewind.

We watch a somewhat grainy video, starting at midnight and zooming onwards. There's nothing for a long while, the building near silent. A couple lets themselves in through the front door, kissing in the elevator. They exit.

I don't dare glance at Tem.

She grabs my shoulder when Reese enters the elevator.

I slow it down to real time, leaning forward. He weaves a little, seeming out of it. Lost in his thoughts? Tem's hand turns into a claw when he exits the elevator at the lobby. He glances around the open space—new angle, now—and stumbles on his way out the door.

"Oh my God," she whispers. "How much did you two drink?"

I grunt.

I click on the camera feed that points outside.

Reese exits and stops on the sidewalk, his chest heaving. Suddenly, he stops.

He pivots and punches the wall, and it must bite him back, because he shakes out his fist. For a moment, it seems like he's going to stride away.

But then—

Tem gasps.

Someone comes behind him from the left-bottom side of the frame. It's grainy, and kind of hard to see with the shadows, but the glint of an object rising in the stranger's hand, coming down hard and fast at Reese—

He shifts, getting a look at his attacker a millisecond before he's hit in the head.

Reese crumples.

I pause it and try to reel in my anger. While this was happening, I was fucking sleeping?

"Don't," Tem warns. "Now's not the time for the blame game. Keep going."

Fuck. I don't want to admit that she's right, but her words ring true. I hit 'play' again, and we watch the guy stand over Reese for a long moment. He then bends down and gets Reese slung over his shoulders, like a fireman's carry.

He walks off-screen, heading across the street, with Reese slumped and unconscious.

Not good.

"Is there another angle?" Tem's voice is desperate.

I click through, but there's nothing. I stand, and her hand slips from my shoulder. I face her, the guilt that I've been feeling low in my stomach now burning through me.

"We'll find him." It's a promise. "Could that have been Kade?"

Tem presses her lips together, quickly shaking her head. "No. Too... slim? Kade is bulky."

I grimace.

"We need help," she adds. "Kade or someone else—"

"How about your brother?"

She hesitates. Scowls. Then, "I don't know if he'd take it seriously."

Yeah. Apollo holds a grudge, especially since our first introduction to Reese was Tem fainting at the sight of him. Although their prior relationship still evades me, I always figured it was wrapped in trauma or some shit.

A regular old breakup wouldn't make Artemis *faint*.

"We're not going to Kade." I cross my arms.

She raises an eyebrow.

I know that look. I also know that her mind is set, and I missed my opportunity to volunteer someone better than *her brother*. I find myself nodding along to her unvoiced idea, silently accepting that Kade and I were bound to clash sooner or later.

I mean *meet*. We were bound to *meet* sooner or later.

"Let's go," she says quietly. "I got my car back from Apollo, so..."

"Great."

I follow her to the parking garage. Her car is in the spot right next to Reese's truck, the block lettering painted on the concrete floor denoting it as her two free spaces. She gets in the driver's seat, and I wrinkle my nose getting into the passenger seat.

The car smells like her, though. She uses some sort of lavender-scented shampoo that I used to loathe. But it's grown on me, and now I take a deep breath. I try to let it settle me.

"What happened earlier..."

I glance over. By the time we pull out of the garage, the sun has risen. It truly is a contrast to how much time we spent watching the footage, and... *other*. Fucking. Which brings my attention back to my dick and how it felt to sink into her.

Thoughts I shouldn't have but cannot stop.

It's what she's bringing up anyway, isn't it? She startled me awake with ice-cold water, I leapt on her, and the burning urge—what I had been dreaming about, not satiated with the icy water dripping from my face—took over. Sue me.

"Go on," I goad. "Gonna try to walk that back?"

"You're using me," she accuses.

I frown. "Am I? Any more than you're using me, Artemis?"

"No, I—"

"Tell me how it's different." I twist to face her, ignoring where we're going. "Tell me how you didn't have any reaction, that you didn't spread your legs. Tell me you said stop and I missed it."

"Saint." Her cheeks redden. "No, I didn't say stop."

I hum.

"We're using each other," she decides. "We're distractions."

"Reese kissed you." *That* unpleasant memory comes snapping back to the front of my mind. "Did you ask him to do that?"

She shifts. "I did."

That silences me. She goes from freaking out around him to—to making out with him? What the fuck is that? It's not like I want monogamy. Actually, it's the last thing I want from her. Or anyone.

Not her.

I mean—

Just stop thinking.

I lean my head back and close my eyes. I blow out a long, slow breath. Inhale. Exhale. It should be easy to get myself back into the mindset, but she seems to have obliterated my calm facade.

"We're here," she says quietly. She shuts off the car.

She gets out before my eyes open. But when I do, my heart immediately stops.

I knew he lived here. I knew... I knew, and I fucking forgot.

We're in front of the mansion that Kronos once took refuge in. The mansion made of glass and steel, that sits on its own private beach in North Falls. There are dunes to the left, the ground rising farther beyond. The sandy beach disappears into cliffs. The reservoir is beyond that, and the church...

I suppose it's not a church anymore. It was an evil place.

But this ground is evil, too.

I get out, unwilling to even let Tem deal with Kade Laurent on her own. His car is in the driveway, nearly covering the spot where...

I swallow.

It nearly covers the spot where I last held Elora.

"Come on." Tem doubles back and takes my hand. "We've got this."

My stomach turns, but I let her lead me anyway. Up the driveway, around the solid wall that was once riddled with bullet holes. It's been repaired, patched, and painted.

How long did it take them to get Elora's blood out of the driveway? Concrete is porous... they might've had to dig up the whole square.

There's a side door that Artemis aims for, but I'd bet anything that it's locked. She releases my hand and pulls a knife from a holster strapped to her ankle.

I stare at her. "How long have you had that?"

She brushes her braid back over her shoulder. It swings across her back, and she eyes me. "I always have it."

Noted.

The sweatshirt, at the very least, isn't Kade's. It's black and boxy, the bottom elastic cut off. It has Bow & Arrow's logo—the neon sign above the club's door just a symbol, essentially—across the back. The edges are all frayed, but it just adds to her aesthetic. A mix of badass and *I don't give a shit*. The sweatshirt hides the gold shirt and the necklaces she wears. Layers and layers of them.

Instead of using the knife to jimmy open the door, she drops into a crouch and continues along the wall.

We have to duck under windows.

"Are we in danger of being shot?"

She frowns. "You probably are. Stay behind me."

Great.

We reach the back of the house, and she straightens abruptly. I almost crash into her and catch myself at the last moment. She stows the knife and motions for me to stick close. My gaze lifts from the back of her head to the ocean.

The very same beach I stormed down, throwing myself into the waves in a fit of grief and shock and rage. I see it now, the way Kora and Wolfe chased after me and dragged me out...

The echo of gunshots rings in my ears.

Tem's elbow lands in my gut.

Kade is waist-deep in the white, frothy water. His tattoo-free torso glistens with droplets, hair wet. His back muscles flex and tense right before he puts his hands together and dives under the waves.

Artemis marches down the beach, stopping at the edge of the water that rolls up to greet her. It recedes without touching her boots.

We wait for Kade to pop out on the other side of the break. He glances back at the shore mid-stroke and pauses.

Appraises, in a single look, the two of us.

Then he dives again, and Artemis lets out a little sigh.

He returns to shore. The waves tug at him, and my eyes widen when the water finally releases him.

He's naked.

And pierced.

What a pair he and Artemis make. The thought strikes me without warning, and I glower at him. While still wondering why the fuck anyone would pierce their dick. Tattooing mine was a long, torturous process that I barely felt because it was in the aftermath of Elora's death. I don't think I could handle it in a normal frame of mind.

I wrench my gaze away before I can examine it further, but when I meet his eyes, he's smirking.

My scowl deepens.

He stops in front of us, hands on his hips. "You've been avoiding me, sweetheart?"

Tem mirrors my expression. "Can you put some clothes on?"

His abdomen tightens, dragging her gaze—shit, no, *my* gaze—down again. I turn away and stalk toward the house. His towel and shorts are on one of the chairs. I pick them up and whirl around, but he's right behind me.

"We fought," he says plainly.

Yeah, we did. And he got the best of me.

Another reason I grit my teeth. I shove the shorts and towel at him, and he laughs in my face. It's loud and abrasive, and will Tem care if I just murder him right here?

With my bare hands?

"Stop." Tem grabs my arm.

Am I really the issue, here? I glare at her, trying to convey that this dickwad is naked *and* laughing at me.

"Kade, Saint. Saint, Kade."

She positions herself in front of me, forcing me a step back. With breathing room between him and I, the weight on my chest lessens. I take a breath, then another. I imagine myself back in Elora's house, hitting my head against the wall. *Thump, thump, thump.* It matches my slowing heart rate.

"We've met," Kade says. His voice is low, but no less powerful than his stance. Or his posture.

I immediately hate him more than I did five seconds ago. The preening peacock.

His unspoken *duh* is obvious. She was there, too. She was also there when I forced myself to enter this house the first time and drag her out.

The urge to do the same is only tempered by the knowledge that he can help us find Reese. Or... well, Tem thinks he can. And that means putting aside my massive trust issues.

It's my fault he was taken.

I didn't tell her about the drinking game. The questions.

"Great," Tem says. "Because we need your help."

34 ARTEMIS

SAINT AND KADE do not like each other.

And yet... well, they're going to have to get along for at least today. We go inside, which is just as bare as the last time I was here. Kade has put on his shorts, rinsed his feet, and now we're in his kitchen. I tug off my sweatshirt and set it aside, then jump up onto the counter. I grip the edges. Saint claims one of the barstools at the island.

I should have changed my shirt before Saint and I left. It's the one I wore to Olympus, then Bow & Arrow, and the one Saint shoved up to lavish attention on my breasts...

Stop that.

There are bound to be hickeys on my breasts from the way he bit and tugged at them. Just thinking about it sends a rush of desire straight to my core. Now is not the time to be thinking about sex. But at least the ones Kade left on my neck from the dance floor have faded. They got lost amongst the bruises after the bike crash incident.

I lean forward so the gold material isn't stuck tight to my chest. My nipples feel sensitive, and I am braless. The last thing I need is for either to spot them pebbling, or...

I should just put the damn sweatshirt back on.

But I don't.

Kade grabs a bottle of water from the fridge and offers one to me. I take it, setting it beside me. When he doesn't offer one to Saint, I take a quick sip from mine and toss it across to him.

Saint grimaces. But he drinks at least half of it.

Is he hung over?

"Well?" Kade asks Saint.

Not me.

I narrow my eyes at Saint Hart, who fucking *flushes*. I don't know that I've ever seen the man so much as get a pink hue in his cheeks...

"Reese has been staying with Artemis and me," he says after a beat. "And last night, he was taken."

Kade straightens. He looks at me, and damn it, now *my* face heats without warning.

"You had him?" he says in a quiet voice. Not a nice quiet. It's downright sinister.

I lift my chin. "Yeah, I did."

"And you *lost* him without telling me—"

"You went behind my back." I hop off the counter and ball my fists. "You went to the *sheriff*. Why even ask me?"

He rolls his eyes. "Artemis—"

"Save it," I hiss. "Save it for after we find Reese. Did you know he was involved with the Cyclopes in Emerald Cove?"

He freezes.

"I'd take that as a no," Saint drawls. His chin rests on his hand, doing a great impression of being fucking bored.

"How do you know?" Kade demands. He yanks one of the barstools around and sinks into it.

"He told me. That's why he came up here..."

"Reese said that?"

I nod. Pause. Did he say that? In so many words?

"He said he wanted to stop them from settling in Sterling Falls," I hedge. Although I'm pretty sure when I guessed that, he just said, *Something like that.* "Either way—"

"We'll table it," Kade says. His expression, which was already serious enough, turns downright terrifying. "Tell me what you know about him being taken."

Saint and I lay it all out on the table. The video, the man coming from off-screen. The fact that, besides the back of this guy's head, we've got nothing. Kade leaves the room, returning with a laptop. I hop down from the counter and circle behind him to get a better view. He pulls up my building on a map and jumps to street view, slowly panning the camera around.

"There's a bank across the street," he points out. "Banks always have security."

Saint frowns. "What do you want to do, bulldoze in there asking to see their video feed?"

Kade considers it for a moment, then shakes his head. "Nah."

He types, then leans back. A second later, a low *ping* makes Saint straighten.

"What did you just do?" Distaste and apprehension run thick in Saint's tone.

Can't say I blame him for it.

"I've got someone who will hack their system. We should have eyes soon." Kade swivels in his seat and gets up. "Anyone hungry?"

My stomach lets out an untimely growl.

I'm not even *that* hungry, but apparently my body has

other ideas. I find myself nodding along, my cheeks heating, while Saint grunts an affirmation.

Kade rubs his hands together. "Tem, keep an eye on the computer, would you?"

I don't hate that he calls me by my nickname. Saint wouldn't dare.

I take the stool Kade occupied. He busies himself pulling stuff out of the fridge, laying out ingredients, then fetching a pan. I glance at Saint, who seems to be torn between watching him and me.

Who took Reese?

And why?

Kade alluded to the fact that Reese might be running from someone—but Reese made no such mention. Either he didn't trust us with it, or he didn't think it was relevant. Maybe he tried to outrun his past, and it caught up with him.

Or Kade's information is wrong, and someone else took Reese. One of the Cyclopes, maybe. But it still brings me back to the *why*—and what they're doing to him.

"We don't know who has him," Saint says in a low voice. "It's no use panicking. Stay rational."

"Easier said than done," I murmur.

I focus on the screen. There's a chat window up, the relevant details sent, and a user with a long string of numbers in their name replying that it was possible.

"Who did you ask for help?"

Kade glances over his shoulder at me. "An old friend."

"Like how Reese was an old friend?" Saint asks.

Kade huffs. "Yeah, he knew Reese and I from the same place. Except when we got out, Reese went his own way and I stayed close with some of the guys."

"Military," Saint guesses.

Oh, shit.

"Reese said he was a former Marine." I narrow my eyes. "Is that where you two met?"

Kade nods. He doesn't even look at us anymore, fixated on whatever he's making. His broad shoulders block my view.

Saint taps the table. "How long ago?"

"Few years."

Saint and I meet eyes, and for once, I think we're on the same page.

"Now isn't the time to hold back," Saint argues. He steals the words right from my lips. "Especially since we're trusting you with this."

"You could've done this already," I add. "Why ask me for help if you have someone who can hack into security feeds—"

The laptop *pings* as a message comes through, proving my point. Saint gets up and circles around behind me.

Kade comes to the table with three grilled sandwiches stacked on a plate. He puts it down and leans in, clicking the link his friend sent. It downloads a file, which pops up as soon as it's done.

Security footage. The street is visible, as well as the front door to my building.

"He sent the whole night," Kade says under his breath.

He plays it double time until I grab his wrist. He slows it down, and the three of us watch Reese come out the front door. He weaves, clearly not super steady on his feet.

This image is much sharper than my building's. Wonder who I have to bribe to update them...

Reese punches the wall. He shakes out his fist and faces the street, giving us a clear view at his face. Someone moves out of the shadows behind him, and he catches sight a moment too late. The stranger raises a pipe and smashes him in the head.

Reese falls. The stranger picks him up.

I want to check Kade's expression, but I'm too fixed on getting a better look at this guy. He's not as big as Kade, that's for sure. And if it *was* Kade, he wouldn't have gotten us this video.

He crosses the street toward the bank, and recognition stabs at me.

I gasp and grab the edge of the counter, leaning forward.

He goes to a car and pops the trunk, folding Reese's long limbs into it.

Slam.

There's no audio, but I hear an echo of the trunk shutting nonetheless. He glances around, then straight at the camera.

Kade hits a button and freezes it.

The hood is up, obscuring his hair. Clearly male, though, just from the build and his face—which is uncovered.

I wet my lips. "I know that face."

"Who is it?" Saint demands. "Someone from Sterling Falls?"

I meet his gaze, doing my best not to flinch. "Not really. He left town years ago... But I think I know why he came back."

"Who is he?" Saint asks.

Just say it. Say where you know him. Say his name.

"His name is Gabriel."

There's so much more to it, though, because just speaking it out loud shoots a weird mix of guilt and fear straight down my spine. Gabriel was imprisoned in Terror for so much longer than me. Not weeks or months—*years*.

He was my first rescue from that web, and my biggest failure.

"How do you know him?" Kade asks.

"I got him out of Terror." I face them, confused about their confusion. Or lack of horror. They haven't heard of Terror? Or if they have, they couldn't know the extent.

I wave them off, feigning indifference, and make up a lie about Terror just being a club.

When we were fifteen and sixteen—no big deal. I don't mention our ages, or the innocence ripped away from both of us at different times. And in vastly different ways.

Kade still eyes me with suspicion, while Saint moves right along. I ignore the questioning expressions. Kade and I trade places, and I take the chair beside Saint, picking up one of the sandwiches.

They watch the video again. They ask me if I'm sure, to which I nod.

My thoughts turn to Gabriel. It's been years since I last talked to him, although I assumed Antonio kept up contact. He's better about that than I am. He likes to keep tabs on everyone and everything. It eases *his* conscience.

Antonio was involved in Terror in a different way, and it's caused him different scars than it left on me. But back to Gabriel—why would he take Reese?

Why is he back in Sterling Falls at all?

Sandwich polished off, I leave Kade and Saint squabbling over the best way to find Gabriel and Reese and retreat upstairs. There are no beds, which is peculiar. Kade has been here for over a month, hasn't he?

There's a cot in one of the rooms, though, with a nest of folded clothes around it. Only the essentials, I suppose. The room has balcony doors of glass thrown open wide, allowing the sunshine and salted air to sweep into the room. The cot is positioned in prime space right in the opening. It's like sleeping outside, almost.

I drag the drapes across the opening, leaving the doors open. A breeze still slips past the heavy blackout fabric, but the room is now considerably darker.

I am so fucking tired, and we're nowhere closer to finding Reese.

Climbing onto the cot and closing my eyes is automatic.

I'm asleep in seconds.

35 ARTEMIS

"TEM." A hand touches my shoulder and immediately releases me.

My swing touches empty air.

"I knew you were going to do that."

I crack my eyes open. My body aches, and I slowly push the blanket off my shoulders. I didn't cover myself, but... now I'm covered.

And Kade crouches just out of reach, a smile playing on his lips.

"Did you find him?"

He shakes his head once. "No, but we're going out."

"We as in you and Saint?"

"We as in the three of us." He tips his head. "Unless you think Saint and I should be alone together."

I narrow my eyes. "You wouldn't hurt him, would you?"

"Only if he strikes first, little goddess."

A chill runs down my spine. *The good kind.* Not sure where he came up with that nickname, but I'm not terribly opposed. He doesn't say it mockingly. There's a softness in his gaze that doesn't reconcile with how he usually acts.

Tough. Almost cold.

He just feels sorry for you.

"Okay," I finally say, swinging my legs out of the cot.

He steps closer and holds out his hand, helping me to my feet. He tugs me closer without warning. My chest bumps his. Immediate butterflies fan their wings in my stomach, and I meet his dark eyes in confusion. He uses two fingers to catch the mussed hair at my temple. He tucks the strands behind my ear, then releases my hand.

I step back, letting out a shaky exhale.

That shouldn't have been sensual.

It definitely wasn't sexual.

Was it?

"Right." I clear my throat. "Let's go, then."

He grabs a folded sweatshirt and thrusts it at me. His gaze drops to my chest, and I follow.

Yeah, those fucking nipple piercings are prominent.

"You've got piercings, too," I blurt out.

His eyebrow rises. Just one, a little tick up before it smooths.

"You saw that, huh?"

"We interrupted your skinny-dipping." My face flames.

I snap open the hoodie, ready to drag it over my head, when Kade reaches out and stops me. Two fingers, the same that tucked my hair, now just barely graze the still-visible piercing.

I just barely stop myself from reacting audibly.

"Come over early more often." His voice is hoarse. "We can continue that interruption in a more positive note... or maybe you can join me in the water."

My mouth dries. I step back and finish putting it on, letting the dark-gray fabric hang down to my mid-thigh. It has the same logo on it as the other one—that I still need to return to him at some point—and I frown as I pluck it away from my chest, examining the eye and the snake.

"Is this your company logo or something?"

Kade sighs. "No, my sister drew it. We used it as a fundraiser."

"For...?"

"Her hospital bills."

We stare at each other, and I try to decide if I need to apologize for overstepping or...

"Let's go," Saint shouts from downstairs.

"He has impeccable timing," I say with a hesitant smile.

Kade returns it, and I exhale my relief. He goes to one of the locked boxes next to his clothes. I hadn't paid much attention to them, but now he unlocks it with his thumb print and pulls a handgun.

"Here," he says, holding it out to me.

I take it. The holster and magazine come next, along with a spare one. I slide the extra magazine into my pocket and load the weapon, checking it over. It fits nicely in my palm—it doesn't seem like the kind of gun Kade would own, much less take with him.

"You expecting a firefight?"

"Better than to be unprepared." He loads his own and attaches the holster to his pants. They're the kind that go on the inside of the waistband for concealed carry, and as soon as he pulls at his shirt, it disappears from sight. "Saint?"

I think I've seen him with a gun. "He's shot before."

Kade nods. We go downstairs, and I finish fiddling with my holster. I own a similar one, so I'm not unfamiliar with it. Jace and my brother taught me to shoot when I was sixteen, and the lessons continued until I was able to master large distances with a range of weapons.

"Why do you wake up so violently?" Kade asks.

My chest tightens. "Doesn't everyone wake up swinging?"

He snorts. "No."

"Product of having a volatile family," I murmur. Although that's really only half of it. The rest comes from trauma. Saying that seems like a step in the wrong direction, though, and would only open myself up to pity.

Reese knows.

Kade and Saint can treat me like a normal person. *Human.*

We get downstairs, and Saint straps his weapon on. Outside, it's practically dusk. I slept for way too long, and I don't know how to feel about them letting me take the nap... if it can still be classified as such.

We got here in the morning. Reese was taken last night. It's been almost a full day.

We pile into Kade's SUV, me in front and Saint taking the backseat. He slides into the middle to see straight ahead.

"Why did you let me sleep?" I ask in a low voice.

"You needed it," Kade replies. "And we were working with my contact to track Gabriel's car's movements."

I sit up straighter. "Did you find him?"

"We found where he parked it," Saint says. "There were some gaps in the footage, and it doesn't appear like he removed Reese from where it is now."

"So he stopped, took Reese out of the trunk, then parked his car." I sigh. "Why can't it be easy?"

"If it was easy, we could call the sheriff and be done with it," Kade says.

I feel my hackles rising. "We're not trusting the sheriff with shit now. You understand that, right?"

He just looks at me.

I get it, in a way. Kade thinks that the sheriff is loyal because he did something for him. But it's not people Bradshaw is loyal to—it's the money that Kade paid him. It was proven again and again before my brother and his friends put an end to the war.

Even before the war, the sheriff had his fingers in all the pots.

"Artemis is right," Saint says. "Brad should be our last resort."

Kade huffs. "Guy really fuck you over, or something?"

I narrow my eyes. "Yeah, Kade, he has. Not to mention, last night he executed a search warrant of my club. No idea what he was hunting for, but he tied it back to the guy who was murdered and left outside it."

They both look at me. Kade only briefly, since he's currently speeding toward West Falls, but Saint's gaze lingers.

"What?" I mumble.

"You didn't mention that, is all," Saint replies.

"We were busy." I try not to think about the main distraction. Before we realized Reese had been gone for too long. "So, where is his car parked?"

We've come down through North Falls into what was formerly called the neutral zone—the gangs didn't fight in this area, which is comprised of the schools, downtown area, and financial district. There comes a line where downtown becomes West Falls, which was run by the Titans.

I was just here. Day drinking my problems away at Madness.

My skin prickles when Kade turns onto that street, and he rolls to a slow stop in front of the bar.

"Seriously?" I breathe. "You're joking."

"Nope." Kade gazes up at the buildings. In this area of town, it seems like Sterling Falls is falling inward. The buildings all kind of slope together, leaning over the street. The buzz of neon signs—another club opened up down the way, more bars and restaurants, smoke shops and cigar dens—hums on the air, and their color splashes the ground.

I've always felt like Sterling Falls was alive, and this part of the city is its teeth.

The gun makes me feel better. Barely.

Kade shuts off his SUV, and we climb out. There are more people around at this time of evening, which isn't too surprising. People are leaving work, going out to dinner. The sun just set. Later tonight, the more volatile citizens will emerge. But that's not for us to worry about.

Saint jerks his chin toward a car parked farther down. My lungs stop working, and I grab his wrist. To go check it out or...

"Come on," Kade says. "He might be watching it."

Saint nods.

I frown.

We go into Madness.

Half the barstools are filled, as well as some of the tables. Busier than I would've guessed. We take seats at the bar, although Saint sits with his back to it. He gazes out at everyone like they're a threat.

Maybe they are.

I'm sandwiched between Saint and Kade, so close that my arms brush both of theirs. It gives me a modicum of security, surprisingly. Saint watches our backs while Kade flags down the bartender.

He comes over immediately, but he doesn't smile. No warm welcome. "What're you having?"

"An old fashioned." Kade tips his head. "And whatever these two are having."

I clear my throat. "Um, water."

"Same," Saint echoes.

Kade scowls. "Give them what I'm having."

An old fashioned appears in front of me. I don't say what I'm thinking—that I've had enough whiskey to last at least a year—but I take a sip all the same. Kade does, too.

Saint tosses his back like a shot.

"You heathen," Kade mutters. "You don't just gulp down—"

"I wanted water," Saint interrupts.

"You stand out in a bar if you just order water."

Saint raises his eyebrows. "Are we trying to blend in? You didn't really tell us the plan when we strolled in here."

Kade snarls. "Seriously? We're trying to blend in. It's common sense."

"You don't blend in anywhere, outsider," Saint retaliates.

I put my hands up in front of their faces. "Stop it. Both of you."

I can only imagine what would happen if I left the two of them alone. They'd probably tear each other's throats out.

"Saint, calm down and stop riling up Kade." My gaze switches to the big man on my other side. "And you should be more forthcoming about what we're doing, since you're not flying solo anymore."

He goes still. His dark eyes bore into mine, and I kind of hate how transparent I feel around him.

"Okay," he finally says. "You're right."

Saint scoffs. He leans forward and flags down the bartender. "We're hoping to speak with Gabriel."

Kade glares past me.

The bartender hesitates. He's young, probably in his early twenties, with floppy blond hair and a handsome face. He doesn't seem like the type to be caught up with the Cyclopes or Gabriel...

Wait.

Are they related? Gabriel and the Cyclopes? I hadn't considered it. Didn't really think it was any sort of possibility. But if Gabriel came here, then...

I keep my expression carefully neutral and hope the bartender doesn't clock my sudden nerves. We're in West Falls, in an area that has definitely been taken over by Cyclopes. Just because I managed to drink here one morning—yeah, it sounds bad in my head, too—doesn't mean that I can just come and go.

I'm marked, isn't that what everyone has been saying?

And they're not talking about my bike. They're talking about me.

Twice now, I've been attacked. Saint saved me once. I saved myself the first time, which was really more like a warning than anything else.

"Gabriel," the bartender repeats, his expression freezing in place. Like he isn't sure what to do with the question and he's never heard the name before.

Saint stiffens. He nudges me, just the barest graze of his elbow along my ribs. I look at him, and in the peripheral I spot someone rising from their booth. Not just one. The stares of several men burn the back of my neck.

I grip Kade's knee under the bar.

"If you don't know..." Kade purses his lips, easily taking over the conversation. "I'll just go smash up his car while we wait."

Saint grabs my arm and pulls me from the stool. He drags me into his side just as someone throws a bottle. It sails through the space I just occupied, smashing into the glass behind the bar.

"Oye," the bartender yells. "Not here!"

Kade swivels around slowly, not even shoving to his feet until someone is right up in his space. The guy punches, and Kade easily evades it by leaning back. He grabs the front of the guy's shirt and yanks him forward.

Kade's forehead cracks into the guy's nose, and he takes the moment of his opponent being stunned to draw him farther forward. And down. The guy's head rebounds off the lip of the bar, and he falls to Kade's feet.

"Anyone else?"

There are seven of them.

Big, burly assholes.

They share looks, seeming to get on the same page, and my gut twists.

Saint slowly uncurls his fingers from my arm. He puts some space between us, edging toward the door. I'm not concerned with him leaving us high and dry—I'm not running. I wouldn't do that to Kade.

And I'm not drawing my gun until he does.

All at once, they charge. One comes for me, two for Saint and two at Kade. Two hang back, but I ignore them as soon as the guy in front of me throws the first punch.

My blood roars to life at the challenge.

I duck, and his arm sails through empty air over my head. I leap forward, into his space, and slam my fist into his gut. He's one of the younger ones fighting, barely a trace of facial hair on his chin. And he picked *me* to fight.

He thought he could get off easy, maybe?

Defeat a girl?

I hammer two more punches into his stomach before he manages to shove me away. I dance back and grin at him.

I miss fighting.

It's been too long since I've fought at Olympus. Since before the war, I think... I didn't want to fight for fun after all the fighting that was for survival.

"Come on, then," I goad.

He lunges. He's not a natural fighter, which makes his movements a little hard to predict. He catches me on the jaw once, and my head snaps to the side. That's all I need to really wake up, and we collide again. Pain echoes down my arm with each hit I drive into his face, and it isn't until hands grab my arms and haul me up that I realize I've been punching an unconscious man.

His face is a bloody mess, barely recognizable anymore.

Saint and Kade have similarly dispatched theirs, and the other two are long gone.

As is the bartender.

Kade grimaces, touching my jaw. "He hit you."

I lick my lower lip and taste blood. "Only twice."

He growls. Before I can stop him, Kade pulls his gun and shoots the unconscious man in the head. The bar goes deathly quiet in the wake of the gunshot, and my mouth opens and closes.

Did he seriously just do that?

"You didn't—"

"I did." His voice is clipped. "No one touches you. Let's go."

Shit.

Okay, then.

I exchange a look with Saint, whose eyebrows are nearly in his hairline. We follow Kade out and down the street to Gabriel's car.

He circles to the front and turns away, shooting the glass

of the driver's door. He reaches in and unlocks it, then pops the trunk.

I catch on to his thought fast—that Reese could still be in the trunk.

Dead or alive, I don't know.

I hurry forward and fling it open the rest of the way, immediately expecting a body.

But the trunk is empty.

"Damn it," Kade roars. "Where the fuck is he?"

I wish I knew.

"There's another place."

We whirl around.

The bartender lingers in the doorway of Madness, his fingers twisting his apron and releasing it, over and over again.

"Another place?" Saint asks. "What are you talking about?"

"Where they meet. Where he feels safe—" He chokes. Blood bubbles out of his mouth, dribbling down his lips.

I start, and Saint moves in front of me. I crane around in time to see him fall forward with a knife protruding out of the back of his throat. One of them inside killed him for talking. What would they have done to us for asking questions?

"We need to get out of here," Saint says.

"Not without someone to tell us where Reese is." I squeeze Saint's arm.

Kade is already nodding his assent, and he moves past me with sure steps. After a long moment, he remerges from the bar dragging an unconscious man behind him. He hauls him over the bartender and to his SUV. Without our help, he pops the trunk and hoists him in.

Saint and I circle around in time to see him taping the

guy's ankles and hands. He places another strip over his mouth.

"Let's go," Kade orders.

Holy shit.

Saint and I climb into the car wordlessly, and I can't help but wonder what the fuck we're doing.

Besides kidnapping a gang member...

That's a given.

36 KADE

I WIPE my hands and emerge from the lower deck of the boat. Flecks of dried blood coat my arms, my shirt, my pants. It's hidden on my black clothing but stands out like a sunburn on my skin.

Artemis and Saint wait for me at Bobby's Eats. He's returned to the marina for the night and seems to have no problem entertaining my guests on his houseboat. They're seated at the same picnic table Artemis and I sat at the last time—granted, there is only one, but still.

I take a knee out of sight and scoop salt water in my cupped hand, splashing it along my arms. I use the stained cloth to scrub and dry them, satisfied that Bobby won't ask any questions about the state of my appearance.

Finished, I tuck away the cloth and wave to Bobby. He's just now serving them food, and I let myself onto his boat with a smile.

Shrugging off what I just did and turning on the charm takes practice, but I fall into it with ease. It's that permanent switch from work to civilian life that doesn't work so well. Charm is just a bravado anyway.

"Hey. How'd it go?"

Artemis chews on her plump lower lip. She and Saint sit across from each other, and choosing who to sit beside is... well, not quite the no-brainer. I want to feel her pressed up against me, but I also like poking the tattooed man's buttons.

And he doesn't seem to like physical contact.

Not from me anyway.

It's why I drop into the space beside him. I spread my legs until my knee brushes his, and he recoils.

I smirk, then announce, "I've got a location."

Bobby returns with a bowl for me. Today, fishnet tights cling to his tanned legs, with black cargo shorts over them. His white button-up shirt is covered in orange and blue birds. His hair is up in a bun on top of his head, and the fallen pieces at his nape are caught in the hairnet he always wears.

His style is distinct, and I struggle not to laugh at the way Saint appraises him. If only I had been here for his reaction when they first saw him...

I thank Bobby, pay him for the food, and he retreats back into his houseboat. I dig into the nachos. He's covered the corn chips with pulled pork, cheese, and a mix of other stuff. Corn, black beans, salsa, guacamole, sour cream.

"You've got a location?" Tem asks. "And you're eating?"

"Torture makes me hungry," I say through a mouthful.

Saint frowns.

"What?" I knock my knee into his again. "Did you think I was going to ask him nicely? You wanted to find Reese. This is how we do that."

"Okay." Tem swallows. "Okay, fine. Where are they?"

I don't answer until I've eaten most of the nachos and drank most of the water Bobby brought with it. Artemis's burger is three-quarters gone, and Saint's paper plate is empty. Satisfaction fills me that they were able to put aside their queasiness over what has to be done.

It's like this in war, too.

Eat when you can.

Sleep when you can.

I wipe my mouth and drop the soiled napkin into the bowl.

"There's an abandoned church up near the reservoir," I say.

Artemis groans.

"What?" I glance at Saint, then do a double take.

The bastard is naturally pale—it makes his tattoos, which climb up his throat and frame his sharp jaw nicely— but right now, he's downright green.

"The Titans held him there," Artemis manages. "You don't have to go."

Saint shakes his head. "No. If you're going…"

"It was blown up," Artemis adds. "Unless it was rebuilt."

I take in that information. I didn't get a lot from the asshole in the boat—just the location and a general idea of the layout—but what the *fuck* goes on in this city? Gang wars, people being taken, buildings blowing up?

"We were rescuing Saint," Artemis says. "We blew up one of the propane tanks to cause a distraction and get a clean escape."

"Clean," Saint repeats. "I don't remember the clean part."

"You were stabbed." She crosses her arms over her chest. "Of course you don't remember it."

He idly rubs at the center of his chest.

I stand. "You two should stay, then. And I will go collect Reese."

Here's the part where I don't give them a chance to argue. I get up and hop over the side of the boat onto the dock and stride back to my car. I get there and slide into the driver's seat, locking the doors right as Artemis and Saint arrive. They both pull at the doors, and I give Tem a look through the window.

She can't come.

Saint can't either.

Knowing what I know now, they'd just be liabilities. While they both held their own in the bar—and the little goddess even going feral, which went straight to my dick—I can't risk it. Their states of mind could be the difference between surviving and dying.

Not an option when it comes to Reese.

I'm going to get my former friend back, and my debt will be square.

I TAKE my time picking through the forest. Three times, I have to hide myself from men patrolling. If they're out this deep in the woods, it means there's more at stake than just one man being held hostage.

Hostage.

No one has demanded ransom, which kind of negates the hostage theory.

Reese doesn't have any money to his name anyway. It's why he's so good at staying undetected. He has a single bank account that receives a government check once a month, that he occasionally draws cash from in Emerald

Cove. Other than that, no credit cards, no mortgage or rent, no car.

There's another use for hostages, though.

To protect themselves from an outside force.

And this double-edged sword is a message to us.

I reach the tree line and eye the sloping ground down to the church. It's not so much a church as a warehouse, everything shiny and new. Fresh wood beams, a metal roof and siding. The smell of sawdust lingers, as well as traces of the heavy equipment they must've hauled up here to handle construction. There's deep grooves in the dirt along the side.

I check my night-vision goggles. They paint the world in gray-green, and I crouch while I watch the building. It's quiet, which is fine by me. My weapon gets a once-over next, and then I move from my position. I scramble down the slope and stay low until I get right up to the building.

The door is unlocked, and I step through fast, gun raised. I swing the goggles up, the hallway lit well enough to see. A line of fluorescent tubes hung at angles down the length of it.

Someone rounds a corner, and I fire without a thought. I don't fucking care about killing someone—and he would just as soon shoot me for intruding.

My gun's suppressor dampens the noise, but it doesn't fully eradicate it. A shiver of sound echoes down the hallway, and the man drops a second later. I step over him, sparing only a glance for the bullet wound that found its mark in the center of his forehead.

After a long moment of silence, I grab him and drag his body with me. I can't have him discovered before I've completed my rescue mission.

I follow the path the man on the boat described, to a

stairwell that goes down. I leave the man tucked in the corner, behind the door and out of sight.

The stairwell deposits me into another hallway that's nearly identical, minus the knowledge of being underground. It smells older here, the air humid. There's a long row of closed doors on my left, and more to my right.

I check each one as quietly as possible, clearing the rooms until I reach one at the end. The door is made of metal, and the handle doesn't move.

Which is usually a sign of something valuable behind it.

I kick at the door on the side of the hinges, and they give way easily. I burst into the room, clearing the corners, before turning my attention to the man hanging in the middle of the space.

His wrists are bound and attached to a hook over his head, although it's low enough that he sags on his knees. His head is bowed forward. He's shirtless, and his brown pants are stained in dark blotches down his thighs.

I lift his head by his hair and stare into the face of Reese Avery. He's not conscious—doesn't appear to be anyway, unless he's faking—but there are still little scowl lines between his brows.

"Come on." I hoist him up, undoing the chain from the hook. He weighs a ton, but I get him over my shoulder.

It feels too similar to how his attacker carried him.

Except I don't have the ability to throw him in a trunk—we've got to escape to the woods. My nose wrinkles. He smells of sweat and the sour stench of fear.

Who knows what happened here?

I carry him back up and stop at the mouth of the stairs. The man is still there, dead and out of sight. I glance up, and a camera with a blinking red light catches my eye.

I flip it off and continue. Double time, now, jogging out of the warehouse and forcing my legs to drill into the ground faster. Up the hill, into the trees.

We stop twice more to evade patrols, but they don't seem to know what's happened. They're not on high alert, they don't even have radios to check in with each other.

My unease is sharp and hard to ignore.

I move more cautiously back to my vehicle. It's parked near the waterfalls—not where I met the sheriff but farther up, tucked out of public sight on a near-invisible service road.

I set Reese down on the backseat, positioning him so he's horizontal. The time to check him for injuries will come soon, but the pressing urge to get out of here is a gut instinct I cannot shed.

So I do.

On the road, I dial Artemis's number. Another gift from the sheriff.

"Hello?"

"It's me," I say. "I have him."

She exhales. "Thank you, Kade. Can you bring him—"

"My house," I interrupt.

She's quiet.

I wait it out as we bump along the gravel ruts. I readjust my rearview mirror to see Reese, wincing when his head bounces on the seat. He's fully limp but still breathing. That's the important part.

"Okay," she finally says. "See you there."

I hang up and hit the gas. My vehicle groans in protest, and my tires skid on the loose rocks around a corner.

There's no one chasing me, but I drive like an asshole down through South Falls anyway. The warehouse district is quiet, the roads nearly empty. I take my time winding back up to the main road that will take me to the heart of Sterling Falls, and then continue past the university north.

To the house I've been calling home.

All the while, Reese doesn't so much as fucking stir.

37 ARTEMIS

"I DON'T LIKE THIS," Saint says.

We're sitting on the beach behind Kade's house. Our other option was breaking a window to get in, but I vetoed that. Instead, I looped around the side of the house and planted my ass in the sand.

I dig my bare feet in, searching for warmer sand.

The moon hangs huge above us, the smattering of stars nearly washed out in comparison. I hug my legs and rest my chin on my knee.

"I know you don't like it," I mumble. "You've said it already."

He almost drowned here. That's what I heard anyway. Because while Nyx was dying and Saint was going through his first abrupt stage of grief, I was with my brother in the center of town. Miles away.

I didn't have to sit with her and watch her die.

Instead, I witnessed the aftermath. Laid her out on a table in my club, sheltered my brother and his friends from their enemies. Kept her safe while we figured out a proper funeral for her and dealt with the danger.

Saint and Nyx made themselves part of that fight.

"You can go," I say suddenly, turning my cheek to stare sideways at him.

I didn't expect him to lower himself down to the sand beside me, but he did. I pictured him scowling and pacing by the door until Kade arrived, not... commiserating.

He blinks at me. "Why would I go?"

I sigh.

He reaches out and touches my shoulder. He prods at the skin until my brows lower.

"You never mentioned the tattoo," he says.

I scoff. "And give you the satisfaction? No, thanks."

But I do pull my arm out of Kade's sweatshirt and lift the fabric until we can both examine my bare shoulder in the moonlight. There's no trace of a tattoo. The scratches that were left by the machine have long since healed, the marker washed away.

"What was it?" I ask now.

"Just a flower. Nothing special."

Nothing special. Not like what he would put on Nyx. She didn't have any tattoos when I first met her, but five years later she was covered. I imagine every tattoo he gave her was special.

This wasn't a tattoo.

It was a prank.

Or punishment—whatever he wants to call it.

I push my arm back into the sweatshirt and resume my earlier position. The whitecaps of the waves catch the moonlight. Watching them is soothing, although nothing can truly calm the riot in my chest.

My eyes burn, and before I can stop it, a tear slides down my cheek.

"Why do you have to be such a dick?"

I'm honestly upset about this? I wipe at it and stand, leaving Saint to sit in the sand and contemplate my abrupt question. The sound of a car in the driveway forces me to move faster, and I collect my boots and meet Kade in the driveway.

He tosses me the keys and carries Reese out of the back. I scramble to unlock the door, then step out of his way. Reese's head lolls, his eyes shut. He should look peaceful, shouldn't he? But he just seems to be in pain. Sweat dots his brow.

"What's wrong with him?" I demand, following Kade into the kitchen. He sets Reese on the island—literally, he needs to get more furniture in here—and steps back.

Saint taps on the sliding glass door.

I yank it open, then return to the island. I touch the back of my hand to Reese's forehead and wince. "He's burning up."

"I don't know," Kade says. "I found him strung up in a lower room and got him out of there. He hasn't woken up since."

"Strip him," Saint orders. He comes up close behind me. "He could have an injury we can't see."

Kade and Saint make quick work of stripping him down to his boxers. His torso is a mottled patchwork of bruises, some much darker and fresher than the rest. Kade probes at his rib cage.

If it hurt, Reese would react, right?

Kade grabs his phone from his pocket and tosses it to me. "It keeps buzzing."

I scroll through the notifications, recognizing the unsaved Sterling Falls number.

"Why is the sheriff calling you?"

He shrugs and continues his examination.

I shrug, too, and hit the button to redial.

"Laurent," Nathan Bradshaw snaps. "I've been trying to get a hold of you."

"Nice to hear your voice, Nathan." I turn away from the three men and heading quickly into the front room. "What is so urgent?"

"I—" He pauses. "Why do you have his phone?"

"He handed it to me and asked me to figure out why it kept buzzing." My tone is sarcastic. "I told him it was because you kept calling, and then I took matters into my own hands."

The sheriff huffs. "Great. Put him on, would you?"

"No."

"No?"

"I know what you did for him, Nathan, okay? So just cut the bullshit. If he asked you to do something else—"

"Jesus, Tem."

The sheriff's voice gets softer, like he's pulled the phone from his ear. He's just muttering a string of curses at this point, most of which are *not* directed at me. Which is good, because otherwise he'd get a knee to his dick the next time I see him.

"I received a message for Kade. It came through our security system and wasn't processed right away, but—"

"But, what?"

"It's about Reese Avery. I know he was looking for him. And he had you looking, too."

I stop pacing. My grip on the phone gets harder, my palms suddenly sweating. "Tell me."

"I'm sending his phone a picture of it. As far as threats go, Artemis, I cannot ascertain how serious this one is. If Avery is still missing, or—"

The phone buzzes against my ear. "Got it. We'll call you back."

I hang up on him and open the text, enlarging the photo.

Envelope—typed, addressed to Kade Laurent care of the sheriff at his office's address.

Letter...

My blood goes cold.

I am the darkness that greets you each night.
    Reese Avery is a pawn to sacrifice... or save.
    But I cannot release him until I get what I want.
    -Hypnos

THINK, Artemis.

Hypnos.

The god of sleep...

My mind flashes to Olympus. Standing in the crowd watching a lean, dark-haired man destroy one of our regular fighters. Demanding not for a favor, but for Sterling Falls to fall to ruin.

He promised war.

No one took him seriously—and then he spotted me.

Sticking to the shadows like always. Your demise will be the sweetest. Always the hunter. But now, you will be the hunted.

I shiver as his words root in my chest.

Hypnos is Gabriel.

And Gabriel...

I lurch and sprint into the other room, where Saint and Kade are staring down at Reese like they don't know what the fuck to do.

"We need to get him to the hospital," I gasp. "He's been poisoned."

"TALK TO US," Saint demands.

We're in the waiting room at the hospital. Saint, Kade, me. I open my mouth to explain when my brother bursts inside.

He grabs me up in his arms, hugging me tightly.

I hug him back and slowly relax into his chest. I hadn't realized how much I needed Apollo until he's here. He rubs my back and stays silent, and I can only imagine the look he's giving Saint and Kade.

Wolfe follows close behind, and he hugs me next. It's not the same as my brother, but it's damn similar.

"Thanks for coming." My voice is hoarse. "I, um, I didn't mean to make you come here in the middle of the night—"

"It's mid-morning," Apollo says. He ruffles my hair. "And it was no trouble."

His dark hair is wet and spiky, the collar of his soft white t-shirt a little damp. It gives away how fast they left the house.

Wolfe stops in front of Kade. Kade is taller, bulkier, but

I have no doubt that Wolfe could take him in a fight. If it came to it.

Which it won't.

"Kade Laurent, you know my brother, Apollo. This is Wolfe."

Saint snickers. "Good luck, asshole."

I hold my breath. Apollo already hates the guy, which is easy to tell in the way he holds me back. He's ready to chuck me aside to save myself, which is kind of rude but also endearing.

Saint has done the same thing.

Do not think that about Saint Hart.

They appraise each other. Wolfe and Kade.

And finally, Wolfe narrows his eyes and sticks his hand out.

Which Kade takes.

I glance up at my brother. His eyes narrow, but he doesn't do anything beyond that slight motion. He releases me and steps back, his gaze taking in my appearance.

"You look like hell," he informs me.

I roll my eyes. I don't need to tell him that I've only caught a few hours of sleep in the past week, that everything seems to be tumbling ass over head around me, and Reese being poisoned is par for the course.

The paramedics questioned us incessantly about what he was poisoned with, but none of us knew. And beyond the bruises, we couldn't find any puncture marks. So they fast-tracked him to the hospital and immediately began running tests, and we've been here ever since.

I cross to the row of chairs and drop into one.

"Can you tell us what this is about?" Wolfe asks me.

I bury my face in my hands. I feel them drifting closer, sitting beside and around me. It isn't until the silence burns that I lift my head and woodenly tell them the story.

The same one I told Kade and Saint...

"I met Reese in Terror," I confess to my brother and Wolfe.

This time, it gets a much different reaction.

Apollo springs to his feet, and Wolfe immediately grabs my hand.

Both Kade and Saint seem confused.

Hurrying on, I continue, "Hypnos is Gabriel."

"Fuck," Apollo grunts. The *crack* of his fist through the drywall follows.

Wolfe's hold on my fingers tightens.

"I'm missing something," Kade murmurs.

Saint nods in agreement, but we ignore them.

"Gabriel..." Apollo comes back to me. "That name sounds familiar."

"It should." I sigh. "He was one of the first that we managed to get out. Him and..." My throat closes. "Antonio," I finish. "Remember?"

Wolfe nods gravely. Antonio has been with us, in our circle, for far longer than anyone else. He's as much family as Wolfe and Jace.

"Drugging Reese would make sense, then," Wolfe murmurs. "Because of the history."

"So this has nothing to do with the Cyclopes?" Saint interrupts. "And can someone fill us in on why someone who used to go to a club is now a raging psychopath?"

Wolfe and Apollo exchange a look. They're doing their mind-reading thing again, having a conversation without words. They're probably saying something like, *Wow, Artemis didn't tell them about Terror. Must be for some good reason. We should keep it a secret, too—*

"Terror's nightclub was a cover for a sex trafficking ring," Apollo says.

So much for that.

Someone chokes. Sputters.

They'll connect it to me in a moment.

I shove out of my chair and leave them to piece it together. I can't *wait* for the realization that my own fucking parents sold me into Terror when I was fifteen to hit them. How I was moved around so my brother couldn't find me.

When he did...

"Miss?"

I cringe.

The nurse who called out eyes me with concern. I wave her off and continue to the stairwell. In it, the placard on the wall catches my attention.

Roof access.

Good.

Yes.

I hurry up the steps, bursting free and taking in a big gulp of air. The wind snatches at my hair, most of which has come loose from my braid. I take it out and comb my fingers through it, simultaneously walking to the edge of the roof.

The sun is up.

Sometime between us getting Reese here and now, we missed the sunrise. I raise my hand to block the sun and squint out across Sterling Falls.

It's gorgeous.

Gorgeous and terrifying, once you know the threads that run under the city and the monsters that pull the strings.

Saint demanded that I talk to him, but he doesn't really know what he's asking. He doesn't realize that the pain I show the world is only a fraction of what I've buried deep down in my bones.

Terror doesn't define me.

Being forced into a sex trafficking ring doesn't define me.

My brother saved me from dying there, and I vowed to do the same. It's why I recruited Antonio. Why I rescued Gabriel—although I have spent so many sleepless nights wishing I could change the circumstances. Why almost everyone at Bow & Arrow has been a victim of human trafficking in one way or another.

They find shelter with me.

And Gabriel, like a hurricane, is coming to wreck the town I hold most dear.

He doesn't want to root out the evil. He's not coming to do good.

He's coming to destroy everything—including the innocent.

NOTHING IS WORKING.

When the doctors tried to bring Reese out of what they described as a medically induced coma, he started seizing. They quickly reversed the drugs, and now we're back to square one.

He was transferred out of the ICU early this evening because he's stable. As far as they can tell anyway. There are little stickers with wires on his head and chest that go to two monitors. One for brain activity, another for his heart.

They're saying that, with time, he'll wake up. He has an IV of fluids keeping him hydrated, with the goal of flushing out whatever was given to him.

Besides being in a coma, he also has a cracked rib and severe, deep-tissue bruising.

We're in a private room. My brother splurged on that, I think. It's on the top floor of the hospital. It's actually kind of nice, all things considered.

We stayed for hours in the waiting room, and when he seized—well, more like when they told us they needed to run more tests but were backing off for now...

My heart stopped working, and I've been cold ever since.

I slide my hand into Reese's. He doesn't squeeze. Doesn't do anything to tell me if he's actually here. Mentally, I mean. The doctors did a test for brain activity, which he does have. That means he's not a vegetable. He's not on any sort of breathing equipment either.

I ache.

Gabriel did this because of me. Because I ruined his life —this has to be retribution, doesn't it?

Kade arrives. He makes some noise of disapproval, probably because I've kicked off my shoes and fully plan on spending the night here.

"Do you think it was too easy?" I run my finger down Reese's forearm, looking for some sort of response. Not even a twitch. I glance sideways at Kade.

He frowns. "What?"

"You got in and out without a hitch."

"I had to kill someone, Artemis." His expression is incredulous.

Yeah. Kade gave us a brief rundown of what happened, and it hasn't sat well with me. There's a niggling idea that it was too simple—that one soldier sacrificed to lay the trap might be worth it in the end.

"I think you were meant to find him." I face Kade. "You got in and out—"

He's already shaking his head. "No. There was patrol—"

"And no one in the building? No one who heard a gunshot, suppressed or not? There was only one guard between you and Reese?" I scoff. "Don't delude yourself. You were meant to find him."

He pauses and considers his friend. Former friend? I don't know.

"I'm going to stay here with him," I say. "Maybe you should make sure Saint doesn't pitch himself off the roof of my building."

Kade stops. "Is that a likely scenario?"

"Maybe." I lift one shoulder. "I don't know what goes through that man's head."

He considers it, then finally nods. "My phone is on. Call me if you need me."

"I will." I force a smile. "Now go away. The least we can do is take shifts..."

Something flashes in his expression, but it's gone before I can decipher it. He raps his knuckles on the end of the bed in farewell, and then he's gone.

I release a breath.

The urge I have to climb up into the bed with Reese is nearly unmatched. Yet somehow, I remain in my seat. My phone is charging across the room, a bag that someone delivered this afternoon with a change of clothes, snacks, and my toiletries.

A toothbrush, especially.

My kingdom for a toothbrush.

I crack a smile at that insane line of thought. The quote

from Shakespeare, no less, although subverted a bit to fit the context.

But my smile quickly wanes when the silence continues. When the monitors don't change in the slightest.

"You're going to wake up, right?" I ask Reese.

I wait for him to squeeze my hand, but there's nothing.

It's kind of funny—one kiss and a dangerous moment changed my perspective on him. He gave me panic attacks, I hated his guts, I just wanted him *out* of Sterling Falls... and now I'm worried about him.

Now, I won't leave his side.

Why?

Because I... I'm getting to know him?

Because it's taken me until now to realize that he was as stuck in that position as I was?

I close my eyes.

Reese's parents put us in the room together. They paid whatever price Terror set on my head—or rather, my body—not once. Not even twice.

And here we are.

My skin doesn't crawl when he touches me. In fact, he's not even reciprocating and I haven't taken my hand away from his.

"It's okay," I say to him. Or myself, I guess. I don't know if he can hear me. "We're going to figure this out."

We have to.

I have to.

39 REESE

RAPID GUNFIRE ECHOES in my mind as I'm dragged into consciousness. It takes me a moment to realize that I'm not crouched behind a half-blown-out wall with my squadron fanned out around me.

"There he is."

A scraping noise reverberates around me, bits and pieces of awareness slotting back into place. The first thing I notice, beyond the noise, is the pain. My chin is on my chest. I'm seated, but my muscles ache.

My head throbs. I lift it and force my eyes open. There's a single bright light directly over me. I squint until my eyes adjust, and the person who spoke comes closer.

He drags with him a chair, which he drops down into, just out of my reach.

I jerk, quickly realizing my arms are tied behind me. My legs are bound to the chair.

"Do you know who I am?" His tone is curious. He wears a bandana over the lower portion of his face.

I focus on his eyes. Light, sky blue. I don't know that I've ever seen such a shade. They're fringed by dark, thick eyelashes. His dark hair is buzzed short. I've done that before, when Kade and I were deployed. It just got to be a hassle with the dust and sweat...

"I don't." What's meant to be a normal voice comes out croaked. "Should I?"

He makes a noise of disgust. "This town forgets."

"I'm not from here."

He eyes me, then drags the bandana down.

I'm not sure what I expected, but it wasn't a handsome face. The world opens up for beauty, and this guy clearly has it. In the same way Kade uses his broad stature to cut through a crowd, or Artemis bats her eyelashes.

Ha, now I *know* I have a concussion.

That girl has never batted her eyelashes in her life.

"Did you ever go to the lower levels of Terror?" he asks.

I open and close my mouth. *Lower levels?*

"I went where I was told," I say quietly. "But I didn't know there were... lower levels."

The man in front of me sneers. "Oh, yes. It's where they let the deviants do whatever they wanted to us. They used drugs to keep us compliant."

The room tilts a bit.

He's getting angry now. He jumps up from his seat and circles around it. I hiss out a breath when he fists the front of my shirt.

"You were there," he says. "You went to Terror. Consumed product that wasn't yours to enjoy."

I look away, because I did. I was a teenager under my parents' direction, but I did it anyway. It's one of those things that drove me to join the Marines. I needed to atone for my sins, and I thought protecting our country would do that for me.

It didn't.

And now, looking into the eyes of someone who was on the other side—and it's truly a remarkable difference from looking at Artemis, who survived it with her mind intact—the old guilt comes rattling back.

I hate it.

I hate what I did.

He hits me. *Hard.* I don't even see it coming, really, his movements brutal and efficient. He hits me until I fall, the chair coming with me, and I crash into the ground hard.

But he follows, crouching beside me and yanking at my hair.

"You and I are going to have some fun together," he swears. "And I'm going to send a little message through you."

I breathe through the pain. I think he cracked one of my damn ribs. "How?"

He smiles. His teeth glint, truly the mark of a fucking madman. "I'm going to put you to sleep for a long, long while."

Fear slices through me.

His grip on my hair tightens. "No, no, easy. This isn't a euphemism for death... although it might feel like it. I don't know what will happen to your mind while your body sleeps. Will it be awake and aware? Will you be dreaming? So many options to consider..."

I fight against his hold, while he just laughs in my face.

"Easy," he murmurs. "There's still plenty of time between us before I cast you to your fate. After all, they're still trying to find you."

He releases me and jumps back, leaving me with my

cheek pressed to the floor. Everything is at an uncomfortable angle. After a long moment, he cuts me free from the chair and yanks it away. My hands are still bound behind my back...

"Let me go," I say. "I'm not who you have an issue with."

He laughs. "No? I think you are. But Sterling Falls needs to burn. That's the only way to remove the rot. Burn it down, start over fresh. But for now, let's see how you do in my own version of Terror."

The door slams shut behind him, and silence fills the room. I wait agonizing seconds, then push myself up to my knees. From there, it's easy to get to my feet. I cross the room and put my back to the door. My cold, tingling fingers grasp at the handle.

It doesn't turn. The thing doesn't budge, even though I yank and yank with all the strength I have left. This room is small. The chair I was on and the one he used are the only pieces of furniture. Tape still hangs off of the legs of the tipped one.

And then, the lights go off, plunging me into complete darkness.

I DON'T KNOW how long I sit in the darkness before the light comes back on and my captor reappears. He seems distracted as he moves around the room, ignoring me completely. Straightens the chair and drags it away, then the other. He puts them against the wall.

"Do you think about death?"

I straighten. "Do I...?"

"Death, Reese Avery," he snaps. "Do you consider it?"

"No."

He goes to the door and hauls in a chain. It's long and looks heavy, although his movements remain easy. Loose. There's more muscle packed on his lean frame than I would've originally given him credit for. His t-shirt is loose and baggy, his pants don't quite fit right. But it doesn't matter.

There's a hook on one end.

"How about we contemplate it now?" he offers. "Rather, that in-between."

When he glances over, his eyes gleam.

"The in-between?" I frown.

"We should discuss it now," he says. "Because that's where you're going, and I'd very much like to know how it differs when we meet on the other side."

Pause.

"*If* we meet on the other side."

I stare at him. My fate doesn't seem concrete. At least— I can't grasp what he's saying to me.

He gets a loop of the chain and swings the hook around, gaining momentum. When he releases it, it sails up to the ceiling and over one of the pipes. It comes down to just over his head. He grabs at it, drawing it down to chest level, and nods to himself.

"Go on," he murmurs. "What did your parents believe? How were you raised?"

I...

"We were agnostic."

I'm in the corner of the room. There's a hollow space at my spine, but both my shoulders touch the walls. It made me feel a modicum of safety in the darkness, enough to doze, but that haze of sleep has vanished entirely.

My mouth is dry, but I continue, "I never believed in

God or anything like that. Just figured the end would be like sleeping. Maybe a dream or two, but... nothing else. Darkness."

He chuckles. "Wouldn't that be nice? Rather than facing the prospect of Heaven or Hell... well, I suppose your parents wouldn't have wanted you to face such a thing, right? After what they get involved in? The Devil always wins."

"It wasn't like that," I protest. "My mom's side is Catholic. My grandmother tried to take me to church, and it just didn't stick."

"So the in-between... Tell me about that." He's wrapped the excess chain around a cleat bolted to the wall. "Your Catholic grandma, would she be worried about your soul?"

"She died." I press back harder against the wall when he stops what he's doing and comes closer. My hands, at this point, are completely numb. I don't think my legs have much feeling in them either, after spending too long in this position.

He pulls a syringe from his pocket and squats over me. So close he's practically sitting on my lap.

"This will just help a little bit with the transition," he says.

I slam my head forward. It collides with his, and he very nearly falls away. But at the last second, he grabs my shoulder. His fingers dig into my skin. Stars dance in my eyes, and blood drips from his nose. He doesn't even touch it, just shoves me back to the wall and leans in closer.

"This isn't it," he promises. "Not the end of our fun."

His smile is stained red, and he licks at his lips. I don't expect him to jam the needle into my neck. He aims for the artery, the injection not meant for muscle. His thumb presses down, injecting who-knows-what into me.

Then it's gone, and I thrash at the sensation of it sliding free. The coldness it leaves behind.

"Shh," he whispers. "Give it a second."

A second is all it takes. Euphoria spreads under my skin, a rush that is indescribable.

"That's it," he breathes. "Ride the wave."

Holy shit.

It's good.

It's devastatingly good.

He grips my chin, keeping my face aimed at his. "Yes. That's right." He reaches behind me and cuts the binding on my wrists. He guides my hands around, leaving them in my lap.

I can't even move.

My body is floating, all the pain and every worry somehow miles and miles away. My skin is warm, but the concern isn't there. Not in the slightest. My eyes close of their own accord, and I sink into thoughts of a girl with golden skin.

While I drift, I'm aware of shifting shadows around me. Something cold touches my wrists, and then I'm lifted. It barely registers until my arms are drawn up over my head. My body sags, but my wrists catch me. My shoulders strain, although even that doesn't hurt.

"How's this?" he asks.

My lips and tongue and teeth aren't coordinated enough for words, and he laughs at my attempt. There's another prick, this time in my arm, and that rush comes back over me. My back arches, and every sensation on my skin seems to double.

"What a sight." He touches my face. "You sit tight, Reese. I'll be back when reality returns to you."

The lights go out. The door shuts.

The dark holds me close, though, and even that is agonizing on my skin.

Slowly, my mind comes back to me.

The reality of my position—on my knees, with my wrists above my head—filter in. How long I've been like this, I couldn't say. Time seems to have stopped moving entirely. I use the hook my wrists are locked on to stand, but as soon as I get a leg under me, my body fails.

I fall.

My wrists and shoulders catch me, and my joints scream.

I might let out a noise, too.

The door opens, and the man who took me appears. He's silhouetted from the hall, and it takes a long moment for the light inside the room to flicker back to life.

"Your friend is going to rescue you," he says. "But I need you to promise me something."

I stare at him.

"We didn't get to finish our talk. When I come back and revive you, you'll tell me where you went. Promise me that." His gaze hardens. "If you don't, I'll just leave you asleep forever. Your muscles will atrophy and your skin will wrinkle, all while you're caught up in a mental cage..."

I lick my lips. There's no saliva in my mouth—I can't remember the last time I had water or food, don't know how long I've actually been here—but I run through the motion all the same.

"I promise," I mutter hoarsely.

He smiles.

"This shouldn't hurt," he adds. "But... if I'm wrong, please let me know."

He brings the chair over and lays out a hard-shell case. Inside are glass bottles, capped syringes.

"A few injections to make it stick," he says. "A paralytic, of course..."

That fear is back, but it's not as potent. It's like the drug he gave me earlier still lingers, even though I can think more clearly. It holds on to my muscles. I want to thrash and kick and fight, but I can't seem to move.

I just stare at him.

"Why are you doing this?"

He sighs and rubs at his eyes. "We talked about this."

"We did," I agree. "But why me? Why—"

"No more talking," he interrupts. "This one might burn."

He comes close and injects me. Straight into my neck. The liquid is cold. My heartbeat is slow, it has been steadily thumping since the initial rush wore off, but now it drops again. He watches me, and I watch him.

My anger—hot and bubbling—fizzles as dread takes over. I'm so cold, but it's coming from the inside. Like he put straight ice into my veins. And with the ice comes the freezing of my body. I try to move. To ball fists, to shift my weight. Even blinking, after a long moment of silence, becomes difficult.

It's all I can do to keep my eyes open.

And then... well, is it better to watch him or close them?

"This cocktail was developed by a friend of mine," he says, filling the next syringe. He taps at it, pushing the plunger until there's no air left in it. A little spurt of liquid comes out and runs down the long, tapered needle. "It's similar to how hospitals put patients into comas."

Similar.

"But with a twist." He offers me a vicious smile. "I hope you know that this is just a safeguard. If they try to wake you up..."

He injects me with the next one. And before that even has time to root, there's another.

It's quick. Too quick. My body and mind separate, which is the strangest thing. I can only watch his face get closer to mine, until he's practically nose to nose with me. He breathes in my shallow exhales, which no longer feel like mine.

He reaches up and drags my eyelids down, and, well, that's the last I see.

40 SAINT

KADE HASN'T STOPPED WATCHING me, and it's getting on my last fucking nerve. He showed up about ten minutes after I got back to the condo. I planned on drinking myself into an oblivion and passing out.

But *no*. He insisted we make dinner, saying that we hadn't had a decent meal since the sandwiches he made for us after we showed up at his house. So, grudgingly, I let him raid the fridge and pantry and put together a meal worthy of a two-star diner.

Okay, fine, it was better than that.

Good, even.

He followed me to the gym.

To the fucking *gym*.

Needless to say, it only wound me tighter instead of burning off the energy I desperately wanted to shed. By the time I was done, my body glistened with sweat.

I forced him to leave me alone long enough to shower, and that seemed like a small miracle. The door remained locked, although he knocked at the five-minute mark and demanded an answer.

Was my answer in the form of a string of curses? Maybe.

He deserved it, though.

Now, we sit across from each other in the living room, and it feels oddly familiar to sitting across from Reese. Except now, I'm not tempted to pull out the whiskey and make him answer questions. Mainly because the idea of *Kade* prying into my life is infinitely more invasive.

If only he would stop staring.

"What?" I finally snap.

He sighs. "Are you suicidal?"

"What?" Hoarser, without the power behind it. I press my palms flat to my thighs. "Why are you asking me that?"

"It's not a no," he mutters.

"Fuck off."

He rolls his eyes.

It clicks, then, that this was Artemis. Whether she was just trying to get him out of the hospital, or she really does think I'm going to do something that will end my life—

My throat closes.

"Let's talk about something else," I manage. "Why are you looking for Reese?"

Kade eyes me and doesn't answer.

Infuriating.

I'm not going to admit if I do or don't want to kill myself. I think about it sometimes. I like to flirt with death. But over the last month or so, I've been... smiling.

Which is so strange, and completely at odds with the last year. Elora's absence hasn't been constantly pressing down on my shoulders. It's only when I'm alone that I consider how she would be perceiving this.

So... *was* I suicidal?

Probably.

Now, I'm not so sure.

"I'm not going to kill myself this week." I think that should be enough for now. Enough commitment. "But I think you owe us something. You met Reese in the Marines, you said."

"We were in the same squadron," Kade says. "He saved my life, so when he went off the radar two years ago, I knew something bad happened. We stayed in contact up until then."

I frown. "You're how old?"

"Twenty-seven."

"When did you join?"

He leans back, seeming to settle in.

"Fresh out of high school. I didn't know anything about anything, and my pops thought it would be a good idea for me to have more structure." His expression darkens. "He and my mom got divorced when I was eight. I lived with her, and he had vocal opinions about that. It did create the drive in me to go make something of myself... and I wanted to impress him. Or at least prove that I could do something with my life."

Huh. "And you deployed."

He dips his head.

"While you were fighting for your country, we were..." I gesture around. "I guess Sterling Falls doesn't really seem too bad to you, does it?"

He sighs. "Every war is different, Saint. Doesn't make it any less barbaric."

That's what we are, then. Barbarians.

We fight tooth and nail for this town, to make any sort of progress, and we chip and splinter our bones on the asphalt to gain any purchase we can.

It's not fair.

"We should stretch our legs," Kade says. "Come on."

I glare at him, but I still follow. To the elevator and downstairs. We head out, and he takes a right. We pass out of view of the security camera, past the blood Reese left behind. If we keep going down this street, we'll end up at the university. And on the other side of that is the sheriff's office.

Two blocks over is Starlight.

And, surprisingly, that's where Kade goes.

He stops outside of the glass storefront, then glances at me. "Do you have a key?"

I scowl and jerk my head in the form of a nod. I open it up and step through, ignoring the way he follows close behind. I turn on the lights, and my skin tingles. I don't like him as my shadow, I don't like *him*, period. The fact that he came here—

"Are you trying to poke around my head? Psychological shit?" I plant my hands on my hips. "I'm not falling for it."

He appraises me. "It's not getting to you?"

"No," I snap.

His dark eyes bore into mine for too long, and then his attention shifts. Like a gust of wind knocking the tension out of my muscles, I exhale. Relax.

He takes his time looking around. The wall of framed drawings, photos, newspaper and magazine clippings. The cover I was on for a tattoo magazine, framed dead center, now seems ostentatious and reaching.

The white couch has sat many people waiting for their appointments. Even some hockey players and their wives, which was a pretty cool experience. Mainly because they're about as crazy as my friends—not openly, but they just had that vibe.

Like Kade.

He plops himself down in my tattooing chair, then leans forward and pulls off his shirt.

Muscles.

I stare at him, trying to comprehend how someone can have so many muscles. His abs have abs.

"Like what you see?"

My face flushes. He's smirking at me, leaning back and crossing his ankles like he has every right to sit there.

"I want a tattoo."

I scoff. "No."

"Why not?" He glances around. "It's the line of people begging to get in, isn't it?"

"For fuck's sake," I groan. "I'm not—we have better things to worry about."

He just waits, and he seems too fucking comfortable in the chair. Like he has all the time in the world.

Finally, he adds, "It'd be a good distraction."

I narrow my eyes. "Do you have any tattoos?"

"A few. I'm not an amateur."

And yet, I don't see any ink on his upper torso.

"Here." He hooks his thumb in the waistband of his pants, right where his abdomen forms one side of a V, and drags it down an inch.

There's a line of script. But before I can get a chance to read it, he releases the waistband and smiles wider.

"I'm not tattooing you," I say. "In fact, I'm going home."

I make it to the door before he replies, "Oh, so you're referring to it as *home*, now?"

Fucker. I hold it open and point to the street. He slowly gets up from the chair and shrugs back on his shirt.

"I had a friend who said getting tattoos was the ultimate way to remember a place." He moves past me, his gaze lingering on the ink visible on my throat. "I like his philosophy. Sterling Falls is growing on me."

I grimace. "Maybe you should consider therapy."

He laughs. Full-belly, open-mouth *laugh* that goes straight into my ears. I grit my teeth and close the door behind us, locking it quickly. Suddenly, he cuts off.

I face him, only to find his somber face staring down at his phone screen.

"I've got to take this," he says.

He answers it and gives me his back—but not only that, he puts distance between us.

My brows furrow.

When he returns, his easy smile is back in place. "Tem said she needs her laptop from Bow & Arrow to work while she stays with Reese."

Oh, jeez. Artemis tends to be a workaholic at the best of times. Hearing that she wants to catch up on spreadsheets or some shit is not surprising in the least.

"You okay?" he asks me. "You kind of look like shit."

I scowl. But... yeah. Exhaustion weighs on me, plus a healthy dose of guilt. While Artemis got some sleep before Kade went to find Reese, I stayed awake. I filled Kade in on everything I knew about that place, although I felt uniquely *un*qualified. After all, I was pretty much unconscious when Elora and her friends came to get me out.

I don't sleep much as it is, but I'm paying for missing hours.

"Fine," I admit. "I'm going to go crash."

He pats my shoulder. "Good decision. Don't burn out before we've even begun."

It isn't until we get back to Artemis' building and part ways that I pause, staring off after Kade. His SUV is parked a block down, his keys swinging around his index finger.

He's the picture of *not bothered*, even though the situation with Reese should bother him a lot.

So either he's the world's best pretender, or he really isn't as attached to Reese—or worried about him—as he made us believe.

And what does he mean, *before we've even begun?*

41 ARTEMIS

I GAVE IN.

I climbed up into bed with Reese, weariness pulling at me, and I think I fell asleep. I must've, because getting comfortable is the last thing I remember, and now a nurse is shaking me awake.

"Sorry," I mumble to her.

It's midday. Not an acceptable time to sleep.

She apologizes, then explains about needing to take him for another test. A scan that will take a while. She holds out a voucher for the cafeteria, which I accept carefully. I tuck the piece of paper into my front pocket and hop off the bed.

While she and another orderly prepare Reese to move, I duck into the bathroom. I brush my teeth and hair—well, I try to for the latter one, although it's so tangled and in need of a wash that I settle for *good enough*. I braid it, then change my clothes.

Kade gave me one of his sweatshirts. A pair of jeans from my closet at the Bow & Arrow apartment, fresh under-wear, and a soft t-shirt. I clutch them to my chest, because only Antonio would've gone in and picked out these clothes.

He knows me best, after all.

Once changed, I unplug my phone from the charger and call him.

"Hey, kiddo," Antonio answers. "How are you holding up?"

I release a slow breath. "Managing the guilt."

He tsks. "It's not your fault."

"Feels like it is." I stand at the window. "I'm to blame for Gabriel."

"Saint said you're on shift," Antonio says. "When one of them relieves you, come to my house. Vittoria and I will take care of that guilt."

My eyes burn. I blink rapidly, trying not to fucking cry like a baby, but all the other telltale signs tumble after each other. My throat closes, my chest tightens. Tears fill my eyes.

"Okay," I whisper. "I've got to go."

I wipe the tears away and hang up. The room is a lot emptier without Reese's bed—and the man, himself—in it. It's unsettling.

Maybe I should try to eat something...

"Hey." Kade pops his head into the room. His brows furrow. "Where's Reese?"

"A scan." I push myself out of the chair. "I'm heading to the cafeteria, if you want to join me."

He moves out of my way, allowing me to exit first, and follows me down the hall. I glance over my shoulder at him. "Thought I told you to watch Saint."

"He said something about sleeping," Kade answers. "And I figured it might be hard being here all alone."

That's true.

The vibe in the cafeteria is... depressing. We glance around, and my panic climbs. There are people here, all eating in fucking silence. It's more like a funeral home than a hospital down here, and it doesn't help that the cafeteria is located in the basement.

I use the voucher to get two sandwiches—one for him, one for me—and two bottled drinks. Instead of choosing a seat, though, Kade tips his head toward the door.

"Let's eat outside on one of the benches."

"Sure," I agree.

He picks one. I don't even care, really. Now that I have food in my hand, I realize how hungry I am. I dig into one of the sandwiches, and we eat in silence.

Kade exhales. "I don't think they're going to be able to wake him up."

I frown. "What?"

"I think he's too smart for that."

"What are you saying, Kade?"

He glances at me. He's barely touched his sandwich. It sits beside him on the bench. "I think Gabriel wouldn't allow him to just wake up."

I scoff. "He's not God."

"No, he's not," he agrees.

A vehicle turns down the street, trundling toward us, and I draw my legs up to my chest. Not that I particularly care about strangers witnessing the hot mess that is me right now, I just... well, okay, fine. Even though I feel relatively put together with the fresh clothes, I'm still exhausted.

That nap on Reese's bed only seemed to make me more tired. But curling up next to him...

Why is Kade being negative all of a sudden? The doctors said Reese will wake up as soon as whatever he was injected with gets out of his system. Their drugs reacted negatively, but they said brain activity was okay.

"Artemis."

I meet Kade's gaze. He holds out his hand, and I automatically put mine in it. His whole hand engulfs mine, warm and dry and calloused. I smile at him, trying to reassure him without words that things will be okay.

"I'm sorry."

"For being negative?"

He frowns. "For choosing Reese."

My gaze drops to the syringe in his free hand. With mine caught in his grip, he quickly tugs me forward and stabs it into my upper arm. Straight through the sweatshirt —his sweatshirt—and t-shirt, into my muscle.

"What the fuck?" I jerk back and kick out. My heel connects with his thigh. The movement puts me off-balance, and I topple off the bench.

Fuck.

Ouch.

Little rocks bite into my palms. I push myself up and glare at him.

"Seriously, Kade, what the fuck?"

For choosing *Reese?* What does that even mean? Why would he feel the need to pick? I didn't know there was such a choice to be made.

Him or me. Who knew?

Kade rises and advances. "Just take it easy. You're going to feel light-headed in a second."

I scowl. "Fuck off."

I turn and head back to the hospital. But it only takes a few steps for my feet to be numb. Somehow, I retain my balance, stay upright, until I lose more feeling. My head swims.

He catches me from behind and scoops me into his arms. "I'm sorry."

I blink at him, but even that is slow. I lose seconds while my eyes are shut, and suddenly I'm being put into the back-seat of a car.

"I'm sorry," he says again. "It'll all be over soon."

The door slams.

"A little something to make her more compliant," a long-dead woman whispers in my ear. Flashes of vulnerability swarm my memory. As much as I try to think of anything else, everything comes back around to Terror.

And my helplessness.

Finally, that light-headedness overtakes me. I close my eyes, and they stay closed. I don't know who's driving the car, if it's Kade or someone else—and I don't want to know. Not like this.

42 ARTEMIS

I MUST'VE PASSED out or been dragged into oblivion by the drug. But waking up is worse, because there's a fabric bag over my head. Every inhale pulls it against my lips and nose, making it hard to get a true deep breath.

As a result, I hyperventilate. I can only focus on that, my frantic breathing and the blood rushing in my ears. White spots dance in front of my eyes.

The bag flies off my head.

It's in the grip of a man who is at once foreign and familiar. Dark hair that's recently been buzzed short, cold blue eyes. Beauty still clings to him, although maybe it's just my perception that's warped.

He grips my chin, tilting my head up. "As much fun as it would be to see you pass out, we need to have a chat. So slow it down, Madden. Deep breaths, now."

With the bag off, the oppressive, claustrophobia removed, it's easier to do that. To follow his direction and slow everything down. As soon as my chest loosens, and that crushing panic abates, he releases me.

I'm bound to a chair. My wrists are secured behind my

back, my ankles attached to the legs. I jerk, testing the hold, and Gabriel laughs in my face. He's so close, I can't tell much else about the room. I can't seem to look away from the madman in front of me.

My muscles tremble.

"Still weak," he says. He's got a hard-shell case on a chair behind him, and the gleam of different bottles under the fluorescent lighting speaks of terrible things. "Kade handed you over. How do you feel about that?"

I narrow my eyes.

"Betrayal has never sat well with you." He approaches again, leaning in and bracing his hands on the arms of the chair. His face comes in close to mine. He has a bandage across his nose. "Kade gave you up to save Reese Avery. Did he tell you that before he stabbed you in the back?"

"He apologized," I say stiffly. "And I have a feeling it was more your fault than his."

Gabriel laughs. "Yes, yes, it was all my fault. I didn't give him much of a choice, did I? The cocktail I gave Reese... well, it's designed to interact with those pesky drugs they give to bring patients out of comas. It just dragged him deeper into the depths of his own mind." He pauses, examining me. "There's something beautiful about that, don't you think? It was a nasty concoction to begin with, everything crafted to put him under for a long time. But it worked perfectly."

"So what he said was right." I sigh. "Reese wouldn't wake up without you fixing it."

"Giving him the correct combination of drugs to unlock his mind? Correct. It's like a key to the cage trapping him in his own body. Delightful to watch you all moan and squirm..." He leans in even closer. We're nose to nose. "How I love to watch you moan and squirm."

"So what's your plan with me?" I demand.

He smiles.

"Well, that's simple, dear Artemis. We're going to reminisce about the good old days."

That does not sound promising.

He nods encouragingly. "Yes, yes, exactly right. Here."

He moves aside, and I get my first good glimpse at my surroundings. So focused on him, I didn't look around when I should've. We're in the amphitheater at Terror.

My heart sinks. We're somewhere in the middle of the rows, positioned above the dark stage. This booth has been cleared of seats. It's just the chair I'm tied to and the one he has that hard case sitting on. He moves the case to the floor and drags it closer, sitting right beside me.

"Begin!" he calls.

The stage lights turn on with a bang, someone, somewhere throwing a heavy switch to illuminate them.

The stage seems to almost glow white for a second, and I blink rapidly to allow my eyes to adjust. It's then that the curtain on the far side is pushed aside, and someone is shoved through.

"Oh!" Gabriel leans in to me, his lips at my ear. "Oh, do you know her?"

I stare.

I do know her.

"The woman..." My mouth is dry. "She helped me get you out."

"Correction," he snarls. "She was *supposed* to help you get us out, and she failed to protect us."

I dip my head.

His fingers curl in my braid, and he jerks my head back up. "What do you think her punishment should be?"

The woman stumbles around the stage. She's in white

lingerie, her body pale and emaciated. I could count her ribs. Her shoulder blades stick out, and her skin is practically translucent.

"I think she's been punished enough," I answer carefully. "Perhaps you should let her go."

He laughs. It's loud enough to draw her attention. Her glazed eyes coast over us without recognition.

"Here are some options," he says. "We could stab her in the gut and watch her bleed out in the corner while we continue our game. Or you could choose to kill her now and put her out of her misery."

I bristle. "Excuse me?"

He reaches down, pushing up my pant leg. The knife I always keep on me slides out of its sheath easily.

Without warning, he presses the blade to my side. Then keeps going.

The knife bites, entering my body slowly. Everything flashes white-hot inside me, and pain chases it. I clench my jaw against the scream rising up in my throat, and only a lone whimper escapes past my teeth. I can't control my hands from spasming, clenching on the arms of the chair, until he stops.

He leaves the blade there. It protrudes from my side, but my mind cannot comprehend it. If my hands were free, I'd yank it out and stab *him* with it.

Gabriel examines my face, then reaches up and swipes his thumb across my brow. "Sweat," he says, more to himself than me. "Interesting."

His attention swings back to the woman I had to bribe, nearly a decade ago, to help me. She worked in the bowels of Terror. It took weeks of watching the place to figure out who worked in the building, and even longer to convince her to help.

In the end, it wasn't her moral compass that made the decision. It was the money I shoved at her.

He makes some sort of motion, a sideways ticking of his finger, and a man with a bandana covering the lower half of his face strides out of the shadows. He grabs the woman by the back of the neck and forces her to her knees.

He drives a knife into her back.

The scream the woman releases is earth-shattering. It goes straight into me, and I yank against the constraints. She falls forward, on her hands and knees, and tries to shuffle away. Her legs don't work, though. She can barely drag herself away from him, her fingernails digging into the platform.

"Got her in the spine," he whispers in my ear. "Even if she survives this, I don't think she'll walk again. Poor bird."

He clucks.

"I don't see the point of this." My voice rasps like I was screaming, even though I didn't make a sound. "You've held a grudge this whole time?"

"No." He taps the knife handle.

The pain radiates through my stomach, the blade shifting, and I groan.

"But I met someone who incited violence in me. Who made it possible." He raises his hand, another signal, and then he pinches my chin and forces me to see who next comes through the curtain.

The figure stumbles before they make it to the edge of the stage lights. I lean forward, straining, even as the knife moves again and my body screams to stop.

Antonio steps into the spotlight and lifts a hand to block the glare.

He first looks to the woman coughing up blood in the

corner, then to us. Recognition flares, then horror, across his face.

"No," I choke out. "No, please."

Gabriel claps. "I love choices, don't you? You or him, Artemis? You get to pick. Who to save? Who to sacrifice?"

My heart breaks a thousand different ways, because there's no way I can't choose him.

Tears fill my eyes, and unlike in the hospital, they spill down my cheeks without restraint.

"Don't," Antonio calls. He moves forward, his expression stern and familiar and full of fear. "Don't you dare pick me, Tem."

I can't speak.

"Oh?" Gabriel's breath hits my ear. "A little needling, then."

He slides the knife out.

I scream. It hurts worse than it did going in, the pain growing until I'm nearly blind with it. But he drives it back in. A different spot, carefully found, and my voice just gets louder. It shreds, and I thrash in place. My vision flickers, the pain almost overwhelming.

"I'm curious how you convinced a Terror guard to betray his employers. Was it his guilty conscience? Money? After all these years, I was never able to figure it out." His breath hits the side of my face, but his words pull me away from passing out. "He was solace when I was in there, Artemis. The only friendly face. But he was still the one left holding the key to my cage at the end of the day."

No. "He's not who you're making him out to be, Gabriel."

He hops up. I barely track him moving down the row, then the aisle. He practically skips down to the stage, where he stops just in front of Antonio. He towers over the older man. My heart lurches.

"Bring her down here," he calls suddenly.

The man who's clearly helping him, or working for him, comes up the aisle. He cuts me free of the chair and lifts me. He ignores the knife blade stuck in my stomach, although every fucking step vibrates through me. He carries me down to the stage and drops me on my feet.

My knees buckle, but I somehow stay standing. Somehow, even though the pain coursing through me is unlike any I've known before. My hands are still bound behind my back. But then a knife slices through that restraint, too.

My hands flutter around the handle of the knife protruding from my stomach. The war between needing it *out* and knowing I shouldn't move it rages in my head.

Gabriel watches me with a small smile.

He enjoys chaos and destruction.

"Here's what we're going to do." He comes closer and, without warning, draws the blade from my skin. Again.

It's *agony*.

I go down to my knees. *Hard*.

My throat locks up tight, not letting a single sound out. At least I can press my hands to the wounds. Both of them. Blood drips and oozes out, more with every beat of my heart. Kade's sweatshirt is soaked through in a matter of seconds, and blood stains my hands.

Suddenly, the knife at my throat makes me pause.

Gabriel grips my hair and stands behind me, the edge of the knife pressing into my skin. There's a prick of pain—a drop in the bucket—and wetness rolls down my throat.

"Antonio," Gabriel says. "Such a pleasure to see you again, old man."

Antonio grunts. He's pale, frazzled. More scared than

I've ever seen him. Unflappable Antonio. He stepped in and protected me when I was fresh out of Terror, vulnerable and flayed open.

"I'm going to give you both a moment to talk over this opportunity. The chance for one of you to walk out of here alive." He pauses. "Well, perhaps not walk... but you'll be alive. Isn't that kind?"

"Like how Reese is alive?" My voice does not sound like the sure, confident woman I pretend to be on a regular basis. It sounds more broken than anything.

Gabriel brightens. "What a good idea, Artemis. A trade. One of you sticks a knife in your heart, and the other gets a little shot. It's like taking a ride. Around and around you'll go. When it stops, nobody knows."

He takes the knife, dripping my blood across the stage, and grabs his kit. He prepares a syringe, recaps it, and brings it back. He sets it between us, along with the knife, and winks at me.

"We'll shoot anyone who comes out," he warns, his expression serious for a split second. "And if you haven't decided when I return, we'll shoot you both." A broad grin overtakes his face, his whole body language changing and tone lightening. "Good luck!"

He leaves, taking his henchman with him.

The woman in the corner is silent—dead, maybe. She was going to die. There's a pool of blood under her. Antonio shifts, and I tear my gaze away from the woman. I focus on him.

"How'd they get you here?" I ask him.

He shakes his head. There's at least twenty feet between us. Ten to the knife and syringe. A good lunge wouldn't do it. My head spins. I just need to get to the knife before him.

"He said he had you," Antonio says quietly. "I was already here. The power went out, and suddenly he was in my office, in the dark, telling me all the things he was going to do to you if I didn't come with him."

"Please. I know what you're thinking—"

"You don't. I should've done better by him, Artemis. This is more my fault than yours."

He says I don't know what he's thinking, but I know he's going to go for the knife. He's unharmed, everything in place. Gabriel didn't have to rough him up to get him here— Antonio came because of me.

He walked into this place, this familiar place, with the knowledge that he might not walk out.

We're not delusional. We both know that Terror still lives in the heart of this building. And we've been desperate to try to hide it, to cover it up with paint and gilded edges, but it doesn't work like that.

"Artemis." He's steady. So fucking steady.

I blink, and he's got both the knife and syringe in his hand.

Another blink, and he's kneeling in front of me. I'm still on my knees. In all this time, I haven't managed to move. Hadn't tried. My limbs are heavy, the blood seeping between my fingers. I've got no fight left, except for the desire for Antonio to walk out of here alive.

"I don't regret saving them," he says to me. "And I do not regret saving you. Because you saved me, too."

My eyes burn. He's gripping both so tightly, his knuckles white and hands trembling.

"Don't do it," I beg him. I latch on to his arm, staining his jacket with blood. "I need you."

He rolls up my sleeve and slides the needle into my arm. A sob bursts out of me, and I fall forward. He catches me, putting my forehead on his shoulder, as his thumb depresses the plunger. He waits a moment, then shifts me onto my side. All the way down, until my head touches the floor.

"Close your eyes," he says. "I don't want you to see this."

I can't.

The drug is already latching on, making it harder to think. I try to reach for him, and my hand barely trembles along the floor.

He turns the knife around, the point aimed at his chest. Under the ribs, angled high.

No, no, no.

I can't lose him.

I can't look away.

The drug is dragging me down into ice water. Everything is cold, nothing else matters. I lose my body in the process. Just a floating consciousness trying to figure out how to fix this, how to stop him from killing himself.

He grits his teeth, hands shaking, and glances around. He says something in Italian under his breath. Maybe a plea or a prayer, but either way, there's no one riding in to save us.

"I love you, Artemis. See you on the other side."

I try to scream, but my vocal cords aren't responding. Nothing is.

With that, he drives the knife into his chest.

TO BE CONTINUED...
In *Warrior*: http://mybook.to/sfr2

WHERE TO FIND SARA

Thank you so much for coming along on this crazy journey with me.

If you like my stories, I'd highly encourage you to come join my Facebook group, S. Massery Squad. There's a lot of fun stuff happening in there, and they're who I go to for polls about future books, where I share teasers, etc!

My Patreon is also an awesome place to connect and get exclusive content! On release months, I do signed paperbacks. Plus, get ARCs, audiobooks, and artwork before the rest of the world. Find me here: http://patreon.com/smassery

And last but not least, here are some social media links for ya:

Facebook: Author S Massery
Instagram: @authorsmassery

Tiktok: @smassery
Goodreads: S. Massery
Bookbub: S. Massery

ABOUT THE AUTHOR

S. Massery is a dark romance author who loves injecting a good dose of suspense into her stories. Originally from Massachusetts, she now lives in Southern California with her dog, Alice.

Before adventuring into the world of writing, she went to college in Boston and held a wide variety of jobs—including working on a dude ranch in Wyoming (a personal highlight). She has a love affair with coffee and chocolate. When S. Massery isn't writing, she can be found devouring books, playing outside with her dog, or trying to make people smile.

ALSO BY S. MASSERY

Hockey Gods

Brutal Obsession

Devious Obsession

Secret Obsession

Twisted Obsession

Fierce Obsession

Hockey Titans

Into Ruin

Ruined God

Shadow Valley U

Sticks & Stones

Heart of Thorns

SVU 3

The Christmas Playbook

Standalone Hockey

The Pucking Coach's Daughter

Fallen Royals

Wicked Dreams

Wicked Games

Wicked Promises

Cruel Abandon

Vicious Desire

Wild Fury

Sterling Falls

#0 Thrill

#1 Thief

#2 Fighter

#3 Rebel

#4 Queen

Sterling Falls Rogues

#0 Terror

#1 Nemesis

#2 Warrior

#3 Martyr

#4 Saint

DeSantis Mafia

#1 Ruthless Saint

#2 Savage Prince

#3 Stolen Crown

Broken Mercenaries

#1 Blood Sky

#2 Angel of Death

#3 Morning Star

More at http://smassery.com

www.ingramcontent.com/pod-product-compliance
Lightning Source LLC
Chambersburg PA
CBHW021242190726
48289CB00005B/1444